Suzette wasn't exactly *kinky,* but she had enjoyed plenty of sex during her college years, and sometimes that sex hadn't been entirely tame. From her first sexual experiences, Suzette had enjoyed a wide range of sexual interactions, and bondage had been a part of that here and there. She had been tied up by three—no, four—of her boyfriends, and each time she'd enjoyed herself immensely, wanting to go further. Her fantasies, more often than not, centered around some kind of restraint, imprisonment, or sexual service. She had never really thought that was unusual, but now she supposed it might be. She never would have thought of herself as someone who was interested in SM or anything like that. As Mrs. Aldridge had read off the list of deadly sins, however, Suzette had felt a little curiosity, a little excitement flowing through her. She knew that her breath was coming more quickly, and she felt a little warm. She could feel sweat forming on her back. Nervously, Suzette crossed her legs....

Also by N. T. MORLEY:

The Limousine
The Parlor
The Castle
The Contract

THE OFFICE

N. T. Morley

The Office
Copyright © 1998 by N. T. Morley
All Rights Reserved

No part of this book may be reproduced, stored in a retrieval
system, or transmitted in any form, by any means, including
mechanical, electronic, photocopying, recording or otherwise,
without prior written permission of the publishers.

First Masquerade Edition 1998
First Printing April 1998
ISBN 1-56333-616-2

First Top Shelf Edition 1998
ISBN 1-56333-919-6

Manufactured in the United States of America
Published by Masquerade Books, Inc.
801 Second Avenue
New York, N.Y. 10017

Chapter 1

"Bondage," said the woman, and Suzette shifted uncomfortably.

The woman tossed her head, looking very intently at Suzette's face. Suzette noticed briefly—once again—just how young the woman seemed to be. Mrs. Aldridge. That was her name. She looked much too young to be a "Mrs.," thought Suzette. And, perhaps, too attractive.

"Bondage," said Mrs. Aldridge again, more firmly this time. "Domination. Whips. Chains. Restraints. Manacles. SM." Her eyes held Suzette's, and even if Suzette had wanted to look away, she would have been unable.

"Yes," said Suzette. It was the only thing she could think of to say.

"Leather underwear," the woman continued. "All manner of sex toys." She leaned closer to Suzette and looked at her very carefully. "Perhaps I should be more specific—*penetrative* sex toys." She said it "Pen-e-TRAY-tiv," so that it took Suzette a moment to understand what she meant, and to form a clear mental image.

"Oh," Suzette mumbled nervously. "Of course. Yes. Certainly."

Mrs. Aldridge was leaning against the edge of her desk, her already somewhat tight skirt riding up a little on her thighs. Suzette could—just barely—see the lacy tops of Mrs. Aldridge's black stockings, and could see that the woman wore a garter belt rather than stay-ups or pantyhose. For some reason this embarrassed Suzette, and she caught herself looking just a little too long at the hem of Mrs. Aldridge's skirt. Mrs. Aldridge saw it, too, and demurely tugged the hem down to cover the tops of her stockings.

Suzette blushed as she looked up at Mrs. Aldridge, who waited for several long seconds before letting Suzette see the barest hint of a smile at the corner of her mouth. Then the smile was gone, and Mrs. Aldridge had shifted again, casually letting her silk business jacket fall open a little. Suzette's blush deepened. Mrs. Aldridge leaned forward, very close to Suzette, and the shadow of her cleavage deepened slightly.

Mrs. Aldridge was wearing a somewhat low-cut beige

camisole under her black business suit. The camisole's light color made the outline of her breasts that much more evident.

Suzette usually didn't take such notice of the details of other women's wardrobes. But she was so concerned at making a good impression—she ran through her own wardrobe over and over again in her head. This was Suzette's first job interview out of college, and she had almost no idea what would be expected of her in the corporate world. Certainly she had gone through a lot of stress trying to figure out what she should wear to the interview. Why, she had changed clothes three times just this afternoon, each time soliciting an opinion from a very sleepy Samantha—her roommate, who always went to bed at dawn. Each time Samantha pronounced Suzette beautiful and then buried her head under the pillow.

Even now, with the interview proceeding, Suzette was wondering if she shouldn't have worn the black suit, rather than the blouse and skirt. She had opted for the white blouse (borrowed from Samantha) and knee-length black skirt (borrowed from her friend Susan)— she didn't want to look like too sexy for her first job interview. That would be undignified. It wasn't like she had all that much choice—she only had the clothes she had been able to borrow, and the black suit had come as a loan from her sister Amelia, who was a size smaller than

Suzette. The black suit looked great on Suzette, even if it *was* just a hair too tight—but it was a power suit, made for an aggressive businesswoman who commanded all she saw, and Suzette wasn't sure she was there yet.

From the way the office looked, the suit would have been *much* more appropriate. It was a very small office on the fortieth floor of a downtown skyscraper. But it looked very professional. The receptionist out front was dressed extremely well, in a fitted business suit and high heels—even if the woman's blouse was a bit more low cut, the jacket of her suit was quite a bit tighter, and its skirt a bit shorter than Suzette had expected to see in an office.

Mrs. Aldridge's clothes were also power broker all the way, plainly very expensive, and not as provocative as the receptionist's. And Mrs. Aldridge wore those clothes beautifully; she looked like an advertisement for the high- powered, corporate executive lifestyle. Suzette was more than a little fascinated by the commanding Mrs. Aldridge. She wondered for a moment whether perhaps— if she got the job—Mrs. Aldridge would be willing to give her a few tips on assembling her corporate wardrobe. Suzette knew she certainly needed some advice—all through college she had gone completely casual, and her job at the campus paper didn't require her to dress up at all. Suzette had spent the last four years of her life wearing jeans, T-shirts, and sneakers. That would have to change, she knew, if she was ever going to compete in the corporate job market. She felt a vague sense of excitement as she thought about all the things she would do to beautify her corporate image. But Mrs. Aldridge's voice brought her interest back to the matter at hand.

"Leather restraints, ropes, manacles—steel ones. Whipping posts, stocks, pillories." Mrs. Aldridge looked very hard at Suzette. "Cages, Suzette. Cages. Women in cages, collared like animals, on their knees. Women depicted in all manner of sexual submission to men— and to other women. Of course," she waved her hand dismissively, "there's no actual penetration *shown,* or anything of that sort. But it's certainly implied by the sorts of things we sell."

"Yes," said Suzette nervously.

"And men shown in submission to women," Mrs. Aldridge continued. "Men on their knees, their genitals bound in complicated fashions, licking the boots of the mistresses they serve. Pleasuring them orally." Suzette listened, fascinated and somewhat horrified—horrified more by the obvious relish with which Mrs. Aldridge spoke, rather than the things she was saying. In fact, Suzette's fascination grew less and less academic as the conversation—if it could properly be called a "conversation"—continued. "Men being…penetrated. Do you understand?"

Suzette thought about it, but she wasn't sure. She

could figure it out, sort of. But then she decided she wanted to hear Mrs. Aldridge saying it, even though she had a rough idea what the woman meant.

"No," said Suzette breathlessly. "Tell me what you mean."

The look on Mrs. Aldridge's face expressed deep concern, even trepidation.

"Women wearing dildos," said Mrs. Aldridge. "And penetrating men with them."

"Yes?" whispered Suzette, as if she didn't understand.

"Anally," continued Mrs. Aldridge, with overwhelming seriousness.

"Oh, yes," said Suzette quickly, her face brightening. "I see what you mean." She was quite sure there was going to be a point here somewhere, but she couldn't imagine just what it was going to be.

Mrs. Aldridge leaned very close, so that Suzette could even smell her subtle perfume.

"Cock-and-ball torture," she said distinctly.

"Oh, my," said Suzette. "Uh, yes," she continued nervously. "Definitely. Of course. Certainly." This was a job interview, after all.

Suzette was getting a little concerned. She wasn't sure what Mrs. Aldridge was getting at—but, thankfully, the woman made herself clear with her very next sentence. Mrs. Aldridge looked intently into Suzette's eyes and watched her reactions very closely.

THE OFFICE

"Does any of this...*disturb* you?"

Suzette thought about it a long time before saying, "No."

It was true. She had never really thought about it all that much, at least not in this context. But she certainly wasn't offended by all the things Mrs. Aldridge had mentioned. The way Suzette saw it, any sort of sexual game was more likely to be interesting than offensive, as long as both parties were enjoying it. And everything that Mrs. Aldridge had mentioned certainly sounded—to the admittedly inexperienced Suzette, at least—to involve enjoyment by both parties.

Suzette wasn't exactly *kinky*, but she had enjoyed plenty of sex during her college years, and sometimes that sex hadn't been entirely tame. From her first sexual experiences, Suzette had enjoyed a wide range of sexual interactions, and bondage had been a part of that here and there. She had been tied up by three—no, four—of her boyfriends, and each time she'd enjoyed herself immensely, wanting to go further. Her fantasies, more often than not, centered around some kind of restraint, imprisonment, or sexual service. She had never really thought that was unusual, but now she supposed it might be. She never would have thought of herself as someone who was interested in SM or anything like that. As Mrs. Aldridge had read off the list of deadly sins, however, Suzette had felt a little curiosity, a little excitement flowing through her. She knew that her breath was coming more quickly, and she felt a little warm. She could feel sweat forming on her back. Nervously, Suzette crossed her legs.

Well, the job sure sounded more interesting than shuffling papers at a law firm or something.

"Does it...*interest* you?"

Suzette felt a little nervous at the way Mrs. Aldridge asked that. She managed to stay casual, however. She answered with a shrug and a matter-of-fact, "Oh, yes." She added quickly; "Just a little. Not *too* much. I mean, sure it interests me. But...uh...I don't think I would find it distracting or anything."

"You don't think you'll be...*offended* by the subject matter?"

Suzette's mind filled with the images to which she might be subjected. She almost burst out laughing. She felt sure that whatever she would see on the job would be less bizarre than the mental images she had just conjured up.

"No, not at all," said Suzette, laughing nervously, remembering what her guidance counselor had said about being relaxed. "Oh, it takes a whole lot to offend me. A whole lot. Lots and lots..." Suzette's voice trailed off uncomfortably.

Mrs. Aldridge smiled. "Women in submission? In service to men? On their knees, performing tasks that some might find...degrading? You don't find that bothersome or offensive? Not even a little bit?"

Suzette nervously shook her head. She suddenly felt a little afraid that Mrs. Aldridge could see her nipples through the blouse she wore. *Oh shit*, she thought. *I should have worn a bra instead of this stupid camisole.* In fact, she was sure her nipples were quite evident through the thin silk of the blouse. Why had they gotten so firm all of a sudden?

Suzette desperately wanted to cross her arms in front of her chest, but she thought that would draw more attention to it, make it more obvious. So she sat still with some difficulty, tensing when she noticed that Mrs. Aldridge's eyes dropped oh-so-briefly down to the level of Suzette's breasts. If anything, Suzette felt like her nipples were now that much *more* obvious.

"And—importantly—women making love with other women? Perhaps on their knees, dominated, humbled, worshipping another woman? That doesn't bother you?"

Suzette had a fair amount of difficulty answering, with the intense way Mrs. Aldridge was looking at her.

"Not at all," Suzette finally said, calmly. Then, nervously, she added, "My roommate's bisexual. And my best friend from college is gay. It doesn't bother me at all. I'm very open."

Mrs. Aldridge looked at Suzette for a long moment before turning away. Suzette felt the tension drain out of her body, and she nervously shifted, turning to the side so that her breasts were less evident. It was very warm in here.

"Very well," said Mrs. Aldridge, walking around the desk and seating herself behind it. "I don't by any means insist that you be a devotee of the sorts of things we sell in our catalogs. But I do insist that you approve of it. The majority of our customers are men, but a very large number of them are women—fully 30 percent, by our most recent survey. The catalog is geared toward both sexes. But as you probably know, photos of women usually encourage sales more than photos of men—in our market, at least. Therefore, many of our photo scenes involve two women, though they're certainly not aimed exclusively at lesbian women. Our strategy is to show our equipment being used in hot scenes, thus encouraging the customer to buy it—and reenact her own hot scenes. Or his."

Suzette was a little less nervous now that Mrs. Aldridge was behind the desk. But she had begun to think about how exciting the job would be. She would get to learn all about different kinds of sex—things she had never experienced! She shifted uncomfortably, feeling her inner thighs giving off little tingles of excitement.

"And to present those exciting experiences as convincingly as possible, we need an accomplished layout artist who can put together a top-notch catalog. Our catalogs are eighty pages or more, and so, as you can imagine, it's a lot of work putting one together."

"I can imagine," said Suzette quickly, trying to keep her mind focused on the conversation and not let it stray off into what the "hot scenes" depicted in the catalog might entail. She wasn't entirely successful.

"Wh—where do you get the photographs?" blurted Suzette, and immediately wished she'd kept her mouth shut.

Mrs. Aldridge smiled faintly.

"I supervise all of our photo acquisitions," she said. "And I work firsthand with all our photographers. We have a dedicated stable of commercial photographers who have worked with us before, know what we like, know what we're trying to achieve in our photos. I personally supervise every photo shoot to ensure that it meets our business objectives."

Suzette couldn't stop herself from asking the next question. "And the models?"

Mrs. Aldridge's eyes seemed to betray a hint of mischief as she let long moments pass before answering.

"All our catalog photos show the actual equipment, being used exactly as it would be used by the consumer, in a scene in her—or his—home—or dungeon. Our models are often commercial models, but they are also real people—who enjoy what they do. On and off camera."

Suzette felt a tingle go through her body as she tried

to decipher that answer. In a way it didn't leave much to the imagination—but in another way, it did.... Suzette's heart pounded.

"There are three employees at this location. Sasha, she's the receptionist, you met her. She's very nice. She handles some of our general office work, and takes phone orders. Then there's Katrina Bixby, who is our sales representative. She takes our business to consumer establishments—a wide variety of shops, not just your garden-variety sleaze joints—and handles our commercial accounts and bulk discounts. Then there's me—I'm Executive Director, and I run things. You would be the fourth employee—I'm afraid we've been without a layout artist for some weeks now, and the catalog is very overdue. We'll start losing business if we don't get a catalog out within the next month or so. That is going to be quite a challenge. Do you think you would be up to that sort of thing?"

"Definitely," blurted Suzette. "I love a challenge." That was the sort of thing her career counselor had told her to say, and it sounded wooden and awkward coming from her mouth, which felt uncomfortably dry at the moment—had she been mouth-breathing?

"Ah, yes," said Mrs. Aldridge. "And then there's my husband, David. He is involved at a number of different levels, but most days he's off-site, managing our other business."

The Office

"Your other business," said Suzette, remembering something the guidance counselor had said about sounding interested in the totality of the business, not just the part that affected you. "Which is?" she asked brightly.

Mrs. Aldridge looked very serious.

"Goat cheese."

"Goat cheese?"

"Goat cheese. There's a big future in it."

Suzette was so nervous, she wouldn't have been able to laugh even if her brain had been able to comprehend the absurdity of that statement. Luckily, it wasn't, so it was a moot point.

Mrs. Aldridge quickly changed the subject. "I don't mind telling you," she said, "I was quite impressed by your portfolio. You've done a lot of excellent work," she said. "Work with real commercial potential. My main reservation is that you haven't done any work in a sexually-related industry."

Suzette's mind raced. *Oh, no*, she thought. *I should have put it on the résumé. I'm not going to get the job because of that...* but she could hardly tell Mrs. Aldridge now! Well...maybe she had to. She made a split-second decision.

Suzette blushed as she quickly said, "I—well, actually I have."

Mrs. Aldridge seemed surprised. "Really? Of what sort?"

Suzette figured she may as well give the whole story, rather than trying to filter out what Mrs. Aldridge wanted to hear.

"I used to be a dancer," said Suzette. "I mean exotic dancing—I did a lot of ballet, too, when I was younger, but…what I mean to say is that I did exotic dancing. When I was in college, for the first two years. I did bachelor parties. Bar openings. Auto races. That sort of thing."

Mrs. Aldridge looked visibly impressed. "Auto races?"

Suzette shrugged. "Well…only one of those. Mostly bachelor parties."

Suzette wasn't really telling Mrs. Aldridge the whole story. The *whole* story was a little more sordid than that —but Suzette wasn't ready to go into it just yet. Maybe later.

Mrs. Aldridge nodded. "Well, that certainly counts as sexually related work, in my mind at least. Why didn't you put it on the résumé?"

Suzette was about to give her a serious answer when Mrs. Aldridge smiled and winked, and Suzette realized the woman was kidding her.

"Well, that experience can be very important here. It's crucial that you be completely comfortable with the kinds of sexuality that we display in our catalog. We encourage consensual behavior, and negotiation. But sometimes…well, we've had a number of layout artists who simply got offended once they started laying out the catalog. I would hate to have that happen again."

"Oh, it wouldn't," said Suzette, too quickly. "I'm sure it wouldn't."

"Yes," said Mrs. Aldridge, reaching out to press a button on the side of the desk. In a few short seconds, the door opened and Sasha, the receptionist, appeared.

"Yes, Mrs. Aldridge?"

"Sasha, would you be so kind as to bring Ms. Sullivan a few of our back catalogs? So she can see what she's getting into?" Mrs. Aldridge gave Suzette that faint, enigmatic smile.

"Right away, Mrs. Aldridge." Sasha hurried off to get the catalogs.

"You've seen our documents about benefits, sick days, salary reviews, that sort of thing. You'll find that we're a very professional office, so your dress is of paramount importance. We obviously don't see most of our customers in the office, but we do occasionally have national sales representatives come by, and it's critical that you dress with the professionalism that shows pride in your work." Mrs. Aldridge glanced over Suzette's clothes, and Suzette shifted nervously. "What you have on is acceptable, though you might want to… spruce it up a bit. Go for the power suit look."

Suzette was mortified, but she managed to hide her embarrassment even as Mrs. Aldridge looked her up and down more carefully.

"We can talk," said Mrs. Aldridge. "Ah, here's Sasha

with your catalogs. Anything else you would like to ask me?"

Suzette shook her head as she took the catalogs from Sasha. She widened her eyes and tried to look away from the photos on the covers of the catalogs. She quickly dropped the catalogs into her valise. Sasha disappeared back into the front office, but left the door open.

"Excellent," said Mrs. Aldridge, standing up and extending her hand for a handshake. "We're interviewing several other candidates, and we'll get in touch with you within a week."

Suzette shook the woman's hand and said, "Thank you, Mrs. Aldridge."

Mrs. Aldridge looked puzzled for a second, then smiled. "Oh yes, of course, Sasha. You see, we like to maintain a professional image, a corporate demeanor. She's afraid she'll forget to refer to me as Mrs. Aldridge on the phone, so she calls me that all the time." Mrs. Aldridge's eyes sparkled. "But you can call me by my first name. Which is Candace. Or better yet—Bunny."

Suzette could almost feel her hair curling. "Thank you," she managed to say without laughing. "Bunny."

"I'll be speaking with you soon, Suzette."

"Thanks. Uh, Bunny."

Out in the front office, Sasha was seated behind the reception desk. She motioned Suzette over.

The Office

"She likes you," said Sasha with an emotionless tone to her voice. "Did she mention cock-and-ball torture?"

Suzette looked at Sasha, who was perhaps a couple of years older than she, redheaded, and quite attractive. But she seemed so cold, distant, aloof—even now, with her conspiratorial whispers, she was without emotion.

"I think so," said Suzette. "Yes, she did."

Sasha went back to stuffing envelopes. "Then she likes you. Good luck."

Nervously, Suzette left the office and closed the door behind her. It all came down to cock-and-ball torture? That was hardly the most shocking thing Suzette expected to see.

Waiting for the elevator, Suzette felt the tension flooding out of her. She had made it—she had survived her first interview! She felt a giddy excitement, even felt a little drunk. She had that euphoric feeling she used to get when she pulled an all-nighter and turned a paper in at six in the morning and then knew that she wouldn't sleep all day. It was as if she was *made* out of energy. As she waited for the elevator, she went over the interview in her head, wondering if she'd done everything right. There was no question that this wasn't your usual job—certainly the bondage and SM angle made it different than what Suzette had expected. But the money was good, and Suzette felt more than a little excitement at the prospect of working with all those naked bodies. Laying out those dirty photos, trying to get the maximum sexual charge out of them for the reader—to encourage him to buy the company's product. Or her.

Suzette stepped into the elevator. She was alone, and for a second her mind flitted over the catalogs in her valise.

As the elevator descended slowly, Suzette opened her valise just long enough to catch a glimpse of the lurid photos on the cover of one of them. She looked up nervously, then reached down and began to page through the catalog, leaving it in her valise. Immediately Suzette felt a sexual charge growing in her body as she flipped through the pages upon pages of naked women, restrained in various complicated ways, in a variety of submissive postures. Suzette caught one spread that particularly intrigued her, and before she knew what she was doing, she'd slipped the catalog out of her valise and was staring, wide-eyed, at the photograph.

The elevator bell went off, and Suzette gasped as the doors opened. She almost had a heart attack as she threw the catalog back into her valise and clutched it to her body. She was only on the thirty-fourth floor, and two staid-looking businessmen in suits were getting on the elevator. Damn, this thing was slow! She realized that as the door had opened, the two men might have gotten a glimpse of what she was reading. Her embarrassment must be evident—she could feel her face flushing hot. One of the men, in his midforties, with graying hair at the temples but not at all bad looking, didn't seem to notice, but simply stood behind Suzette reading his newspaper. The other guy, younger and with darker hair, gave her a knowing look and then glanced at her valise. He stood a respectful distance, but Suzette's embarrassment deepened as she stood, trying not to look at the man. She realized how cute he was. The cut of his suit accented his athletic body. She wondered if he worked out. She noticed again how cute he was, and that he was staring at her. She looked down.

Another floor, and three more people got on, all men. Damn. Suzette had forgotten that it was rush hour, so it would be hell getting home. The elevator began to smell faintly of male flesh, something Suzette, to her horror, found herself liking. She had gone to school in a small college town hundreds of miles from the city, and hadn't been in elevators all that much. They made her nervous, in part because she sort of liked them. It excited her to be in a small, enclosed space, close to people she didn't know and would never know. Since she had moved to the city, Suzette had had more than a few fantasies about elevators. In fact, fully against her will, she was starting to have one right now.

I wonder if you could stop one of these between

floors, she was thinking. *With a guy, I mean. Maybe Rob. Or Paul.* Suzette was a little shocked at herself, thinking about Samantha's boyfriend like that, but it's not like she hadn't done it before. *Stop the elevator between floors. Sometime when the building is really crowded, so everyone has to wait for you to finish. But you could take your time. He could come up behind me—*she had switched from the theoretical "you" to the concrete "I," and even though she was horrified, she couldn't stop the fantasy that was forming in her mind—*And press me against the wall. I would be wearing a little black dress, something really short, nothing on underneath, and he could enter me from behind...while everyone on every floor is waiting for the elevator, but they would just have to wait for him to fuck me, fuck me right, fuck me nice and slow, taking his time sliding it in...pushing it in me from behind while everyone waits...and they know what we're doing in here...they know it's me...*

The fantasy flowed through her mind in seconds, fully-formed, and the image of her ass under the dress, pushed back to take her lover's thrusts, echoed in her mind.

Suzette's fantasy vanished with the loud bell of another floor—thirty-two. Jesus Christ!

But the excitement still flowed through her. Now she was *certain* her nipples were showing through her blouse! But she couldn't cross her arms without putting down her valise, and that would call attention to it. Better to just stand here and endure it. Endure the gaze of the man across from her—was he looking at her?

Suzette glanced up and saw with nervousness and a little pleasure that he *was*. But he looked away, embarrassed, the second Suzette looked up. So she watched him for a second or two as the doors opened.

Four more guys got on, filling the elevator almost to capacity. Suzette was crowded a little toward the corner with the dark-haired man. She blushed deeper, her skin getting so hot it felt like it would burn her clothes. She was pressed closer to him, and she wished with all her might she hadn't indulged herself with that brief elevator fantasy. She could feel that she was getting more than a little wet. Suzette kept her eyes averted, not looking at the dark-haired guy, but she wondered once again if he was looking at her. She glanced over and saw that he was not—he was averting his eyes respectfully. But as she looked down at her feet, shifting nervously, she wondered again if he was looking. Watching her. Maybe noticing the way her nipples showed through the blouse. If they were, that is. She was sure that they were. She looked down and saw that, indeed, her nipples were quite visible through the thin silk. The blouse clung to her breasts, moist with sweat and heavy with the elevator's humidity.

Several more people got on the elevator, and Suzette

was jostled roughly back. She couldn't be sure, when she thought about it later, if she did this on purpose— but somehow, she ended up being pushed up against the dark-haired guy who had seen her reading the catalog. The press of bodies was so tight and hot that there was nothing she could do to pull away from him. But now her ass was pressed against the guy's thigh, and if she shifted just ever-so-slightly, just a bit—it could easily be an accident—her buttocks were pressed up against the guy's crotch, and suddenly Suzette was horrified with herself. She shouldn't be playing around like this, this was totally disgusting. After all, she was still going out with Rob, even if they had agreed not to be exclusive or anything (and Suzette figured he probably still slept with his ex-girlfriend when she was in town). Suzette chided herself. What did *that* have to do with it? This was a million times weirder than cheating on Rob; she was rubbing her ass against a stranger in an elevator! God, she had to stop this—but when she tried to pull away, she found that the press of bodies was too tight, and she couldn't move. She managed to reposition her hips so that her ass was an inch or so away from the guy—but then a lurch of the overburdened elevator made her sway and press back against him, and this time Suzette didn't even try to move. For the second she had pulled away, she felt a sudden surge of decadent nastiness.

God, she should stop this. She had just gotten carried

away with that fantasy for a few seconds, and now her mind was playing tricks on her. It felt like the guy was starting to get hard. *Oh, God,* thought Suzette, horrified. *Now what have I done.*

Suzette managed to catch a glimpse of the guy's face in the shiny elevator doors, and saw the look of horror and embarrassment on it. She was embarrassing him by pressing up against him. The guy probably thought this was an accident—it sort of *was* an accident, just an accident that Suzette liked a little more than she was supposed to like it—and he was horribly embarrassed that it excited him. That he was starting to get a hard-on. Suzette tried to lean forward, but the lurching elevator kept making her press back against him, as the elevator moaned, rocked back and forth. Now she was sure the guy was hard. God, she was horrible. She felt embarrassed herself, horrified at the situation she'd forced this guy into without his consent. Maybe in another situation he'd think this was hot, sure—but what about his girlfriend, his wife? Or if he didn't have one, what about him? This wasn't exactly his idea…even if he might have had this very idea the moment he and Suzette looked at each other, right after he'd seen her looking at the catalog.

How much had he seen, wondered Suzette. Enough to give him some ideas? Enough to put some fantasies in his head, like the ones that had gone through hers?

Stop it, she told herself mentally. *This is not OK.*

The elevator lurched, rocking back and forth. It moaned loudly and refused to close its doors. The rocking motion pressed Suzette's ass more firmly against the dark-haired man's crotch, and she closed her eyes, praying for it all to be over, even if it was making her wet as can be, even if she could feel her nipples pressing through her blouse, rubbing against the back of the guy in front of her. Even if she was more turned on than she'd been in weeks.

"Somebody's going to have to get off," shouted the gray-haired man in the back.

Suzette couldn't stop herself from looking at him. She glanced over her shoulder and saw the poor guy's face, bright red, his embarrassment obvious. She hated herself for doing this to him. But looking at his face hadn't helped much—she just noticed again how cute he was.

And something about his plight, his embarrassment, really excited her. Her own embarrassment grew as she thought about the dark-haired man's.

Suzette hadn't fantasized so much about bondage and SM, the sorts of things Mrs. Aldridge—Bunny (Suzette suppressed a giggle)—had talked about. But she *had* had a lot of fantasies about public sex, about embarrassment, about—it made her nervous to use the word, but it certainly fit—humiliation. Was that sort of thing what

THE OFFICE

intrigued her about the man behind her and his embarrassment at getting hard?

That didn't help. It just made Suzette *more* excited as she thought about the fantasies she did have. The guy pushed back desperately, trying to disconnect his erection from her backside. She helped him by pushing forward, but as soon as their flesh parted, Suzette felt an acute sadness. God, she wished she could just throw all caution to the winds and do whatever demented things occurred to her.

The elevator doors closed and the elevator started its slow descent through the twenties. At twenty-two, fifteen, and six, the stops and starts were particularly rough, and Suzette felt herself jostled against the dark-haired guy again. By six, she was pleased to note that he'd started to lose his erection.

She still felt horrible. She shouldn't have teased him like that—then again, had she really meant to? Maybe she'd gone out of her way to get jostled back further than she would have ordinarily. Maybe her conversation with Mrs. Aldridge—Bunny—had put a few thoughts into Suzette's head that wouldn't have been there otherwise. Or would they?

The elevator opened and the sea of people flooded out into the lobby. Suzette realized that her blouse was soaked with sweat, and it clung to her breasts even more than it had before. Well, nothing could be done. It was a warm day outside, and as she hurried out onto the sidewalk, she saw the dark-haired man hanging back, obviously not wanting to run into Suzette on the street. He must have known how obvious his arousal was to her, and—she hoped—he didn't know just how extreme her own arousal had been. *Damn*, thought Suzette. *I think I must be dripping*. She was surprised at herself, but she couldn't deny it—she had gotten very turned on by the encounter in the elevator. Despite herself, she found that she couldn't wait to get home and see just how wet she was. Thinking about that turned her on even more as she ran across the street to catch the uptown bus.

Of course, Suzette didn't get a seat on the bus. She even had to lean out over somebody to get a handhold. She balanced her valise between her feet, praying that it wouldn't fall open, as she gripped the handhold and tried to stay balanced with the bus's violent lurching. Suzette realized yet again that she should have worn the bra instead of the camisole, and a couple of guys were taking notice of this. *Who cares*, she thought contemptuously. But she was still a little embarrassed. She found herself wondering whether she could have the same sort of public-sex fantasy on the bus that she'd had in the elevator. But even Suzette wasn't *that* horny.

†††

The Office

On the two-block walk home, Suzette stopped and bought a bottle of red wine to celebrate surviving her first interview. Maybe Samantha would be home to celebrate with her. Suzette couldn't remember when Samantha had to work tonight, but it was usually pretty late. Suzette kind of envied Samantha—but the kind of work Samantha did was very different than the bachelor parties Suzette had done. Well, maybe not *so* different.

Once through the door of the apartment, Suzette immediately began stripping off her sweat-soaked clothes. She untucked and then unbuttoned her blouse, then slipped it off and let it fall to the floor as she tore off the sweaty camisole. She gasped as she reached the end of the hall and saw Paul there, lounging on the couch watching *Blade Runner* for the umpteenth time.

Suzette stepped back quickly, crossing her arms across her chest—but not before Paul had gotten quite an eyeful.

"Sorry," she called. "I didn't know you were here."

"You always strip when you're alone?" said Paul with more affection than sarcasm in his voice.

"You know how we bachelorettes are," Suzette said, trying not to sound embarrassed. "So carefree and uninhibited!" Paul wasn't much of a prude—he couldn't be, going out with Samantha.

Suzette picked up her blouse and buttoned it back up (without the camisole) before walking into the living room. Paul tried to be sly, but she definitely saw him checking out her tits through the sweaty, thin blouse.

"You're peeping, Paul," she said, playfully slapping him as she walked by. She went into her bedroom and shut the door.

God, she thought the second the door was closed. *I thought I was never going to be alone!* She took the blouse off again, tossing it on the floor, quickly stripped off the long skirt, and kicked off her shoes. *My clothes are soaked.* She peeled off her panties, and found that those were soaked, too. *I guess I was more turned on than I thought. Now I get to see....*

Suzette had developed this habit of feeling herself to see how wet she was, more because it excited her to do it than because she needed to know if she was wet. She almost always knew when she was, after all. But feeling it *told* her she was wet, told her she was ready for sex. And that turned her on, more than simply *knowing* she was wet.

Suzette sat on the edge of the bed and spread her legs wide, leaning forward. She wanted to feel how wet she was. She quickly slipped a finger into her cunt, felt her lips part for it, felt her entrance easily accept the intrusion. *God, I'm dripping.* She worked the finger out, then in again, then out. She tried it with two, found that she accepted the two fingers just as easily. She felt

THE OFFICE

the sensations magnify as the two fingers glided in. *I'm totally wet.* Suzette slid her two fingers in and out, then took a moment to rub her clitoris, to feel how erect and sensitive that was. *I'm gushing.* She said it to herself as she toyed with three fingers at the entrance to her pussy. She could feel that two was her limit for taking them easily, even being as wet as she was. Suzette slipped two fingers in and played with her clit, feeling her nipples ache in sympathy as she rocked back and forth on the edge of the bed.

It was too hot in here. Suzette eased her fingers out of her pussy and licked them clean, lingering over the taste. She wondered if all women did that. She hadn't asked anyone, and she'd never read any statistics about it.... Maybe it happened all the time. She wondered lasciviously what other women did in their bedrooms when they were alone after getting all turned on by a job interview. She imagined it wasn't all that common a problem.

Suzette quickly took off the pale suntan stay-up stockings she had on, and stretched out on the unmade bed. It felt wonderful to be naked, even if the room was hot and stuffy from hours of being closed up. She got up again and opened the window, careful to close the curtains. *Oh damn,* she thought. *They're blowing in the wind. Oh, fuck it,* she decided. Her window faced a mostly-empty alley, and the wind felt good, so if the curtains blew open then it was someone's lucky day. She realized that she better put some music on—no telling what kind of noise she'd make once she got alone by herself on the bed. She had a nasty habit of making more noise than she thought she was making, and being embarrassed afterwards by next-door neighbors or roommates who had heard everything in graphic detail.

Suzette put on a noisy grunge-rock album and settled down onto the bed again, stretching out, feeling her whole body ache with the heat and the exhaustion. She hadn't realized how tense she was through the interview. And then that episode in the elevator hadn't done much to relax her. God, what *had* she been thinking? She didn't normally have that dirty a mind. Well, actually she did. Most of the time. But she usually didn't involve other people in her weird fantasies. That poor guy.

Or had he enjoyed it? She was angry at herself for teasing the guy, but then she didn't know that he hadn't liked it. She still shouldn't have done it…but it was kind of exciting to think that he might have enjoyed himself, that he might have wanted to go further.

With all those people? Yes, Suzette told herself as she stretched on the bed. With all those people. She pictured it happening as if it were a vivid memory. The man with the dark hair pushing up against her from behind. Suzette pressed back against him by the crush of the crowd and the sway and jiggle of the elevator. His cock, hard and long, pressing up against her ass, right between her cheeks.

Suzette is wearing that incredibly tight black crepe skirt, the one she wore for Halloween that year. God, that's really slutty. Nothing underneath. Nothing at all. The guy reaches down and lifts Suzette's skirt. He finds she's bare underneath, her cunt open and ready for him. Suzette leans forward against the man in front of her, spreading her legs slightly as her valise opens, spreading its contents over the floor among the people's feet. The guy snuggles up behind Suzette, fitting the head of his cock to her waiting entrance. She presses back against him, lifting her top—she's just wearing the camisole now, no blouse at all—so she can rub her breasts with their erect nipples against the back of the man in front of her. She reaches around him and works open his belt, reaching in to take hold of his cock—he's hard, too, and she starts to jerk him off. The elevator is picking up speed. Suzette feels the dark-haired guy enter her, his cock big and smooth inside her as it penetrates to her very core. Then he starts to fuck her, slowly, taking his time at first, then faster as the elevator hurtles down, faster and faster.

Suzette was spread wide on the bed, rubbing herself furiously with one hand while she played with her nipples with the other. She was incredibly close already, ready to come. She imagined the guy in front of her groaning as he shot off to her insistent hand gestures, shooting streams of come all over her hand. Then the guy behind her was coming, filling her up with his seed. And as she imagined that, Suzette was struck by a vision of the elevator being crammed full of men, all naked, all waiting for their turn with her.

Suzette came, fighting hard to stifle a moan so loud it would have carried over the music. She thrashed back and forth on the bed as her orgasm exploded inside her. She let out a long, even sigh, gasping, "Oh shit!" as the powerful explosions continued to go off inside her. When the intense pleasure had started to dissipate, Suzette took a deep breath and wondered if she shouldn't take the catalogs out of her valise.

Part of her didn't want to. There was something really nasty about knowing they were in there—something that made it seem much dirtier than it really would have been if she just, well, *looked* at them. Her imagination ran away, picturing all sorts of improbable humiliations and complicated submissions. She imagined what absurd postures the women might be in, offering their services to men. Services. *There's something so sexy about that word,* thought Suzette. She began to wonder what "services" might entail.

An image flooded her mind, bringing a surge of

The Office

excitement. She pictured herself on her knees, bound in a complicated way that placed her hands at her ankles, but forced her legs wide apart. She was forced to lean forward, against a padded bar, and while Suzette was at it she made the padded bar a sort of stock—like they used to have for persecuting witches in Puritan times. Oh, yes. She was shocked at herself, but picturing herself with her head in one of those things, her wrists bound to wide-spread ankles, leaning forward, ass in the air, thighs parted, cunt exposed and available for whoever might come along....

Suzette was getting incredibly turned on just thinking about it. She thought more about the position, tried to figure out just what turned her on so much. But the intensity of her excitement was such that she just couldn't think rationally, and she found herself rubbing her pussy again, feeling how wet she was, imagining being wet in that submissive position, wet and ready—

Who had placed her there? Who had bound her in that position?

Rob, the guy she'd been seeing? Maybe...but no, that didn't seem quite as exciting. Suzette liked Rob a lot and he was certainly a good fuck, but he didn't seem the type to put her in stocks and leave her there to suffer.

Mrs. Aldridge—Bunny?

Oh God, thought Suzette. *That's it.* She wanted to stop the fantasy flooding through her mind as she rubbed herself furiously—but she was helpless to do so. She was helpless to stop the exciting imagery of Candace Aldridge placing her in that extreme bondage, leaving her there to suffer. She pictured Bunny locking her into the restraints, bending her forward over a padded bar, locking her ankles and wrists together so that her legs were forced open by...what? Some sort of wooden bar, forcing her knees apart and making her keep her thighs parted wide, open, helpless, wet and ready.... Suzette imagined Bunny fitting her throat into the wooden stock, padlocking it shut...even gagging her, forcing a rubber gag into her mouth and locking it in, so she couldn't even cry for help....

And *then* what would Mrs. Aldridge do to her?

Suzette was so turned on she felt like she was going to explode any second. She rubbed herself in perfect rhythm, almost ready to come—but she held back, not letting herself hurtle over the brink. She didn't want to come yet. The fantasy was too delicious. She couldn't believe she was having a sexual fantasy about this woman she wanted to work for—but then again, here it was, raging through her mind and her body—

She saw Bunny running her hand down the insides of Suzette's exposed thighs, teasing her...letting her hand come to rest on Suzette's exposed, willing pussy—

And then Suzette moaned, louder than she meant to, coming hard, coming wildly, gasping for air as her

THE OFFICE

orgasm thundered through her body. She collapsed, sweat-slick, amid the rumpled sheets of the bed, the image of Bunny Aldridge gently touching her pussy still burning through her mind.

Suzette's mind roved as her orgasm dwindled inside her. She couldn't get rid of the thought of Bunny Aldridge exploring her body with her hands. She was getting all turned on again just thinking about it. She imagined Bunny sliding her fingers into her pussy, teasing her open. God, that was hot. She thought about all the things Bunny had described, and she imagined herself going down on her knees before Mrs. Aldridge, with her wrists tied behind her back. Mrs. Aldridge spreading her legs, exposing what Suzette imagined to be creamy, inviting feminine thighs. Suzette lowering her face between them.

Nervously, breathing hard, Suzette felt her body responding. Felt herself getting excited again. Almost without knowing what she was doing, she rolled over, spreading her legs, lying down on her belly. She put her wrists together behind her back, mimicking the position of her body in the fantasy she was having. She didn't even know why she was thinking about this....

She imagined Mrs. Aldridge in front of her, dressed as she was at the interview, sitting in a big armchair—no, a throne. Suzette imagined herself standing there, with a bunch of other people watching her. Men and women both. All clothed.

Mrs. Aldridge owns me, she thought. *I am nothing but her possession. Her sexual toy.*

Suzette let the fantasy come to her. *Two of the women come up behind her and bind her wrists. Then Suzette walks up to Mrs. Aldridge, gets onto her knees before the throne.*

Mrs. Aldridge lifts her skirt to reveal that she isn't wearing anything underneath. Her pussy is beautiful, exposed, glistening with sexual excitement.

Suzette reached up quickly to grab her pillow and stuff it between her legs. She kept her wrists behind her, pretending they were bound. She moaned softly as she pressed her thighs together, clutching the pillow, forcing its softness against her clit. She sometimes came like that, and it was exciting her so much to have her wrists behind her, she didn't want to give it up.

Suzette, on her knees, lowers her face between Mrs. Aldridge's spread thighs. She begins to lick Mrs. Aldridge's pussy, the way she likes it done when a guy goes down on her. Giving sexual service. Pleasuring Mrs. Aldridge. Owned by her. Possessed by her.

Jerking up and down on the pillow, Suzette came, whimpering softly as she felt the orgasm go through her body. The fantasy dissolved as she finished coming. But she still had the image of the powerful and stately Mrs. Aldridge in her mind.

Why did she keep thinking about that? Why had

she fantasized about Mrs. Aldridge owning her? About being forced to service her orally in a room full of people? Suzette had never made love with another woman—well, she had made out a little bit with her roommate in college—though she did fantasize about them from time to time. What was going on?

Suzette lay there, her naked body washed in the rock music and the afterglow of her own desire. She was more than a little surprised at herself—her sexual fantasies didn't usually run so fast. She had indulged in fantasies about women before—more than a few—but she rarely felt a fantasy take hold of her like that and refuse to let go. She could almost feel the ghostly touch of Mrs. Aldridge's hand on her pussy, restrained in that complicated device…she could almost taste Mrs. Aldridge's pussy, as she knelt there, bound before Mrs. Aldridge's throne, pleasuring her orally.

Suzette shuddered as she remembered it. She was still incredibly worked up, almost ready for another go. But her clit was starting to ache already, so she just lay there for a while letting fantasies float in and out of her mind. Hot days like this always made her horny—there was something about all the sweat, and the smell of all the people on the street, and the knowledge that everyone was just gushing sweat down under their clothes.

Maybe that was some of it. Maybe it was just that her mind turned to whatever was in front of it to get her off. Suzette had certainly experienced that before, having spent more than a few boring classes in college fantasizing about doing her instructor even when she didn't find him—or her—at all attractive. Why, she had even been able to get off in class a few times, coming just from rubbing her thighs together and fantasizing about going up in front of the class, lifting her skirt, and fucking the professor in front of everyone. Professor Kramer, her economics teacher, had been a favorite, not because Suzette found him attractive—she didn't—but because his lecture style was so incredibly boring. Suzette had spent many classes being fucked from behind by Professor Kramer, up against the chalkboard while the rest of the class watched. Or on her knees, sucking his cock while he lectured. In her own mind, that is. She didn't always come—most of the time she didn't—but it did help to pass the time.

Suzette had also eroticized her anthropology teacher, Dr. Robson, whose boring lecture style rivaled even Professor Kramer's. She had enjoyed the fantasies about Dr. Robson even more, though—the doctor was a woman in her late thirties with a pretty face, long black hair, and an intriguing, attractive figure. Suzette had imagined being bound in front of the class and having Dr. Robson demonstrate certain points of sexual anthropology by exploring Suzette's body and showing the class the ways she responded to erotic stimulation.

Suzette had also fantasized about going down on Dr. Robson while she lectured. The more boring the lectures got, the more intense were Suzette's fantasies about the lecturer. It wasn't that she wanted to go to bed with either Kramer or Robson—far from it—but the fantasies helped to pass the time.

Why, then, was she fantasizing about Mrs. Aldridge now that she was alone on her bed?

She just lay there and let the question slip away as she enjoyed the feeling of her naked body, all slick with sweat and tense with arousal.

Chapter 2

The album came to an end just about the time Suzette wanted to get up.

She didn't feel like getting dressed—she rarely felt like getting dressed. She loved to lounge around the house naked, and if she had lived without a roommate she would probably have been naked by far most of the time. But Paul was probably still out there. Suzette wasn't about to put on the sweaty, filthy clothes she'd stripped out of. But she didn't want to get clean clothes dirty by putting them on her sweaty body. And the only robe she had was the little black silk thing she'd bought in Chinatown a few years ago. It wasn't really much of a robe—it didn't hide anything at all. *Fuck it*, thought Suzette. She was too tired and sweaty to worry about being immodest in front of Paul.

That was first on the list when she got a paycheck—a robe that wasn't so damned sexy.

Then again, Suzette really didn't mind if Paul *did* see her. She knew she shouldn't be showing off in front of Samantha's boyfriend, but it kind of intrigued her to know that Paul liked looking at her. Maybe it was exciting to her because it was totally safe—Suzette would *never* dream of coming on to her roommate's boyfriend, or even flirting with him very heavily. That would be totally uncool. And so she could take a little interest in the fact that Paul liked the way she looked, knowing that she never had to follow through with anything more than a casual glance.

Was she being a tease? Suzette didn't really know, nor did she really care that much. If Paul really minded, he would look away.

Suzette was sure Samantha didn't mind her tendency to let Paul get a glimpse of her here and there. After all, Samantha spent her working hours showing her body off to all sorts of men who, for all she knew, had girlfriends or wives. From what Samantha had said, sometimes she didn't just let them look—her lap dances were quite popular, and involved Samantha getting as close to the guy as it was possible.

The Office

So Suzette was sure Samantha didn't mind that she scoped out Samantha's boyfriend—as far as Samantha was concerned, just looking was fair game. Maybe even a little touching was okay. Suzette knew this wasn't even close to being the same thing—Samantha was doing a job, while Suzette was just being an exhibitionist, and a flirt. But the same rules applied—sort of.

Well, I can't help it, thought Suzette sadly. *I like flirting....*

Suzette put on the black robe and went into the living room. She was surprised—and maybe just a little disappointed—to find the apartment empty.

She glanced into Samantha's room and found it a mess as usual, underwear and fashion magazines strewn everywhere. Samantha was nowhere in sight. Paul must have left with Samantha, who had probably gone to work. The kitchen clock told Suzette it was just past seven, which meant Samantha was probably working the swing shift. Usually Samantha worked the shift from ten at night to six in the morning—the club where she danced was open twenty-four hours. But sometimes she was on from the evening—around six—until about 2:00 A.M. So Suzette knew that Samantha probably wouldn't be home until almost three in the morning—or maybe even later if it was a busy night. Sometimes she stuck around if the tips were good.

That meant that Suzette had the apartment to herself

for the evening, except for Samantha's cat, Tabby, who usually didn't get in the way too much. Knowing that she would be alone all night sent a tingle through her body. Suzette unbelted the little black robe and let it fall open, relishing the feeling of being revealed even though there was no one to see.

She opened her celebratory bottle of wine—four-dollar Cabernet Sauvignon, nothing special, but it still felt like a celebration—and poured herself a glass, clicking on MTV with the remote control.

She settled down on the couch and sipped her wine. As she watched, she absentmindedly eased the robe open further, tucking it behind her and lifting it so that her body was completely revealed—no need to be prudish since she was alone in the apartment. She finished her first glass of wine and poured another. It was beginning to give her a little bit of a rosy glow, and was almost making MTV interesting. Suzette was just getting interested in an Aerosmith video when the phone rang.

She muted the TV and picked up the phone.

"Hey, baby. What're you wearing?"

"Not much," Suzette said, slipping the robe off.

"Waiting for company?"

"Waiting for you. To come over here and pay me some attention."

There was a pause on the other end of the phone. "You're serious?"

"Oh, what the fuck, sure, come over. It's not too exciting over here, I'm just sitting around watching MTV."

"In your underwear?"

"My underwear? Not even," laughed Suzette good-naturedly, and hung up.

She shouldn't be so sarcastic with Rob—sometimes he took it the wrong way. But she just couldn't stop herself.

She shrugged the robe back on, then let it fall halfway off again, liking the way she looked stretched out like that on the couch with the robe opened around her breasts and invitingly rumpled down the slope of her belly. Suzette reached down and felt herself—she was still wet. Very wet, actually. She slipped one finger in and felt that she was getting wetter. Must be the Aerosmith video. Or maybe it was thinking about Rob coming over.

Suzette knew damn well that if Rob was coming over it meant he was going to fuck her. They almost never saw each other without at least one of them getting off. Usually they would fuck, but she loved to give Rob blowjobs, too—he had such a nice cock, and he responded so wonderfully when she sucked him off.

Rob was a friend of a friend from college that Suzette had gotten hooked up with after moving to the city. She had been dating him for a few months—"dating" was the polite term. She supposed that "fucking" was more like it, since neither of them ever had money to go out on a real date, and didn't really have much of a desire to do so anyway. Instead, their "dates" usually consisted of Rob's coming over to Suzette's apartment and fucking her several times before heading home. Or sometimes Suzette would go over to his place. Sometimes she just dropped by to give him a blowjob—she liked doing that, it seemed so cheap and sleazy.

It wasn't really a "relationship"—they were just fuck-buddies. Suzette didn't mind the arrangement much—the sex was very good, and it was nice to have a "boyfriend" when she needed one. But Rob and she had an agreement that they could see other people. Or maybe "fuck" other people would be the less polite, more accurate way to say it. She had picked up the clues that Rob still did it with an old girlfriend of his who lived in Santa Barbara. She had accidentally run across some Internet e-mail on Rob's computer that told her as much—and before Suzette knew what she was doing, she had read it—even though she hadn't exactly *meant* to find it, and she supposed she was invading his privacy. But however it happened, Suzette knew Rob was still fooling around with other women. She didn't mind that—she even kind of liked the fact that she was free to go out and play around if she felt like it. But then again, Suzette hadn't had any real opportunities since she moved to the city, which was what made her arrangement with Rob so convenient. It was nice to know that if she just lay around the apartment there was a pretty good chance that Rob would drop by and fuck her.

Is it bad to think like that? she wondered, vaguely pleased with herself. *Oh, who cares,* she decided, taking another drink of wine. *This is the nineties. I can be a selfish slut if I want to be.*

Suzette reached down to check herself again—yup, she was still wet, and getting wetter as she thought about Rob coming over. She found her hand lingering on the slightly-spread lips of her pussy.

Her thoughts wandered deliciously as she touched herself. She liked the fantasy she'd had on the elevator so much, it was hard to get it out of her mind—in spite of the guilt she felt about putting that guy in an uncomfortable spot. But she supposed she had gotten away with it, and she wouldn't do it again. What she did wasn't all that bad. She even found herself wondering if the guy on the elevator had enjoyed it.

And the fantasy of Mrs. Aldridge feeling her up while she was bound and gagged on her knees—a shudder went through Suzette's body. She shrugged the robe off again and began to stroke her wet pussy, feeling her pleasure mount. MTV was showing some hot video with lots of half-naked women and guys in leather, and Suzette focused on that, trying to let the elevator fantasy go. But the elevator kept popping up, making guest appearances between a guitar-stud's flexing pectorals or a bikini-clad, metal-bimbo's jiggling buttocks. Soon Suzette was thinking about herself being fucked by every guy in the elevator, one after another. This was getting ridiculous.

She was getting really turned on. Her nipples were hard and ached with arousal. She teased them, pinching them with her fingers while she rubbed her pussy with her other hand. It took a lot of willpower, but Suzette stopped rubbing herself—she wanted to save her come for Rob. She knew if she stopped now, she would be so horny when Rob came over that she would hardly be able to control herself, and she'd be a raving sex maniac for him. That was just the way she wanted it.

With some difficulty, Suzette took her hand away from her pussy. She still pinched and rubbed her nipples with her other hand—but she wasn't going to get off like this. Instead, she just lay there squirming and getting more and more worked up—when Rob walked in, he was going to have a horny slut on his hands.

Finally, when the sexy video faded into a commercial, Suzette got off the couch and rushed into her room. She wanted to dress the part for Rob. He would like that.

She figured she still had time before Rob showed up—though she would have liked to have time for a shower, she was so sweaty and gross and everything.

No, it was better this way. It was better to be soaked in sweat and grime, the way she had been on the elevator. There was something sleazy about it, and Suzette kind of liked that.

She rummaged through her closet until she found what she was looking for—the tiny crepe miniskirt she had worn for Halloween a few years ago. The one she had been wearing in her fantasy. Suzette slipped it on, noting that she'd gained a pound or two since then. The miniskirt fit incredibly snug now, which didn't horrify Suzette as much as she expected it to. Rather, she liked the snug fit, feeling the tightness of the skirt, even tighter than when she'd worn it before. Her panty lines would be quite visible under the thin, tight skirt, so she would have to wear a thong—something with no fabric to cover her ass, just a thin string going between her cheeks. No, wait—with this skirt she shouldn't wear anything at all underneath. Or maybe she needed something. But not panties. Her pussy would be exposed, wet and ready for Rob. God, that was hot. Suzette could hardly keep still, she wanted to get off already. She was *so* glad Rob was coming over.

Suzette slipped the skirt off and went in to Samantha's bedroom, naked. She was sure Samantha wouldn't mind if Suzette borrowed some things for just for a little while. And Samantha had so many cool sexy clothes—it came with her profession.

Suzette rummaged through Samantha's top drawer—she was a little surprised to see a stack of snapshots showing Samantha in lurid poses. It looked like they'd been taken at the club—but Samantha usually gave those photos away—"gave" them away for five bucks—to her customers. Maybe these were rejects or extras or something.

The provocative poses Samantha took in the photos made Suzette think about the catalogs in her valise, and she felt a tingle of excitement. Now that Rob was coming over, she wouldn't get a chance to look at the catalogs unless she wanted to look at them with Rob. God, that would be embarrassing. Then she'd have to tell him the whole fucking story. No way. Well, she could look at the catalogs before he arrived, if she looked at them right now. She told herself to wait, thinking how much better it would be to take some time to look through them. Besides, she wanted to be ready when Rob got there.

She found the black lace garter belt she was looking for—she'd seen Samantha wear it a number of times—and a fresh pair of black seamed stockings—she'd have to remember to buy Samantha a new pair, since she was probably going to ruin them with what she had in mind. Suzette was in such a rush, in fact, she almost ran one of the stockings tugging it over her sweaty, sticky leg—thank God she'd shaved for the interview. She managed to get the stocking on, and hooked the garters. Suzette stood and looked at herself in Samantha's big mirror, astonished at how rumpled and slutty she looked with the garter belt and her hair all messed up like that. And her skin glistened with sweat. Suzette sighed in pleasure—this was working perfectly. She went back into her own room and struggled into the tight little crepe skirt. It was so short it almost revealed the wispy hair that covered her pussy. It was decent by maybe one inch—maybe less.

Now for something to wear on top. A camisole? Too obvious, maybe too slutty.

No, thought Suzette. *Maybe not slutty enough.* She tiptoed back into Samantha's bedroom and quickly found the black lace bustier with the underwire that pushed her tits up so enticingly. Samantha said when she wore it she got great tips. The only problem was that Samantha was a full cup size smaller than Suzette, so it was kind of difficult getting the thing on, and once it was fastened Suzette's tits bulged and spilled out over the top. Well, that was okay. She wasn't going to be wearing it for long.

She found that lacy shawl thing that Samantha had, the one that didn't close in front. That worked perfectly to accent the revealing bustier. Next Suzette borrowed a pair of Samantha's heels—she was sure Samantha wouldn't mind, and it's not like she was going anyplace dressed like this. She tried the three-inch heels...no, no, not quite right—the four-inch heels worked perfectly.

Suzette looked herself over in the mirror in Samantha's room. *Not slutty enough,* she thought with frustration.

She went into the bathroom and teased her long brown hair, tousled it until it was a wild mop. Then she put on some lipstick and a little blush, and some eyeliner. When she was finished Suzette put on some more of each.

Maybe she was going overboard here. Maybe she should lighten up.

She decided she wasn't going overboard yet, and started putting more lipstick and eyeliner on, making herself look like a total slut. Before she knew what had happened, Suzette looked into the mirror and realized that this was *way* sluttier than she had expected to look. She looked really cheap. *God, maybe I did go overboard.*

There was a knock at the door. *Oh, shit. Well, too late now. Rob's getting a slut whether he wants one or not.*

Suzette quickly tiptoed to the door, unlocked it without opening it, then tiptoed down the hall, tottering in the four-inch heels. She went into the living room and leaned on the edge of the couch with her legs crossed and her back arched to show off her cleavage just right.

"Come in," she called.

Suzette should have known when she heard the familiar footsteps just what had gone wrong. But it took a minute for it to register, so she was still sitting there draped over the edge of the couch, with her best come-fuck-me look on her face, her thighs parted ever so slightly, her breasts thrust out with the arch of her back, when Samantha walked in carrying two bags of groceries.

Samantha's face brightened. "Suzette!" she exclaimed, both surprise and pleasure in her voice. "I see you've been expecting me!"

Suzette's face went blood-red instantly and her head began to swim. She didn't know what to do. She sat down on the couch and crossed her arms, trying to hide her slutty attire. Then, as Samantha stood there looking her over lasciviously, Suzette started to laugh.

"I'm sorry," said Suzette. "I thought you were Rob."

"I can see how you'd make that mistake," said Samantha. "I forgot my keys, that's why I knocked," said Samantha. "If I'd known you were undressing I would have baked a cake. You look good!"

Suzette laughed again, her wounded pride turning to hilarity. "Thanks," she said. "Coming from you, I guess it's a compliment."

"Oh, it is," said Samantha, munching on a celery stalk. "Let me look at you." Blushing horribly, Suzette stood there and let Samantha look her over. "Not bad, not bad. You've got the makings. That skirt is perfect. What are you wearing underneath it?"

"Um…your garter belt," said Suzette. "I hope you don't mind."

"No, not at all. I mean, are you wearing a thong or a G-string?"

"Nope," said Suzette a little nervously.

Samantha's eyes went wide and she smiled. "God, nothing at all? Wow, that's hot. Really? Nothing at all?" Suzette shook her head. "That's perfect. God, that's so sexy. Rob will love it. You really know how to dress the part. Does he know you're doing this?"

Suzette shook her head again.

"How sweet, a surprise! He's going to love it! Guys love this sort of thing. You look great—you make a perfect slut! Perfect!"

"Uh… thanks, I guess. Hope you don't mind that I borrowed some of your stuff."

"Oh, no, no, *mi casa es su casa,* as you know. The bustier's boned so I don't think you can stretch it out with those big tits of yours. Looks good on you. All spilling out like that. Very sexy. *Very* sexy."

"Uh…Rob should be here soon," said Suzette. "I thought you were already at work."

As if on cue, Rob knocked on the door, which Samantha had left open. "Anybody home?" said Rob. As he came down the hall, he caught sight of Suzette's outfit. His eyes were instantaneously the size of saucers.

"Wow," was all he said as he stared.

"Uh...I'm working the ten o'clock shift tonight, but I think I'll go in a little early," said Samantha. "I can put these away later, I never buy anything perishable. I'll leave you to your own private pleasures, okay? See ya..." Samantha hurried off to her bedroom, leaving a very embarrassed Suzette being gaped at by Rob.

"Wow," said Rob, dumbfounded. "You look *great*."

"Uh...thanks," said Suzette.

"How'd the job interview go?"

"Oh...you know."

Samantha got ready for work in record time while Rob and Suzette made awkward conversation in the living room. When Samantha shouted her quick, "Bye! I'm bringing my keys this time!" Rob looked Suzette up and down with his lust even more obvious than before.

"Wow, you look great," he said lamely.

He moved to embrace Suzette, and she was greatly relieved to be able to press her body up against his. His warmth felt good—he was just wearing jeans and a T-shirt, and he had been sweating as much as Suzette. Well, maybe not *quite* as much as she. Rob pressed his lips to hers, and she parted her lips, feeling his tongue sink into her.

She had lost some of the excitement when Samantha had showed up, but it quickly returned. She rubbed up against Rob, feeling her nipples harden in the bustier until they almost popped out. She let Rob kiss her a long time, savoring the feel of his tongue inside her, as she let her arms snake around him and her hands come to rest on his tight ass. Rob had a great body, and never failed to turn Suzette on. She felt Rob already starting to get hard in his jeans, and she hugged him tightly until she could feel his hard-on against her belly. She reached down and began to stroke his cock, flattered and excited to feel how hard he was.

"You weren't kidding when you said you weren't wearing much," said Rob.

"I was wearing a lot less," said Suzette. "I put this on after you called."

"Aw...just for me? I'm touched."

"Just for you," said Suzette, a hint of sarcasm in her voice. Her hand on Rob's hard cock, she quickly lowered herself to her knees. Rob let out a hungry groan as Suzette pressed her mouth to the bulge in his sweaty jeans. She massaged his cock through the thick material, working on his belt with her hand while she stroked his ass with the other. God, she wanted to taste him. She got his pants open and took a long time stroking his cock through the sweat-soaked jockeys. Then she tugged the waistband down, pushing his jeans over his ass and bringing them down to his knees while she took hold of his cock and guided the head between her parted lips. She slipped it into her mouth, then began to caress the sensitive underside with her tongue. She whimpered as she swallowed him, sliding his shaft into her mouth until the head pressed against the entrance to her throat. Holding her breath, Suzette swallowed it down, pressing his cock into her throat neatly until her lips clamped around the base of his hard shaft. Rob moaned, running his hands through Suzette's messy hair. She reached between his legs and gently stroked his balls, teasing them with her fingernails. She remembered the sound of Mrs. Aldridge saying that phrase, meant to be shocking—"cock-and-ball torture." Suzette circled Rob's balls with her thumb and forefinger, firmly holding them and tugging them down while she held his shaft deep in her throat.

"Oh…oh, God…," gasped Rob suddenly, obviously pleased with the new sensation. "Oh, God…yes…"

Suzette needed to come up for air. She slid his cock out of her mouth, taking a deep breath when she had her lips around the head. Rob's hard shaft was glistening with her spittle and slicked with her lipstick, the slutty shade she'd put on for her little role-play. Something about that turned her on—smearing lipstick on his dick. She rubbed his cock against her face, stroking the spit-slick shaft over her cheeks, not caring that she was smearing her lipstick and blush. Then she swallowed again, tasting the bitterness of the lipstick, taking him down all the way while she pulled harder on his balls, encompassing them with her fingers, savoring the feel of having that much power.

"Oh...oh...God...," moaned Rob as Suzette pulled at his balls and lathed her tongue around his shaft. She was really getting wet; it was amazing how much this was turning her on. Part of her could imagine that this was the man in the elevator, that she was going down on a stranger, and that excited her incredibly. But part of her was just glad to be kneeling before Rob, on her knees and... servicing him. God, something made her so wet when she did that. Suzette had always loved giving head, but right now it was the most wonderful thing she'd ever done. She felt Rob's hands gently pressing on her head as he stroked her hair, and she half-wished he would grasp her more firmly, pull her hair, guide her head back and forth, like she was in bondage to him—just as she had been in bondage to Bunny Aldridge in her fantasy....

Suzette was on her knees, her legs slightly spread, and she didn't need her finger to tell her how wet she was getting under the crepe skirt. She was faced with the dilemma—remain on her knees and suck Rob off until he came in her mouth, or get him to fuck her? Rob was quickly making the decision for her, rocking his hips back and forth as she sucked him. All right, then. Rob was going to come in her mouth. God, she loved that. Suzette eagerly worked his cock in and out of her mouth, not deep-throating any more, just focusing on the sensitive part around the head of his cock, her fingers closed around the shaft as she gave the best blowjob of her life. But as she felt Rob tensing, knew he was approaching orgasm, Suzette slowed, came to a halt, just held him there against her face, her warm breath ruffling his pubic hair, not wanting him to come yet. She wanted to make it last. She wanted to make him wait. She wanted to take her time sucking his cock, to enjoy every minute he had to give. Suzette held his balls tightly and began to squeeze gently.

"Oh…oh, God…."

When Suzette felt that he'd cooled down a little, she took his cock back into her mouth and swallowed it all the way down. Rob's moans grew in volume; he seemed a little unsteady on his feet, so Suzette pushed him back toward the couch, letting him sit down without once letting his cock leave her mouth. Now he was in a better position, Suzette had better leverage to get his cock down her throat, and she could better enjoy the feel of his hard prick in her mouth. The only real disadvantage of having Rob on the couch was that she couldn't really get to his balls—but there would be plenty of time for that later. "Cock-and-ball torture." She remembered the way Mrs. Aldridge had formed the words, as if she expected it to shock Suzette. The memory sent a surge of lust through Suzette's body.

Suzette gulped him down rhythmically until she felt

him nearing again, then she took a long time teasing him by barely touching him at all, just letting the very tip of her tongue laze along the underside of his shaft. Rob's cock was rockhard, ready to burst, and Suzette loved the feel of knowing she could now make him come in her mouth any time she wanted to. But she wasn't ready to taste his come—not quite yet. She waited until Rob had cooled down again. Then she tugged down the bustier until first one breast, then the other, popped free. She tucked it down around her rib cage, then rubbed Rob's spit-slick cock over the swell of her breasts, smearing lipstick over her pale mounds. She pressed her tits together and slid his cock between them, rapturously listening to Rob moan—she knew how he loved that. She slid his cock back and forth between her breasts, savoring the feel of his shaft when it brushed against her hard nipples. She teased him like this until she was quite sure that he wasn't going to shoot off soon. Then Suzette took him into her mouth again, using her tongue roughly over the underside of his head—then swallowing it all the way, opening her throat for him. Rob's hips pressed up, his back arching as his fingers gripped her hair. *Oh yes,* she found herself thinking. *Hold me harder....*

Then she was rubbing his cockhead over her lips and face, pumping his shaft with her hand. She took him halfway into her mouth, feeling the swell of his cockhead, and she almost had him at the edge before she realized the time had come. She didn't hold Rob back this time, but pumped his cock with her hand and clamped her lips around the upper part of his shaft, eagerly awaiting the first thick, sharp stream of his come. Then it came, the muscles of Rob's cock spasming and spurting out his fluid.

Suzette rode him eagerly, swallowing the first stream easily and then letting her mouth fill with several more before opening her mouth to let those drizzle over his cock and her hand. Rob's semen dribbled out over her lips, and as he spurted again and again, she clamped her lips shut and swallowed the next mouthful. Then she let the remainder escape around her lips, slicking Rob's hard prick, and Suzette rubbed it over her lips and hands as Rob caressed her hair gently. She was dripping sweat, and dripping in other places too, desperately eager to get fucked. But she knew Rob wouldn't be ready to fuck her for a while—maybe not even tonight. She didn't regret having brought him off in her mouth—in fact, she had loved giving him this blowjob almost more than any she'd ever given—but she couldn't help but pout mentally at the fact that there wasn't a hard cock to fuck her, after she'd gone to all the trouble to struggle into this little skirt without underwear, and totter around on these fuck-me heels all night. What she needed, Suzette found herself thinking, was another guy…so she could enjoy both a sumptuous appetizer and a long, hot main course. She was a little scandalized, but the image of another guy entering her from behind while she knelt before Rob's cock, giving him head, was enough to make her go crazy with sexual hunger.

Rob was spent, utterly exhausted. He sprawled on the couch as Suzette licked him over, cleaning his cock of his savory come. When she'd gotten as much as she could of it, and her face was slick with the stuff, she quickly tottered into the kitchen for a few paper towels, then returned to her knees before Rob to finish the clean-up job. She pulled the bustier, which had gotten a little uncomfortable around her rib cage, back on. She rested there with her head in his lap while he whispered a heartfelt, "Thank you," and Suzette answered with one of her own.

As it turned out, Rob's hard-on returned faster than he or Suzette would have expected. With her head in his lap, and her hand absently caressing his soft cock, she felt him swelling and growing in her hand. She felt a rush of excitement; there was very little she liked as much as feeling a guy get hard in her hand. Feeling his cock go from soft to hard made her think about how much he wanted her, which seemed flattering and incredibly sexy.

Suzette licked the head of Rob's cock just long

enough to get him fully hard. Then she looked up at him, her eyes full with hunger. She glanced around the room; the dining table would do nicely. She stood up and quickly walked over, leaning against the dining table, her legs slightly spread, her ass swaying back and forth in the tight black skirt.

Rob got the idea quickly; he got up and quickly took off his clothes, then snuggled up behind Suzette naked, his hard cock pressing against her ass through the tight skirt.

*Just like the guy on the elevator pressed against me...*she thought, trying to banish the image. But it was too powerful; she felt her arousal surging as she remembered how wet she'd gotten. Then Rob was pulling up her skirt, letting out a sigh of surprise and delight when he saw she wasn't wearing any underwear. Suzette leaned more fully on the table—which was a sturdy, fifties-retro kind of thing, and had been used for this purpose more than once before. She felt Rob kneeling down behind her, pressing his face between her legs as he pulled the tight crepe skirt up over her waist. She moaned loudly as she felt Rob's tongue snuggling between her lips, teasing out her clitoris. Her nipples stiffened against the table, and she pulled down the bustier so she could feel their hardness pressing against the cold linoleum. Rob's tongue slipped into Suzette's entrance, bringing a gasp of pleasure; then he started focusing on her clit, suckling as she got closer and closer. Rob was better at this than almost any guy she had been with. He teased her clit, then began suckling it rhythmically, knowing that that was exactly what could make her come like a rocket. Suzette felt two of Rob's fingers sliding into her pussy, feeling how wet she was—she was wetter than ever, and ready to be fucked. But Rob teased her, making her wait, suckling her clit while he finger-fucked her slowly.

"Fuck me," moaned Suzette softly. "I want you inside me."

Rob slowly stood up, still working his fingers in and out of Suzette's cunt. He used his free hand to tease her clit, listening to the sound of her moans growing louder and louder as she approached her climax. Then he was pressing up behind her, guiding the head of his cock between her open, waiting lips, so that the head pressed into her entrance. She moaned as she felt him penetrating her slowly, pressing in until the thick head of his cock slipped into her, filling her pussy. Rob was more than a little over-endowed, more thick than long, and when they'd first started to sleep together it had taken Suzette a while to get accustomed to his size. But now she relished it, enjoying the feeling of being filled up with his thickness.

She was incredibly wet, and her pussy opened up for him as he entered her. Rob slid into her easily, pushing until his cock was all the way inside her. Suzette snuggled her ass back against him, loving the feel of his hot, sweaty body against her, fucking her from behind. She tottered on the edge of her orgasm. Then Rob began thrusting, slowly at first, but picking up speed as she clawed at the table. Suzette pushed her body back against him to take every thrust. She was whimpering helplessly, lost in her own pleasure, enjoying the knowledge that she was being taken from behind—and the image of the man on the elevator doing it. But it was Rob who was fucking her, and she was glad to have the comfortable curve of his cock inside her, sliding into her rhythmically as she pushed herself back against him.

Then Suzette felt her climax nearing, her pleasure mounting as she whimpered "Oh, God…oh, God…." She leaned heavily on the table, letting Rob do all the work as she rode the ecstasy of her approaching orgasm. She came as Rob pumped into her, his hands firmly holding her ass steady to give his thrusts better leverage. Suzette's body exploded in ecstasy as she relaxed into the feeling of being fucked, of giving herself over to Rob's control. She imagined Bunny Aldridge's hand on her pussy again, and Suzette's orgasm mounted out of control, filling her body so that she thrashed back and forth violently. As she finished coming she began to snuggle back against Rob, pushing him slightly away from her, giving her the chance to thrust back against him. Rob got the idea, and stood firm as Suzette began to move.

It wasn't easy in this position, but Suzette loved to push her body back against Rob's while he was inside her, and do the fucking. It gave her such a thrill to bring him off, to know that her motion was making him come—almost like it was when she got him off with her mouth or her hand. She began to thrust herself back onto him, pushing his cock into her, pumping as fast as she could as she listened to Rob groaning. Then she heard his moans changing, and she knew he was going to come soon. She pushed herself up and down on him, trying to keep the rhythm—but then she realized what she really wanted, and she pushed herself forward, taking Rob out of her body, reaching back to hold his cock in her hand while she expertly jerked him off. Then Rob was gasping, his cock spasming as streams of his semen shot out over Suzette's bare buttocks, the warm jets splashing over her pussy and drizzling down her thighs. The feel of the warm fluid on her flesh was exquisitely erotic, and Suzette pushed herself back against Rob's hard cock when she was sure she'd milked every last drop of come out of him. She pushed him back inside her and leaned forward so she could snuggle against him, feeling his cock slowly go soft inside her. Rob was panting, dripping sweat, utterly spent.

After a few minutes, Rob's softening prick slipped out

of her, and they embraced each other and kissed gently. Then Suzette stripped off her clothes—shit, she'd ruined the stockings with that last little stunt, and she'd have to wash Samantha's garter belt and take the crepe skirt to the cleaners. She toyed with the idea of taking a shower—but it seemed so much more erotic to let the sweat and the semen dry on her body, while she and Rob made out and cuddled on the bed. By the time he'd dropped off to sleep, Suzette realized they'd forgotten all about dinner, and she was getting kind of hungry. But before she could do anything about it, she fell asleep herself, at a more reasonable hour than she was used to.

Even as she started to drift off into sleep, though, Suzette thought about the catalogs in her valise. God, just *having* them there had brought her the hottest sex she'd had in weeks. She couldn't imagine what actually *reading* them would do. She thought about slipping out of bed and taking a look at them in the bathroom—but that seemed so undignified. So she let herself float off into sleep, feeling Rob's warm body pressing against her, wondering if her dreams were going to be more interesting now that she'd had all this unusual stimulus.

Chapter 3

Suzette woke up when Samantha came in from work. Samantha always made a lot of noise coming home from work—it didn't really bother Suzette that much, but it was one of those annoying things. Tabby, Samantha's orange cat who had recently taken to sleeping on Suzette's bed, meowed plaintively until Suzette reached out and scratched her behind the ears. Suzette looked up at the clock and saw that it was about six. Rob was still curled up next to her. They had left the bedroom door open when they went to bed, and she caught a glimpse of Samantha as she stripped off her clothes and walked half-naked down the hall to the bathroom. Suzette saw her again, naked and carrying her clothes in a ball. Then Samantha went back down the hall and Suzette heard the shower running. Samantha always showered when she came back from work.

Suzette was still sleepy, but she knew she couldn't get back to sleep now. She had already started thinking about last night, and about the job interview yesterday, and whether she was going to get the job. She spotted her valise on the floor next to the bed, and remembered the catalogs in there. She felt her body responding immediately to the thought of those dirty catalogs with all their outrageous photos.

God, now she'd *never* get back to sleep. Rob was still curled up behind Suzette, his warm body pressed against her. She could feel his strong arms around her and his hands resting on her breasts. She felt her nipples stiffening against Rob's fingers as she thought about the catalogs. Well, if she wasn't going to get to sleep, she might as well enjoy herself....

It took some doing, but Suzette managed to lean over and get the valise and push the door shut. It didn't click, but it closed enough (she didn't want Samantha finding out about the catalogs, now did she? What would she think? Suzette knew that Samantha would probably be less than scandalized...but Suzette was still a little shy about it). To get the door closed, Suzette had had to ease Rob's hands off her breasts—something she wasn't entirely happy about, they felt good there. But as she settled back against him, she felt his hands returning naturally to their places on her tits.

She froze, remaining perfectly still as she waited to see if Rob was waking up. She didn't want him to get the wrong idea—or maybe she did. Well, in any event, she didn't want to share the catalogs with him yet. She wanted to look at them herself.

Rob's breathing didn't change, so Suzette figured he was still asleep.

She looked at the catalog. *Bondage Creations*. The cover had a woman in a black leather outfit, holding a whip. There was a man, fully dressed, on his knees in front of her. Just seeing the picture made Suzette's temperature rise. She opened the catalog and began to look through.

Mrs. Aldridge had certainly been right. There were all the things she had mentioned and more. Bondage. Discipline. Women in every conceivable posture of submission—to men, and to other women. Men in submission, too. At first Suzette couldn't decide which she liked better. It turned her on to see the women in submission, but it gave her a kind of drunk power to look at the men on their knees. After a few pages, she decided she liked the women in submission the best. She realized she was putting herself in their position, thinking about what it would feel like to be restrained like that. There were also things like clips that went on a woman's nipples—that made her own nipples stiffen against Rob's hand. She wondered if he was going to wake up, but she didn't really care that much anymore. Suzette kept turning the pages, seeing a wide variety of bondage equipment and implements of punishment. They all had prices next to them. She noted with disappointment that the prices were all much more than she would be able to afford any time soon. What had put that thought in her head? She wondered if she would really want to buy some of this stuff, play with it... maybe have Rob tie her up while he fucked her. *God, just the idea is making me wet,* she thought. She snuggled her bare ass back against Rob's body, feeling his soft cock on her flesh. She wriggled her ass a little so that her buttocks rubbed his softness. She wondered if he would want to fuck her when he woke up. Suzette turned her attention back to the catalog.

"Oh, God," she heard herself saying softly as she turned the page and saw women on their hands and knees, wearing black leather bits—like horse bits—and saddles on their backs. A surge of arousal seemed to pour right into Suzette's cunt. She could feel herself moistening as she thought about it.

The next few pages had a wide assortment of dildos that strapped onto a woman's body like a dick—so that she could fuck another woman, or fuck a man up the ass.

The Office

She had heard about things like this, but had never seen pictures. Suzette's eyes went wide as she looked over the pictures, getting more and more turned on as her mind roved over the possibilities of such devices. First, she thought about what it must feel like to have one of those things on, pushing your cock into another woman's body like you were a guy with a big hard-on—except the hard-on could be as big or as small as you wanted. She wanted a big one. Then she thought about what it must be like to wear one of those and fuck a *guy*.

She imagined herself mounting Rob, slathering a strapped-on dildo with lube and pushing it inside him, pumping her hips, fucking him rough as she rode him. Suzette wondered if he would ever want to do that. She didn't think so—but then again, that one time she'd touched his ass when she was giving him head, it had made him shoot off just like that. Right in her mouth, as she just barely touched his asshole with the tip of her finger. Suzette wondered what he would do if she showed up with a strap-on like that and told him she was going to fuck him in the ass with it. She thought he might freak out...but the idea excited her. Maybe she would fuck him even if he *did* freak out. Hold him down and fuck him forcibly. Of course, she would never, *ever* do that, or even think about doing it in reality...but the idea got her so wet she could hardly sit still. Her ass wiggled back and forth against Rob's body, and she wondered again if he was going to want to fuck her when he woke up.

Then she thought about what it would be like for her to be fucked by a woman wearing that. *God,* she thought. *That would be so fucking sexy.* Would it feel that much different from being fucked by a guy? Suzette felt quite sure it would—you would have a woman's body against you, with a woman's energy, not a man's. Suzette thought about both options and started to get even more turned on.

Almost without knowing what she was doing, Suzette reached back and felt Rob's soft cock. She began to touch it, gently stroking it, while she looked at the catalog. She turned the page and heard herself moaning softly in surprise and arousal. These pages showed women and men in cages, like the kind you would see in a kennel or zoo. She was shocked at herself, but the idea of being locked up in a little tiny cage—locked up, and collared like an animal—was more than she could handle. Her arousal consumed her, and she simply lost control of her lust.

The catalog fell onto the floor, and Suzette pressed her ass back against Rob, stroking his cock against her thighs as she felt it getting harder.

She turned her head and kissed Rob deeply as he awoke. She didn't turn around—she wanted him to fuck her from behind. Suzette gently massaged Rob's prick until she felt him stirring, felt that he was hard all the way. She snuggled her body against him and spreading her legs just enough so she could get his cock in between them. She guided the head of his prick to her entrance, and began to work him up and down in her slit, slicking him with her juices, teasing her clit with his cock, all the while kissing him. The pressure of his cock against her pussy was so intense that she could already feel herself mounting toward orgasm. She was incredibly wet, her slit lubricated and slippery with her excitement. She held Rob's cockhead right at the opening of her pussy, savoring the feeling of impending penetration.

Rob was awake now, eagerly kissing Suzette and pinching her nipples as he pressed against her. Her hand cupped her pussy, holding his cock in just the right position to enter her. Rob eased his hips forward, and Suzette felt his cockhead penetrating her tight channel. She let out a wild moan of pleasure and squirmed against Rob as he sank his shaft into her from behind. Still playing with her tits, and holding her close, Rob began to fuck her.

Suzette's head reeled with the intense sensations exploding through her body. She pressed back against Rob, loving the way his warm body felt against her back, adoring how his shaft jutted into her. Rob moved one hand down to her hip so he could hold her steady while he fucked her. Keeping perfect time to match the mounting tension of Suzette's own excitement, Rob began to thrust into her rhythmically. She moaned as the pace increased.

She still had her hand down between her legs, cupping her pussy so she could feel Rob's shaft thrusting into her. It turned her on immeasurably to be able to feel the slickness of his shaft as it slid out of her, then back in, every second bringing a new, powerful thrust into her. With her other hand, Suzette was furiously working her clit, getting ready to bring herself off.

"God...," she moaned. "This is so good...you fuck me so good...so hard..."

Suzette's right hand picked up speed, turning to a blur between her legs as she stroked Rob's thrusting cock with her left hand. Her naked body began to shudder in ecstasy, and she gave in to her orgasm, letting it flood through her naked, helpless body as Rob pounded into her from behind. Her orgasm heightened as she pressed her fingers more firmly around Rob's cock, better to feel its slickness as it thrust mercilessly into her. Soon her entire body spasmed, her climax sending waves of ecstasy through her. As her orgasm shuddered away, draining out of her, she relaxed, limp, against Rob, letting him fuck her at his own pace, knowing that it wouldn't be long before she felt the warmth of his come inside her.

Suzette's eyes fluttered open and she realized with horror that the door to the bedroom was still open a crack. *Oh, God,* she thought, *Tabby must have pushed it open. Oh, God!* Her mouth dropped open and her moans stopped for a moment as she saw that a very naked Samantha was standing there just past the crack of the door, the wet towel around her body having long since sagged, revealing her full, ripe breasts, and parted in front, revealing her pubic thatch. Samantha seemed to be hypnotized, her eyes wide and her lips parted as she breathed heavily, watching Suzette get fucked. Suzette was mortified, but she was so overcome with her own pleasure that she couldn't stop moaning even as she locked eyes with Samantha. Amazingly, Samantha didn't turn and run away—not at first. Instead, she just stared at Suzette, their eyes holding each other as Suzette felt Rob pistoning faster and faster into her. Something about the look in Samantha's eyes sent a new surge of excitement through Suzette's body, and she was shocked to find herself mounting toward orgasm again. *God,* she thought, *I can't be doing this. Not right in front of my roommate like this....*

Then Suzette was moaning louder, leaning her body forward so she could get better leverage to hump her ass back against Rob and take his thrusts with newfound energy. The rapid thrusts into her cunt felt so incredible, fueled as they were by the knowledge that Samantha was watching—and that Samantha knew that Suzette had seen her. Suzette felt her second climax rising inside her, and she looked up at Samantha to see her still staring, her face flushed with excitement. The towel had fallen to the floor, and Samantha's naked body was revealed to Suzette. The sight of it excited her as never before—Suzette and Samantha had seen each other naked before, but never like *this!* The sight of Samantha's breasts rising and falling as she panted hungrily was enough to bring Suzette to the very brink, and she stared, helpless to stop herself, at Samantha, as her climax welled up inside her and got ready to burst. As Suzette rode on the brink of her second come of the morning, Rob threw his head back and moaned, his thrusts turning to great shuddering heaves as he stroked his cock into her. The feel of Rob's cock spasming inside her cunt, spurting, filling her with his warm seed, was enough to send Suzette over the edge, and she moaned wildly as her whole body was taken over by the pleasure. She snuggled back against Rob, letting him finish off inside her as the delicious sensations of her climax echoed inside her body. She looked up, suddenly horrified at herself, and saw that Samantha had disappeared from the doorway.

Oh, God, thought Suzette. *What have I done now?* Rob was trying to snuggle with her, stroking her breasts, but she felt suddenly dirty and ashamed of what she was doing. But the knowledge that Samantha had watched—and the sight of Samantha, naked, obviously enjoying the show before her—had made Suzette so hot that she'd gotten off just like *that.* She couldn't deny how much it had turned her on. She had never thought of

The Office

Samantha in that way—sure, she'd noticed what a great body Samantha had, and she'd noticed how pretty she was, who wouldn't? But, God, she'd never thought of her like *that.* She'd never wanted to go to bed with her—well, maybe the thought had occurred to her a few times....

Suzette blushed red with embarrassment as she thought about what Samantha must think. Then Suzette started to come to her senses. Samantha was a dancer. She took her clothes off for money, in front of rooms full of horny guys who were getting off at the things she was doing. Surely she wouldn't be too horrified at what had happened —after all, hadn't Samantha stood there watching?

Another horrifying thought occurred to Suzette. Did Samantha think that Suzette had left the bedroom door ajar on purpose? That she had *wanted* Samantha to watch? Maybe even that it was...an invitation?

Suzette's horror almost immediately gave way to excitement. *God, that would be so hot.* Suzette tried to stop herself but she just couldn't. She was thinking about how great it would be to get in bed with Samantha and a guy. Rob, for instance. Maybe even Paul. *God, that would be incredible.* She felt her face flushing hot, felt her arousal rising, hitting her hard, filling her body with waves of lust. *God, not again,* she thought as she pressed back against Rob. Her mind raced over the possibility of Samantha climbing into bed with them and holding her as Rob drove into her pussy from behind.

Suzette thought about kissing Samantha. The idea made her incredibly hot. She felt Rob snuggling against her, and she knew her pussy was getting wetter—she didn't have to check.

Rob would surely want to have both of them at once—it was every man's fantasy, wasn't it? She had no question about whether Rob would want to fuck Samantha—did that make her feel jealous? Much the opposite—the thought of her lying there while Rob mounted Samantha and the two of them fucked like weasels made Suzette so hot that, almost without knowing what she was doing, she reached down and began touching her pussy.

Suzette could feel Rob's warm semen leaking out of her pussy, slicking up her lips and drizzling down her inner thighs. The feel of it excited her. She slid one finger into her cunt and was amazed at how good it felt. She began to stroke herself as Rob pressed up behind her.

God, I wish he would get hard again so he could fuck me, she was thinking. Suzette whimpered as she rolled over so she could embrace Rob as she rubbed herself. Rob began to kiss her hungrily, obviously intrigued by the sight and feel of her jerking herself off. Suzette moaned as she rubbed her body up against Rob's, her hard nipples stroking the soft hair on his chest. She rubbed herself harder, concentrating on her clit but then, every few seconds, sliding her hand down to press two fingers into her cunt. Rob got the idea and reached down with his hand, pushing two fingers into Suzette as she rubbed her clit. She was so hot she felt like she was going to burst, and within a few minutes she was slick with sweat again, panting and writhing as Rob finger-fucked her. She squirmed against his body, getting closer and closer to an intense orgasm—and then she whimpered as she came, the pleasure exploding through her naked body until she almost felt pain. "Oh, God...it's so good...," she moaned as Rob continued finger-fucking her. She lay there on her back with her legs spread and let him slide his fingers in and out for a few minutes until she was utterly and totally exhausted. As Rob finished, she leaned up and kissed him tenderly.

Then she was struck again by what she'd just done. Suzette knew from experience that Samantha could hear what was going on in here—and with all the noise Suzette had just made, she had just added to her own embarrassment. And to think that she'd gotten off from thinking about having a three-way with Samantha! She was surprised at herself. She had to go in there and apologize.

"I've got to take care of something," said Suzette as she climbed out of bed. Rob watched after her, his eyes plainly full of lust. She slipped into the little black robe—the one that hid nothing—and tied it in front, holding it shut because if she didn't it hung mostly open and revealed just about all of her cleavage and, sometimes, depending on how she moved, her breasts.

She went to Samantha's room. Samantha had closed the door. Suzette hoped she wasn't asleep. No, of course Samantha wasn't asleep. After all that noise that Suzette had just made?

Suzette knocked.

There was a long pause.

"Yes?" said Samantha. "Come in."

Suzette went through the door and closed it behind her. Samantha was in bed, lying under a single sheet which was pulled up to her neck. Suzette could see from the way the sheet clung to Samantha's body that she wasn't wearing anything underneath.

"Hi," said Suzette, pulling the robe closed self-consciously. "I just wanted to apologize. I didn't know the door was open—the cat…"

"No need to apologize," said Samantha, a little nervously. "I'm just embarrassed that I stood there watching you. I'm really sorry about that."

Suzette sat down on the edge of the bed. "Why are you sorry for that? I'm the one who let the door open…"

Samantha frowned. "Well…I'm the one who stood there watching you…even kind of…getting off on it."

"Really?" Suzette was surprised and a little flattered.

"God! Oh, God, yes," said Samantha. "You two looked like you were having a good time. I mean, I take off my clothes in public for a living, but you two were hotter than *anything* I've ever seen on stage, or on a video."

"Wow...thanks."

"I'm just sorry if I invaded your privacy."

"No...no, don't worry about it," said Suzette. "I don't think Rob even noticed."

"Oh, he noticed," said Samantha, blushing. Suzette was surprised that Samantha could blush so easily. "When you had your eyes closed, he glanced over and saw me. That's what made me leave...I kind of figured you wouldn't mind, but I don't know about him."

"Oh, no," murmured Suzette, horrified. Rob had been in on the whole thing. Now what did *he* think? She decided not to ask him. God, this was embarrassing.

"OK...well...sorry. I'll keep the door closed from now on."

"Oh...well...leave it open if you want," said Samantha, with more than a hint of mischief in her voice. "It won't bother me." Suzette nervously got up, wondering just what Samantha was trying to say.

Suzette felt her own nipples stiffening under the thin black robe.

"Okay," Suzette blurted, as she tiptoed back out into the hallway and closed the door behind her.

When Suzette went back into her bedroom, Rob was propped up on a couple of pillows, reading the catalog.

Suzette's eyes went wide in horror—she had forgotten about that.

"This stuff is great," said Rob breathlessly. "I had no idea you were into this stuff."

Suzette's face reddened as she climbed back onto the bed. "It's a job," she said uncomfortably. "The job interview I had yesterday."

"Was at *this* place?" said Rob incredulously. "The place that makes this stuff?"

"No, just the catalog," said Suzette nervously. "I don't know who makes it."

"Wow," said Rob, looking wide-eyed at the pictures. "I hope they have an employee discount. I had no idea you were into this stuff."

"I'm not!" said Suzette quickly, and Rob gave her a disappointed look.

"I mean...not yet," she said, trying to figure out exactly what she meant. "I've never tried it. Not really. I mean, I think it's kind of sexy..."

"You got that right," said Rob, staring at a picture of a lithe young woman bent over in a pillory. He shifted his body slightly, and Suzette saw that under the thin sheet his cock was rockhard. Despite her embarrassment, she felt a surge of hunger go through her at the sight of Rob's ready hard-on.

"I see it's having the desired effect," she said, her voice dripping sarcasm. She reached out and slipped her hand under the sheet, wrapping her fingers around the shaft of Rob's cock. It was as hard as ever, though still slick with the juices of Suzette's cunt and with Rob's come.

Suzette swept the sheet away and bent forward, rolling onto her stomach as she neared Rob's crotch. She parted her lips and took the head of his cock into her mouth, swirling her tongue around the sensitive underside. Rob moaned softly but didn't put the catalog down. He flipped through the pages as she began to suck him.

Suzette tasted the sharp tang of her own pussy as well as the underlying flavor of Rob's come. That flavor just made her want to taste more of him, to swallow a mouthful of his delicious juice. She opened wide and downed Rob's cock. Her fingers wrapped around his balls as she deep-throated him. Her lips came to rest around the base of his prick, and she held it there, her mouth filled with the taste of their sex. She loved to give head right after she'd been fucked—there was something unbelievably nasty about it, raunchy and dirty. It excited her to be able to taste her own cunt on a man's prick and to know that his come was inside her. She reached down and ran her hand up her inner thighs, feeling the rivulets of Rob's semen that were still running down her legs.

Suzette rubbed Rob's come over her thighs, savoring the sensations. Then she began to stroke her own pussy, loving the feel of the thick fluid leaking out of it. She eased back, off Rob's cock, panting heavily for lack of air. She wanted to suck him so bad she could just swallow him down and forget about breathing. She brought her lips up to his head and swirled her tongue around, kissing and sucking her way down Rob's cock and rubbing his slippery shaft all over her face.

The image from the catalog of a man about to be penetrated by a woman with a strap-on dildo suddenly formed in Suzette's mind. The idea excited her immensely. As she sucked Rob's cock, paying particular attention to the head, thinking about how it had penetrated her, how it would penetrate her again, Suzette let her hand slide down behind Rob's balls, feeling between his asscheeks, until her hand cupped the tightly-muscled curve of his ass, her middle finger slipping into his crack so that the tip just touched his tight, puckered asshole. Feeling that vulnerable spot of Rob's excited her that much more, and she took him into her mouth again, pushing his cock in until the head pressed against the back of her throat, then she opened her throat wide to accept his shaft and deep-throated him all the way. Rob moaned uncontrollably and the catalog fell from his hands onto the bed. Suzette savored the feeling of his cock thrust all the way into her, and toyed with the tightness of Rob's asshole, wondering what it would be like to penetrate him with a strap-on dildo.

Rob's shuddering moans grew louder as she gave

more attention to his asshole; he plainly approved of the new sensations.

Suzette felt incredibly excited by this new sexual game. She eased his cock back out of her mouth and slipped her finger between her lips, licking it and getting it all wet with her spittle. Then she gently slid it between Rob's cheeks again, feeling the tight hole. She began to tease and massage as she licked his cock from base to head, loving the feel of its hardness, knowing that she would take his come in her mouth before long. Suzette glanced up and saw that, much to her surprise, the catalog had fallen open on a page with several strap-on dildo scenes, in each case women about to penetrate men anally. She felt a surge of excitement go through her as she thought of what that must be like. Rob plainly liked the idea; he had almost gone crazy when he turned to that page. And the gentle explorations she was making between his asscheeks brought approving, hungry moans from Rob's lips. Part of that was the expert blowjob she was giving him—but some of it had to be the new, unexpected sensations she was bringing in her boyfriend's ass.

Suzette teased Rob's unyielding opening gently, feeling him tense and then relax as she stroked the finger in. She heard him moan, and the sound excited her so much that she took his cock in her mouth again, running her tongue all over the head, sucking hungrily.

She pressed her finger further into him, and Rob's back arched as his cock began to spasm. Suzette thrilled to the taste of his hot jism shooting into her mouth; she gulped it down and felt the second spurt filling her mouth; some of it dribbled out over her chin but she still managed to swallow most of the precious fluid. She kept sucking until Rob had ejaculated his last come into her mouth, and she whimpered in satisfaction as she licked his softening cock. She eased her finger out of his ass, feeling her own, almost painful, arousal.

"God," he said. "I've never had a chick do that to me. You're some kind of weirdo," he said good-naturedly.

Suzette thanked him and curled up on top of her boyfriend, licking her lips of the last remnants of his delicious come.

Rob had very flexible hours for his job as a computer consultant, so he took his time getting ready and Suzette made him breakfast. They even started to fool around as she fried up a couple of eggs, but she was too afraid Samantha would wake up and happen by—and after what she'd experienced this morning, that would have been one time too many. Besides, Rob was pretty sore from all that activity. So Rob had to content himself with an unobstructed view of Suzette's tits as she let the robe hang open.

Rob finished breakfast and left for work, still wearing

his grungy and sweaty clothes from last night. Suzette envied him—it must be nice to have a job where you can dress however you want. But then again, she wouldn't mind having a job where she got to dress up. She figured it would be a good skill for her to have in the corporate world.

She looked at herself in the bathroom mirror, horrified at what she saw. Her hair was a mess, and her makeup, piled on thick from last night, was smeared and horrendous. She decided to go ahead and take a shower, even though she didn't have anywhere to be today. After yesterday, and last night (and this morning) she felt unbelievably grimy.

She slipped off the black robe and hung it up, then stepped into the almost-too-hot shower and felt the soothing hot water embrace her.

As Suzette soaped up her naked body, she thought about all the weird stuff that had happened over the last day. She didn't really consider herself oversexed, but she certainly had always had a healthy sex drive. However, this was getting ridiculous—since that job interview yesterday, she hadn't been able to get sex off her mind. Was it the excitement of meeting a woman as powerful and commanding as Mrs. Aldridge, or was it just that the subject matter she would be working on—bondage—was enticing to her? Or maybe a little of both?

Or maybe I'm just becoming a hopeless slut, thought

Suzette as she rubbed her soapy hands over her breasts, feeling her nipples stiffen. *A hopeless, insatiable slut.*

There were certainly worse things to be.

Suzette heard the phone ringing. Shit, it might be someone returning one of her calls about a job. She left the water running and jumped out of the shower, dripping suds and water onto the carpet as she ran for the phone. She didn't make it, though—she heard the answering machine click on, heard the short outgoing message, and stood there listening.

"Hello, I'm calling for Ms. Suzette Sullivan. This is Mrs. Aldridge. Suzette, I would like to offer you the position at *Bondage,* and I would like you to start this week. Tomorrow, if possible. Please call me back at—"

Suzette was so stunned she didn't even pick up the phone. She just stood there naked, dripping on the carpet, overwhelmed. She had gotten the job. Now she would spend her days immersed in the images that had so painfully aroused her and in close contact with Mrs. Aldridge, who had figured so prominently in last night's fantasies.

She felt a wave of fear. She couldn't possibly work there. She couldn't possibly work that close to the sexy Mrs. Aldridge, or to those erotic images! She would go totally insane...she would become a raving sex maniac!

Then Suzette came to her senses and got back in the shower. *Of course* she would take the job. The money was good, and there was more to interest her at *Bondage* than at any other place of employment that she could imagine. She would have to be stupid to turn this job down. And if the job turned her into a raving sex maniac... well, then so be it.

Chapter 4

Suzette really only had one outfit she could wear to her first day of work, but it still felt as though she changed her clothes a hundred times. She felt that the black suit was *way* too tight for her—too tight across the breasts, and across her hips and ass—and too short, showing off too much of her legs. But she didn't have anything else she could wear, especially since Mrs. Aldridge had made it very clear that they expected very professional appearance. Suzette finally settled into the suit, just wearing a thong underneath. She borrowed Samantha's black three-inch heels, which, she hoped, would give her the height not to be intimidated by Mrs. Aldridge. Under the jacket she wore a camisole—she had thought she ought to wear a bra, especially after her experience at the interview, but she just didn't have a blouse that would work. So she wore the white camisole with lace around the neck, and hoped for the best. She could just keep the jacket buttoned, at least.

It already felt like it was going to be a hot day. She felt uncomfortably warm taking the bus to work—a fact that wasn't helped by the conservative-looking businessman across from her, who kept looking her up and down hungrily while pretending to be reading his paper. If anything, that made her a little warmer—even as it annoyed her. *I guess maybe the suit is a little tight,* thought Suzette as the man eyed her figure.

Suzette was greeted warmly by Sasha, the receptionist, who showed her to her new desk. The door to Mrs. Aldridge's office was closed, so Sasha gave Suzette a tour of the small office. There wasn't much to it—just a desk in front for Sasha, and then one behind a partition for Suzette and one for the saleswoman—Katrina was her name. Suzette noticed that Sasha was wearing a dress that, even while being reasonably businesslike, was still quite a bit tighter and perhaps more low-cut than prudence would have allowed. Sasha was quite pretty, with beautiful dark red hair and green eyes, and the green dress complemented her looks beautifully. The dress buttoned quite tightly across her bust, making more noticeable the fact that Sasha, while not a large woman, had surprisingly large breasts—and rather nice ones, too. And the dress was a little shorter than usually considered appropriate for business wear—revealing the fact that Sasha had extremely nice legs. Suzette tried not to think about this as Sasha walked her around the office, speaking softly in her faint accent. What was that, wondered Suzette. German? French? She really was quite pretty. My, that dress really was very tight.

"Well, as you can see, Mrs. Aldridge isn't off her conference call yet...so perhaps you could peruse a few of our catalogs while she's finishing up, and then she can see you."

Suzette almost jumped at the opportunity. Sasha directed her to a file cabinet that was absolutely stuffed with the catalogs, every issue as far back as they were published—about four years, it seemed. Suzette settled into her new desk and happily began to page through the catalogs of *Bondage, Inc.* The pictures were a little less risqué at the beginning, and the catalogs shorter. But as she went through the catalogs approaching the current one, she saw a definite trend toward explicit sexual content in the catalogs. It was *very* clear in the recent catalogs exactly what the equipment was meant to do. The quality of the photography, and the attractiveness of the models, also increased as the catalogs got more recent. Soon she was turning pages with wide-eyed abandon, her lips parted and her breath coming quickly. She shifted uncomfortably in her office chair.

God, she thought. *I'm getting completely wet.*

Suzette was overcome with a devilish thought. Was she really wet? One way to find out.

Inching closer to the desk, so that her lower body was well hidden from Sasha, Suzette inched up the skirt of the tight black suit. Expending some effort so that anyone who walked by wouldn't see what she was doing, she wriggled her hand between her slightly-parted thighs and deftly eased the crotch of her tight black thong out of the way. She slid her finger between her pussylips, and felt the slickness of her own desire.

Ooooooh, I'm wet all right. Suzette wiggled her butt against the office chair, feeling the skirt inch up a little further. She didn't take her hand out from between her legs, but left it down there, her fingertip gently stroking up and down in the slickness of her ready slit. She began to tease her erect clitoris with her fingertip, feeling the surge of pleasure go through her. She squirmed a little as her pleasure increased. *I shouldn't be doing this,* she thought even as she tugged the thong away and began to inch it down her thighs.

I can't be doing this, Suzette told herself as she felt her fingertips pulling the thong down her legs. *I should be concentrating on my work.* But as she leaned forward to look over the catalogs, she saw that her work at the moment was a photograph of a woman on her hands and knees in a steel cage, wearing a dog collar and lowering herself onto a twelve-inch dildo mounted on the cage's floor. Suzette lifted her feet and eased the thong down, taking it off over her heels.

Oh, God, thought Suzette when she realized what she'd just done. *I can't be doing this. It's my first day.* But it was too late now; it would be more trouble to get the thong back on than to leave it off. Suzette blushed and tried to act casual as she opened the top drawer of the desk and hid her panties inside.

The front of Suzette's desk was solid, so she was hidden from Sasha's view. That way, Sasha couldn't see that Suzette's legs were slightly parted, and the black skirt pulled up just over the curve of her asscheeks, and up high on her thighs. Suzette pretended to be intently studying the picture of the woman in the cage—and in fact, that was exactly what she was doing. Her hand slipped between her legs as she looked at the photo, and before she knew what was happening she was rubbing her clit rapidly.

Sasha glanced up at Suzette, and gave her a little smile. *God, she's really pretty,* thought Suzette, hoping that the smile didn't mean that Sasha knew what she was doing here. She didn't think it did mean that…but how could she be sure?

Suzette almost didn't care. She was rubbing her clit rapidly now, and almost ready to come as she looked at the picture of the caged woman on her hands and knees. She rubbed more quickly, mounting the hill toward orgasm—and then she came, fighting not to make a sound as she sat there at her desk. The pleasure exploded through her, and she remained totally still as she finished her climax, still looking intently at the catalog.

I can't believe I just did that, she thought as she pulled down the skirt and quickly smoothed it. *I have to put my panties back on,* she told herself, and she was about to take them out of the desk drawer and hurry off to the restroom, when Mrs. Aldridge's door opened and Mrs. Aldridge stuck her head out the door. "Sasha, did the new girl—oh, hello, Suzette. Sorry to keep you waiting."

"Not at all," said Suzette breathlessly.

"Come on in when you're ready," said Mrs. Aldridge. "I'll show you the ropes. So to speak. Ha ha."

Suzette managed to keep her composure while Mrs. Aldridge was teaching her all about the complicated ins and outs of the bondage catalog world. The business had started four years ago with just Mr. and Mrs. Aldridge. Mrs. Aldridge did not indicate whether she and her husband had more than a professional interest in bondage, but Suzette felt a surge of excitement going through her body as she imagined Mrs. Aldridge dominating her husband. For surely Mrs. Aldridge must be dominant in bed.... Suzette's thoughts wandered as she thought about that.

The Office

Mrs. Aldridge talked about the way the distribution system worked, how satisfied their customers were, all the different ways their catalogs got out to the world. The materials were all manufactured by different companies and distributed through a shipping office in Iowa. The restraints and written materials—erotic books and magazines—were their most popular items, with bondage furniture—cages, slings stocks, pillories, whipping posts, racks—being rarely-ordered and very expensive indulgences. But the photos of women restrained with these complicated devices, Mrs. Aldridge said, was exactly what made the catalogs so popular from coast to coast. Men and women both, she told a breathless Suzette, loved to look at the photos of complicated and beautiful bondage and imprisonment, and often they would order items from the catalog even if they would never think of buying an item like a whipping post or a bondage chair. Or at least, never think *seriously* about doing it.

"That's very interesting," murmured Suzette. She shifted uncomfortably, acutely aware that her thong was still in the top drawer of her desk in the front office, which left nothing between her steadily-moistening pussy and the wool skirt. Even the skirt was riding up as Suzette wriggled on the office chair—all this talk about cages and bondage chairs was making her temperature rise, especially with the sensuous way Mrs. Aldridge said those words. "Restraint." "Submission." "Sexual service." It was enough to make Suzette lift her skirt and rub herself to orgasm right here! But, thankfully, she didn't. She managed to sit still and listen politely as Mrs. Aldridge turned to the details of Suzette's job.

"You will be responsible for laying out the magazines," said Mrs. Aldridge. "Now, as I said, I personally supervise the photography—as well as the selection of models—so that I can ensure that the images will be up to our usual standard of quality, the standard of quality that our loyal customers have come to expect. But those photos still have to be selected from a wide variety of shots, and that is really your job. Oh, I may have some input or a strong opinion here and there, but for the most part, it will be your responsibility to go through hundreds—in many cases, thousands—of photos and choose the appropriate images which show our products off to their best advantage. Do you think you can handle that responsibility?"

Suzette was about to burst into tears of joy. "Oh, yes," she said. "I'm quite sure I can handle that responsibility."

"Good," said Mrs. Aldridge. "And then, it will be your responsibility to tweak the photos on the computer, to play with them to make sure that the images are displayed to their best advantage when in the catalog. That means you'll be in almost constant contact with these images, looking at thousands of photographs of women and men in bondage every single day. Do you think you'll be able to meet this challenge?"

The Office

Suzette's eyes widened. "Oh, yes," she said breathlessly.

"Then, you must check the specs and prices of the items, make sure the catalog copy is correct, and give the catalog a final proof—to be approved by me, of course. Suzette, I don't mind telling you that I expect your work to be flawless. When I look over the final proofs of the catalog, I don't expect to find one error. You will be held accountable for the quality of your work, do you understand?" Mrs. Aldridge spoke with the tone of the harsh disciplinarian, but there was a sensuous, rich quality to her speech, as though she was savoring every syllable, savoring the power she had over Suzette. Suzette was fascinated and intrigued by this. She could feel her excitement mounting as Mrs. Aldridge fixed her with a stern, unforgiving stare. "You must anticipate being responsible for the impeccable quality of the final product. You will be held accountable."

Suzette's nipples stiffened in the thin camisole. She nodded respectfully.

"Yes, definitely," said Suzette softly. "I do expect—and hope—to be held accountable for everything I do. Everything. I hope you will settle for nothing less than the best from me."

"Oh, you may be sure of that," said Mrs. Aldridge firmly. "Only the best. Anything less will be met with extreme disapproval. From me—and my husband."

"Oh, yes," said Suzette, the hardness of her nipples

painful under the tight jacket. Even though she had the jacket buttoned, she felt that Mrs. Aldridge could see the firm buds of her erect nipples poking out through the black suit jacket. Mrs. Aldridge's gaze seemed to linger over Suzette's upper body, then returned to her face as Suzette was fixed with that piercing stare.

"I have no doubt that you will not disappoint me," said Mrs. Aldridge coldly.

"I won't, Mrs. Aldridge."

"Call me Bunny."

Suzette fought hard to suppress an uncharitable laugh.

"Madam," she said softly. "If it's all right with you..." Suzette stammered, searching for the words. "I would prefer to call you Mrs. Aldridge."

Mrs. Aldridge watched Suzette closely, as if this request revealed everything there was to know about her. Suzette felt as though Mrs. Aldridge was looking right through her, was undressing her with her eyes and leaving her naked and revealed under that unforgiving gaze.

"Would that be all right?" asked Suzette respectfully.

"You prefer to be more formal with me?"

"Y—yes," said Suzette as Mrs. Aldridge's gaze opened her up, leaving her breathless.

"All right, then," said Mrs. Aldridge. "But I shall continue to call you Suzette."

"Yes, Mrs. Aldridge. Thank you."

The Office

Mrs. Aldridge quickly stood up, showing Suzette just how tall she really was. She wore three-inch heels, which put her over six feet. She was wearing a red power suit. The jacket fit rather tightly across her ample breasts and fit snugly around her waist, flaring over the hips to merge with the midthigh-length skirt that showed the length of Mrs. Aldridge's long, shapely legs. Mrs. Aldridge walked slowly around Suzette, talking as she came to stand behind the new employee.

"Now, from time to time there is some question of authority at Bondage, Inc.," Mrs. Aldridge was saying. "I want you to understand that I am the ultimate authority in all matters. All decisions will be made by me, and supported by my husband. Is that understood?"

"Yes," said Suzette breathlessly. She did not turn to face Mrs. Aldridge, but sat there respectfully, feeling the woman's powerful presence behind her.

"My husband understands that I have full control of this office, but from time to time he drops by to take part in the operation, just to keep himself in contact with it. In all cases, you shall treat him as you treat me. Understood?"

"Yes, Mrs. Aldridge." Just saying the words, those respectful, subservient words, brought a tingle to Suzette's body.

"Working in this office is often difficult work—sometimes the hours can be long. I do not expect you to miss any publication deadlines, or to hold up any segment of production. Your position receives overtime, and I want you to understand that if you need to work extra hours to get the catalog out in time...then you are expected to do exactly that. No matter how long the hours may be."

"I understand, Mrs. Aldridge," Suzette said. "I won't disappoint you."

"See that you don't," said Mrs. Aldridge harshly. "Suzette, I will have Sasha issue you a key to the office—I expect no excuses. You will work whatever hours are needed to get the job done."

"Yes, Mrs. Aldridge," said Suzette.

"Now, because we've been so long without a designer, we are overdue on the production deadline for the fall catalog. I expect that you'll have to work a few extra hours to make up the time." Mrs. Aldridge leaned close to Suzette, her warm breath ruffling Suzette's hair. "Does that bother you at all?"

"Not at all, Mrs. Aldridge." The way Suzette was feeling at this particular moment, she would have done anything for the woman. She had never experienced such complete control at the hands of another person—but such sensuous, concerned control. Suzette could feel the exact place where the hem of her skirt had crawled up the backs of her thighs, and was acutely aware of the thong she had left in her desk drawer.

"If you have *any* questions, *any* needs whatsoever, I expect you to bring them to me or Sasha. Any needs whatsoever. Please don't be embarrassed to ask. You'll find that we can be quite helpful."

"Yes, Mrs. Aldridge."

"But don't forget what I said about commitment. I expect you to work hard to get the job done."

"I'll be happy to work as much as possible," said Suzette quickly, desperately. "Any amount of time that is required. Anything that needs to be done, I'll do it. I won't disappoint you, Mrs. Aldridge."

"Very well. Then I suspect you'll want to start looking at the contact sheets for our fall catalog photo shoots right away. See Sasha about those. I expect to see a mock-up by the end of next week."

Mrs. Aldridge returned to her seat behind the big oak desk. Suzette sat there for a moment, dazed and stunned. Then she quickly stood up, smoothing her skirt down over her thighs.

"Thank you, Mrs. Aldridge. Thank you very much."

"Certainly," she said. "And good luck."

Once Suzette got the contact sheets from Sasha, she got so engrossed in looking through them that she completely forgot to slip into the bathroom and put her thong back on. She only noticed it when she realized that she was getting painfully aroused looking at the photo spread of a beautiful young redheaded woman being tormented while lashed naked to an X-shaped cross. She felt the moistness of her cunt dribbling onto her thighs and soaking the black suit. That was when she realized that she needed to put her thong back on, and remembered what she'd done when she had been looking at the catalogs earlier. *I can't believe I did that,* she thought for the hundredth time as she squeezed the little black thong up into a ball in her fist and went down the hall to the ladies room to put it back on.

When she got into the stall, though, she realized she had to pee, so she sat down and did that, realizing as she relieved herself that she was still excited from looking at the photos. Suzette was horrified—how was she going to keep this job if she kept getting wet every ten minutes? Like now, for instance. How wet was she? When she was finished pissing, Suzette dabbed herself with a bit of toilet paper and then reached down to feel her pussy, to see if she really was all that wet. *I'm pretty wet,* she thought, as she slipped one finger into her pussy. *Oooooh, that feels good. I wonder if I'm wet enough to get two in there.* Suzette slipped two fingers in easily, amazed at how wet she'd gotten already. She bit her lip as she felt her excitement mounting, felt the firmness of her nipples against the tight suit jacket. Almost without knowing what she was doing, Suzette unbuttoned and then slipped off the jacket, reaching up to hang it on the hook on the stall door. Then she slipped her free hand up under the camisole so she could feel the full swell of her breasts and see how hard her nipples were now that she knew she was wet. They were pretty hard. She worked two fingers in and out of her pussy, working her clit with her thumb as she thought about Mrs. Aldridge. *That bitch is really going to work me hard,* thought Suzette. *Hard. Work me hard. Ooooh....* She rubbed her clit faster with her thumb, pushing a third finger into her pussy as she sat on the toilet. She pinched her nipples harder, moving from one to the other under the camisole; finally, she hiked the camisole up over her breasts, exposing them and letting her play with them more easily. She was incredibly hot, ready to come soon. But not too soon. She wanted to enjoy herself for a few minutes before she went back to work.

Suzette teased her clit back and forth, feeling her excitement mount. She wondered whether Mrs. Aldridge knew what kind of effect she was having on Suzette. *God, I hope not,* she thought. What if she did? What if Mrs. Aldridge knew that Suzette was in here masturbating right now? What if Mrs. Aldridge had a hidden camera under Suzette's desk, and she'd been watching her rub herself off earlier this morning? What if she had hidden cameras in the bathroom, and she was watching Suzette right now....

That thought was enough to send Suzette over the edge, hurling her into an explosive orgasm as her ass pistoned up and down on the toilet seat.

She had a hard time keeping herself from moaning, but she managed to keep quiet as she came. She came hard, the orgasm thundering through her body as she writhed and squirmed on the toilet seat. Finally she relaxed onto it, feeling her ecstasy fade away. She took a deep breath and began to pull her camisole down.

I've got to stop this, she thought. *Maybe it'll wear off as I see more of the photos. Maybe I'll get used to it.*

But even as she hoped that would happen, part of her hoped that it wouldn't. And she knew that it never would—that her employment at Bondage, Inc. would be frequently punctuated by episodes like the one she'd just experienced.

Since Mrs. Aldridge had made it painfully clear that she expected Suzette to wear a *very* professional wardrobe, Suzette had no choice but to call her parents and beg to borrow some money. They were elated that she had gotten a job already, and when they asked what it was she told them she was doing layout for fashion-industry brochures. Could they see some of the things she was working on? Oh, no, she said. They were trade secrets. She couldn't show them around.

After Suzette's father had transferred the money to her account, she took a long evening shopping for business clothes. She spent almost the full thousand dollars her parents had loaned her, and found herself trying desperately to select clothes which made her look sexy as well as corporate. She favored the skirts a little shorter, the blouses a little more low-cut, the sweaters slightly tighter, than the saleslady recommended for strictly corporate wear. But Suzette figured it was okay— after all, Sasha was doing it. And no matter what kind of corporate job Suzette might get, she didn't want to become a sexless corporate drone! She didn't mind looking a little sexy.

Suzette also spent some of the money on underthings, since most of what she had were boring white cotton panties—college student underwear. That just wouldn't do under the thin, silky material that was fashionable for business skirts and blazers. So she invested in a few packages of thong underpants— simple cotton, and a few of more expensive satin with lace. They wouldn't interfere with the line of the skirt or the dress, and they worked perfectly under a slip. Plus, Suzette had to keep herself entertained during the long workday, and she didn't want to be too encumbered down there in case she had the chance to...take a long lunch.

Suzette had the feeling she might do exactly that now and then.

Chapter 5

Mrs. Aldridge plainly approved of Suzette's wardrobe. Suzette's professional appearance was very appropriate for the job, Mrs. Aldridge said. Despite this, or perhaps because of it, Suzette found her first week at *Bondage, Inc.* incredibly taxing. First there was the constant sexual stimulation of the erotic pictures she used. There were so many of them—far more than she could use in the catalog, which meant that she witnessed enormous numbers of nubile young women and well-muscled young men in complicated and improbable bondage every single day.

Then, there was the fact that Sasha was a shameless flirt. It had taken Suzette a while to catch on, but she eventually figured out that the somewhat provocative clothing that Sasha enjoyed wearing was intended to be enjoyed by her office mates. Suzette harbored her suspicions for a while, until she caught Sasha giving her an undeniable come-hither look as Suzette bent over the copy machine. She was quite sure that Sasha was interested in women as more than office comrades.

Which made things that much more confusing. Suzette wasn't interested in getting involved in an office romance—even if she *did* fantasize about Mrs. Aldridge almost nightly. But that was different, it was just a fantasy—Sasha was clearly flirting with her, and sometimes even a little more than flirting. Sometimes she thought Sasha might be coming on to her.

But then, on top of that, there was the fact that Suzette had never even been that interested in women until just the other day! It was bad enough being assaulted every night by vivid fantasies of Mrs. Aldridge putting to use all the implements in the Bondage, Inc. catalog. It was bad enough knowing that Samantha had seen her being fucked from behind by Rob, and had gotten into it. It was bad enough knowing that Samantha was more than a little interested in inviting Suzette into her bedroom some time when Paul was over. Now, Suzette had to face the almost constant flirtation of Sasha, had to watch her bending over or kneeling before the copy machine when it jammed, wearing clothes that were progressively tighter and more revealing each day. She hadn't been sure at first, but now she was quite convinced that Sasha's wardrobe was migrating toward the less and less decent, and that Sasha was progressively finding more excuses to lean up against Suzette or put her hand on Suzette's back.

It wasn't even that Suzette minded. She found it kind of flattering. And she couldn't say she didn't take some pleasure from looking at Sasha in those tight suits and skimpy dresses she wore. Sasha was a beautiful woman, definitely, with a great body. And Suzette didn't look away when she was treated to a quick glimpse down Sasha's shirt as she bent over to pick something up, or the sight of Sasha's pert buttocks in those silky slacks she wore. How could she? Sasha was a very attractive woman, and the sexual energy she was putting out was harder and harder to ignore.

But why was she so enticed by all this? Thankfully, before the end of her first week, Suzette got wrapped up in the tasks before her—namely, getting the catalog put together in time to make their mail date for the fall.

She ended up working many long hours to get the catalog laid out in time. At first, it would be Suzette and Mrs. Aldridge alone in the office after Sasha left at 5:00. Mrs. Aldridge would labor away in her office as Suzette worked out front. She found it increasingly hard to concentrate when she knew that Mrs. Aldridge was in there, with no one else around, and the office door was locked. More than once she felt sure that she was going to stand up and walk right into Mrs. Aldridge's office and make a pass at her. Luckily, she managed to restrain herself. Soon, Suzette was staying even later than Mrs. Aldridge, sometimes as late as nine or ten o'clock. But strangely, Sasha began finding excuses to stay, as well. That made Suzette more than a little nervous; sometimes Sasha and Suzette were in the office alone. Sasha would linger by Suzette's desk, doing some banal task—filing or straightening up—while Suzette looked over dozens of pictures of attractive young women—though no more attractive than Sasha, to be sure—bound up in various complicated poses. She was terrified that Sasha was going to throw herself at her—and, more to the point, Suzette was quite convinced that if Sasha did, then she would find herself with a willing partner. Sasha was certainly quite seductive.

By the beginning of her third week, Suzette was sometimes staying as late as eleven o'clock. She knew this wasn't healthy, but she wanted so much to do a good job on the catalog and please Mrs. Aldridge. The worst thing was that when she worked that many hours, she didn't get to see Rob as much, so she wasn't getting laid regularly. In fact, she rarely had time to masturbate anymore, which was particularly trying given the fact that she spent the whole workday almost painfully aroused from the images she worked with. That made Suzette lots more horny than usual, and she felt like a loaded gun waiting to go off. God, if Sasha were to make a pass at her, Suzette would almost explode with desire.

This was all made worse by the fact that she kept running into the guy from the elevator, the one she'd tormented by rubbing up against on that day of her job interview. He looked nervous at first, but then as Suzette saw him more often he seemed less uncomfortable, and she was pretty sure she caught him looking at her. She was ashamed at what she'd done, even though she began to suspect that the guy had enjoyed himself immensely. To feel his heavy gaze on her body was too much, though —Suzette felt horribly embarrassed. She started coming to work early so that she could avoid running into him— but she still seemed to catch him at lunch, and each time he seemed to be glancing over at her. He was really cute, and Suzette had trouble keeping her mind off him when she rode the elevator, whether he was there or not. She almost felt like she wanted to ask him out, just to see what he was really like. But no, that would be totally crazy, she'd never do it. Still, seeing that guy all the time contributed to her general sense of sexual need.

One day in her third week, Suzette was working late—it was about seven, with Sasha and Mrs. Aldridge still there—when she decided that she simply *had* to get fucked. She hadn't seen Rob in a week, and she had barely masturbated in that time, and if she didn't get fucked she was going to go totally insane. She had to, and she didn't care if she had to abandon work to do it. Suzette grabbed her stuff, said good night, and rushed out the door.

Suzette felt newly free as she rode the elevator down— she was so glad she was doing this. She would call Rob, hoping he could drop by or she could come by his place. She just *had* to get some sex or she was going to explode! It wasn't natural for a girl to go without like this, especially not when subjected to the sexual pressures that she was experiencing.

She made it all the way to the bus stop and waited for the bus before she'd realized that she had left her bus pass in her desk. Cursing, she went back to the building, used her key to let herself in, and rode the elevator to the fortieth floor.

Suzette let herself in as quietly as possible—she was embarrassed that she'd forgotten her bus pass, and was hoping she could slip in and out of the office without Sasha or Mrs. Aldridge noticing her. She made it through the door and tiptoed silently to her desk. But she sensed something was wrong—she could hear Mrs. Aldridge's voice, and mixed with it was a clearly male voice. It sounded like they were having some sort of an argument. The voices were coming from back near the copy machine, where the supplies and coffee were.

The Office

She crept around the corner, keeping to the shadows, not wanting to get involved if there was some kind of argument going on. But as she rounded the corner and stood there silently, watching, Suzette's eyes widened—and she wasn't so sure any more whether or not she wanted to get involved.

Mrs. Aldridge and Sasha were in back, along with a man in a business suit whom Suzette didn't recognize. Could that be Mr. Aldridge?

Sasha was dressed typically—with a skirt that was too tight and too short, and a silk blouse that hugged her large breasts like a second skin. Mrs. Aldridge had Sasha bent facedown over the copy machine, with her tight little blouse pulled up to her neck so that her tits were exposed in the little lace demi-bra she wore. Mrs. Aldridge was leaning heavily on Sasha, as if she was holding her down, her knee pressed roughly between Sasha's knees.

"You've been coming on to her, you *whore!*" Mrs. Aldridge was growling bitterly. "You think I haven't noticed what you're doing to her? Of course I've noticed. How can anyone not notice when you're rubbing your tits against her every fifteen minutes. You little slut, you can't wait to get her into bed, can you? Or maybe you don't even want a bed, you just want her to spread you out on the copy machine and fuck you right here. Like this?"

With that, Mrs. Aldridge rammed her knee up into Sasha's crotch, pushing her already-short skirt up over her ass and grinding her thigh into Sasha's pussy. Sasha let out a moan and shuddered as Mrs. Aldridge did that. Her arms hung limp at her side, as if she didn't dare resist her employer—out of fear of reprisal or fear that she would stop, it was impossible to tell. Whatever the reason, Sasha was an obedient victim in Mrs. Aldridge's iron grasp. Mrs. Aldridge got a handhold by putting her arm around Sasha's waist and yanking on the middle of that minuscule demi-bra so that her tits popped out, now unencumbered by the faint strip of lace that couldn't really be called a "bra" or anything of the sort. Mrs. Aldridge leaned on Sasha as she pushed her forward; the leverage pushed the unfortunate Sasha down hard so that her bare breasts flattened uncomfortably against the glass of the copy machine.

"Oh, I see, you little bitch! You want to send her a love letter—like this!"

Mrs. Aldridge hit the COPY button on the machine, and a bright light bathed the two of them as a flawless 11 x 17 photocopy of Sasha's bare breasts came out the far end.

"Ooooh!" moaned Sasha as Mrs. Aldridge sneered down at the perfect image of Sasha's mounds with their dark nipples, all pressed and flattened against the glass.

"Like that! Is that the kind of love note you want to write to your new girlfriend?"

The Office

Sasha moaned as Mrs. Aldridge roughly rammed her knee into Sasha's crotch once more. Crouched in her hiding space in the shadows, Suzette could see Sasha wriggling her ass, pushing her crotch down against Mrs. Aldridge's knee, as if begging her for more.

"You want to feel *her* do this to you, you horny little slut?" Mrs. Aldridge once more ground her knee hard up into Sasha's cunt, and Sasha shuddered and moaned as she felt the pressure against her private spot. Mr. Aldridge stood leaning against a stack of copy paper, a smile on his face, obviously enjoying the sight of his wife disciplining the unfortunate secretary. Suzette noticed with a little bit of a shock that the gray wool slacks of his suit bulged in an obvious hard-on. In fact, it was quite a sizable hard-on. The guy seemed like he must be pretty "well endowed." Suzette noticed for the first time how cute he was, and that he must have been over six-foot-three. The thought of this gorgeous man making love to the exquisite Mrs. Aldridge made Suzette's hormones explode in a rainstorm of lust. Suzette crouched down in the darkness and pressed her thighs together, intently watching the scene as Mrs. Aldridge continued berating the young secretary.

"You spend all your time at work trying to figure out how to get her into bed, you little slut!" Mrs. Aldridge's knee ground rhythmically up and down between Sasha's legs. Mrs. Aldridge leaned heavily forward, her lips curling in a sneer of disgust as she spoke in a breathy, harsh voice, her face very close to Sasha's ear.

"You can't think of anything except how it's going to feel when you finally seduce her and feel her tongue pushing up inside your pussy—isn't that right?" Sasha moaned helplessly in response. She tried to push herself back against Mrs. Aldridge, away from the copy machine, but Mrs. Aldridge was upon her in a second, grasping both of Sasha's wrists and forcing them together, up into the small of Sasha's back. In that position, Sasha was helplessly pressed forward so that her tits were painfully smashed against the glass of the copy machine. Someone hit the COPY button—whether Mrs. Aldridge or Sasha, Suzette couldn't tell—and the bright light lit up Mrs. Aldridge's features demonically as the copier made another perfect black-and-white image of Sasha's breasts.

"Maybe you think she'd like you better if you had bigger tits, huh?" growled Mrs. Aldridge, pinning Sasha's wrists behind her with one hand while, with the other, she reached down to the control panel and started expertly punching buttons. "Maybe *this* big?"

Sasha let out a wail of tortured humiliation as Mrs. Aldridge hit the COPY button, and the white light again washed over Sasha's tormented face. The photocopy slid out of the machine with the image of Sasha's breasts terribly distorted, enlarged so much as to look inhuman in the bland fluorescent light, as Mrs. Aldridge picked up the copy and forced it into Sasha's face.

Sasha tried helplessly to avert her face, but Mrs. Aldridge just pressed the copy closer.

"Look at it, you little slut! *Look at it!* Is *that* how big you wanted your tits, so the new girl would want you? Is *that* big enough for her, do you think?" Mrs. Aldridge started punching buttons again, working the ENLARGE function up to its maximum. "Or do you think she likes *really* huge tits—like maybe *this* big?"

"Ooooh—Aaaahh—Ohhhh, God—" Sasha's plaintive, desperate cries grew louder as Mrs. Aldridge leaned her harder than ever against the copier, forcing her breasts against the glass and hitting the COPY button so that enlarged images of Sasha's breasts started shooting out at breakneck pace, each one punctuated by a bright light and a hum as the copier took the next picture. Mrs. Aldridge held Sasha down as the light quickly rode back and forth under her tits, and Sasha's wails became screams and sobs as she begged for mercy.

Suzette realized suddenly what was going on here. The glass of the copy machine got incredibly hot after a few minutes of copying—the temperature of the glass against Sasha's tits was going up rapidly with each image the machine took. Sasha must be overwhelmed by pain by now, her tits cruelly tortured by the copier games of the devious and unforgiving Mrs. Aldridge.

"Please, Mistress," moaned Sasha as the copier picked up speed. "Please have mercy!"

"Have mercy on you how, you little slut? Get Suzette into bed for you? Or spread you out on the floor so my husband here can fuck your pretty little pussy—like this?"

Mrs. Aldridge viciously rammed her knee up into Sasha's cunt again, and Sasha wailed as she lunged forward, her breasts pressed harder than ever against the glass as Mrs. Aldridge started more copying. Photocopies of Sasha's breasts, so enlarged as to be almost unrecognizable, went flying all over the office. Sasha's moans of torment grew louder and louder as the heat of the glass increased.

Suzette watched from the darkness, wide-eyed. She couldn't believe the effect this was having on her. She could feel the moisture of her own pussy soaking the panties she had on. *Damn it*, thought Suzette. *I knew I should have worn something more than a thong today. Now it's totally soaked through....* In fact, she could feel the moisture pooling between her engorged cuntlips and dribbling down the insides of her thighs. Watching Sasha suffer at the hands of the unforgiving Mrs. Aldridge was enough to make Suzette's pussy catch fire with lust! *God*, she thought, *if I could just reach under there and touch my clit a little bit....*

Suzette managed to keep still in the shadows as she

reached down and hitched up the tight-fitting skirt she wore. It was one of her thrift store finds, and was several sizes too small for her—making it a little difficult to pull the skirt up over her thighs. But she managed, watching in amazement from her hiding place as Sasha's torment continued. Suzette almost couldn't believe she had been so lucky as not to be spotted yet—but then again, both Mr. and Mrs. Aldridge were quite distracted by the pretty and nubile secretary receiving torment at their hands.

Suzette eased her hand between her legs and slipped one finger under the wet crotch of her thong. God, yes. She was wet, all right.

Sasha was sobbing and shuddering as the heat of the glass increased. Finally the copying was done, with huge images of Sasha's breasts scattered all over the floor. Suzette thought for a moment—with shocked disappointment—that now Mrs. Aldridge might stop Sasha's torments! But even after those long, agonized minutes of Sasha's suffering, Mrs. Aldridge showed no sign of slowing down the punishment or easing up her temper on the poor secretary. The devious Mrs. Aldridge had other things in mind.

In fact, in a quick moment, Mrs. Aldridge had snatched an electrical cord from a nearby shelf and quickly bound Sasha's wrists together, placing the longest part of her wrists parallel to each other so that her shoulders were pulled back uncomfortably and her bound wrists were forced up high on her back. This meant that poor helpless Sasha had her back arched precariously and thus her breasts thrust out most evidently. As Mrs. Aldridge pulled Sasha back to finish the job of binding the girl's wrists, Suzette caught her first real glimpse of those delectable mounds—except for the photocopies which covered the floor, of course.

Suzette's eyes lingered over the impressive swell of Sasha's firm tits, much larger than she would have expected on a woman of Sasha's size. Suzette had certainly looked at them many times—the low-cut, clingy blouses that Sasha tended to wear had made sure of that—and Suzette had paid more than a little attention to their striking size and enticing firmness, and to the fullness of Sasha's nipples, which hardened at the slightest provocation. Sasha rarely wore a full bra. She opted some of the time for a low-cut camisole which clung to the outline of her tits. Other times she wore a demi-bra, which only shrouded half of her breasts and thus left her nipples to poke distractingly out around the spray of lace on the cups. This meant that Suzette was treated to the frequent sight of Sasha's nipples hardening through her blouse or sweater every time Sasha walked by or handed over a set of particularly lurid contact sheets. Or, most strikingly, when some vague excuse in the office caused Sasha to squeeze gently by

Suzette in a tight space, thus pressing her tits up against Suzette's body or "accidentally" brushing her with her ass. Other times, Sasha opted for one of the push-up bras, with stiff boning and padding on the underside, which—on a woman of Sasha's bustline—created quite a striking effect. The bra forced her tits up and apart, poising the nipples invitingly so that even if they weren't erect (which they usually were, given Sasha's temperament) they still showed plainly through whatever top Sasha was wearing.

So Suzette had spent more than a few hours of her workdays taking very close notice of Sasha's breasts and even admiring them. Now, Suzette was able to admire Sasha's glorious tits in all their naked splendor.

Sasha's nipples were dark and full and, Suzette noticed with a surge of excitement, entirely erect—almost painfully so, it appeared. But what really drove Suzette overboard was the sight of Sasha's breasts all reddened and painfully heated by the copy machine. Sasha's normally milk-white skin was more of a hot pink color now. Suzette imagined the discomfort Sasha must have been feeling from the merciless torture of her treasured breasts at Mrs. Aldridge's hands. Sasha's torment looked truly frightening—and Mrs. Aldridge's anger seemed unstoppable. But despite all this, Sasha's nipples were fully hard, plainly showing the height of her arousal! God, that meant Sasha was enjoying herself

...which made Suzette realize how much *she* was enjoying herself, and just how envious of Sasha she was. Suzette's pussy moistened noticeably as she realized that she wished it was she there against the copy machine, receiving Mrs. Aldridge's brutal attentions, being the focus of that cold temper, having her tits tormented and teased at Mrs. Aldridge's unforgiving hands.

The thought of it made Suzette's pussy throb with excitement...and, as she rubbed her clit, crouching there in the darkness, it was an easy matter for her to slip one finger inside, then two fingers, then one again, and finally three as her pleasure mounted—but it was *not* an easy matter for Suzette to keep her mouth shut as she did that, so extreme was the pleasure that thundered through her body as she fingered herself in her carnal crouch. She wanted to moan in excitement, to whimper in pleasure—but she managed to keep very still and keep from making any noise at all as she watched the scene continuing in front of her.

Mrs. Aldridge cruelly took hold of Sasha's long red hair, which was pulled into a rather conservative bun, and yanked her upright. Sasha let out a whimper as she squirmed against Mrs. Aldridge's grasp, but Suzette noticed as Sasha turned her head that her lips were slightly parted and there was an obvious look of rapture on her face. Mrs. Aldridge, ever the stern disciplinarian, would do her best to take that look of pleasure off Sasha's beautiful face.

Mrs. Aldridge took hold of Sasha's breasts and shook them vigorously, pinching the nipples.

"I see these big tits of yours are all red now—red and hot, just like your pussy is hot." Mrs. Aldridge pinched the nipples harder and Sasha gave a squirm as the pain shot through her.

Mrs. Aldridge still stood behind Sasha, so the secretary knew that at any moment she might be forced to bend forward and pay homage to the copy machine again. But for the moment, Mrs. Aldridge was enjoying herself by taking a more personal interest in Sasha's breasts. She pinched the nipples harder, reaching around from behind so that she could rub and roll the nipples between thumb and forefinger, increasing the pressure until Sasha's mouth opened wide in a soundless scream of agony. Then she gave a great shuddering moan, and pressed her body back against Mrs. Aldridge—whether begging for mercy or encouraging further torment, Suzette couldn't know. Mrs. Aldridge pinched still harder, and Sasha let out a sob of agony. Then Mrs. Aldridge relinquished her grip on Sasha's nipples. She gave Sasha's right breast a stern slap, making a very loud crack echo in the office. Sasha whimpered in pain. Apparently the whimper wasn't loud enough, for Mrs. Aldridge slapped again, much harder, and then again and again as Sasha squirmed in her grasp. Mrs. Aldridge slapped Sasha's other breast, reddening it noticeably as she brutally punished Sasha's sensitive flesh, and soon Sasha was moaning loudly and thrashing her head back and forth with each of the punishing smacks that Mrs. Aldridge gave her huge tits.

Mrs. Aldridge got hold of Sasha's bound wrists and turned her around to face Mr. Aldridge, who had been watching this whole scene with a cruel smile of pleasure on his face. Mrs. Aldridge held Sasha there firmly as Mr. Aldridge reached out and began to touch Sasha's firm tits with his hands.

"Such easily punished little mounds," he said teasingly as he rubbed his palms over the erect buds of Sasha's nipples. His hands were very large, and Suzette was shocked to find herself wondering what those fingers would feel like sliding into her—maybe while her body was pressed up against Mr. Aldridge's....

"I think they'll be so much nicer without this bra on." Mr. Aldridge reached around behind Sasha and unclasped her demi-bra, revealing her tits still more fully. He tossed the discarded garment onto the copy machine.

Mrs. Aldridge reached over with one hand and hit the COPY button. White light filled the room.

"For our files," sneered Mrs. Aldridge uncharitably.

Now that he had them unclothed, Mr. Aldridge took

hold of Sasha's bare breasts and squeezed more firmly, placing each of her nipples between his thumb and forefinger. Sasha's back arched and she pushed back against Mrs. Aldridge as he pinched harder and harder. Soon Sasha was wailing, her body wriggling enticingly back and forth as Mr. Aldridge tormented her hard nipples.

"Mercy," she begged, her lips forming the word softly.

"No mercy for you tonight, you little slut. How wet are you? Are you positively gushing?"

"Please...Mistress...mercy...."

Hearing Sasha call the divine Mrs. Aldridge "Mistress" gave Suzette's pussy a strong surge of lubrication. She was still playing with herself in her dark hiding place, quickly fucking herself with her fingers, alternating between one, two, and three fingers as she worked her clit with her other hand. But she wasn't going to come yet—not yet, not until she had seen the full torments that Mr. and Mrs. Aldridge had in mind for Sasha.

Mr. Aldridge was concentrating on Sasha's tits, slapping and pinching them roughly, making Sasha squirm and writhe in pain as he grew more and more forceful with every pinch and slap. Sasha threw her head back and said in a desperate, pitiful whimper, "Mercy... please...mercy...."

"I already told you, there's no mercy for you, you little whore. You've been showing your ass off every day to that new girl, and now you're going to put it to work for us. Isn't that right? Isn't that what you want to do?"

"Oh…please, Mistress.…"

"Or do you want to wait for that little slut Suzette to take your clothes off? Are you wet enough to be fucked or are you waiting for her to finally throw herself at you? She's going to, you know. She's going to throw herself at you if you keep this up. One day she's just going to come up behind you in the supply closet and slip her hand up your skirt. Next thing I know, you two sluts are going to be fucking on my desk while I'm off working!"

Suzette could hardly stand hearing herself talked about like this. Not because she was angry about it—quite the contrary. She knew she should have been horrified, been angry at Mrs. Aldridge saying those things. But all they did to her was send a surge of arousal to her pussy, and Suzette picked up speed as she finger-fucked herself. *She thinks I'm going to throw myself at Sasha*, thought Suzette excitedly. *She thinks we're going to do it right here*. And at that moment, Suzette wasn't so sure that she wouldn't throw herself at Sasha—the sight of those beautiful breasts made Suzette want to get closer, take them in her hands, feel the nipples hardening in her mouth…

Mr. Aldridge slapped Sasha's tits harder and faster as Mrs. Aldridge berated her.

"Isn't that right? Aren't you waiting for Suzette to

THE OFFICE

come after you and lift your skirt? You know she wants to do it, you just can't stop yourself from teasing her. Isn't that right?"

"Yes, Mistress," groaned the tormented secretary. Sasha was gasping and sobbing with the torment of her breasts, but Suzette could tell from the way Sasha was moaning that she wasn't really begging them to stop— in fact, she seemed to want Mr. Aldridge to go on with his torture of her breasts. Sasha's eyes widened (and so did Suzette's) as Mr. Aldridge reached out to a supply shelf and brought his hand back holding a box of binder clips—those tiny black clips that you use to hold papers together—to hold them together *tightly!*

Suzette's fingers picked up speed as she slid them into her pussy. She was getting close—but she desperately held off her orgasm, knowing that she couldn't come without making noise, and wanting to see the whole show without interrupting it.

With bitter disappointment, Suzette realized that she couldn't keep touching herself and refrain from climaxing. But if she came she was sure to make some noise that would give her hiding place away—she simply couldn't! With some difficulty, Suzette forced herself to take her hands away from her pussy and pull her skirt down. She desperately wanted to come, but she couldn't take the chance of being discovered! She crouched there in the dark and turned her attention to the scene being acted out at the copy machine—finding that it provided more than enough diversion for her.

When Sasha saw the box of binder clips, she began to whimper and moan wildly, squirming and writhing against Mrs. Aldridge. Mrs. Aldridge held Sasha tightly, one hand on her bound wrists and the other gripping her hair. Mrs. Aldridge forced Sasha to stand with her back arched, presenting her tits to Mr. Aldridge as he took out one clip and took hold of Sasha's nipples.

Suzette had put one of those clips on the web of her hand once—they were *tight!* She couldn't even imagine what it would feel like on her nipple. She had never had any kind of clip on her nipples—her nipples were exquisitely sensitive, and she felt sure it would be intolerable for her to have anything that tight on them. She had seen pictures of women wearing nipple rings in the catalogs, though, and they had made her incredibly excited. The thought of somebody torturing her nipples made Suzette wet, and seeing Mr. Aldridge put the clips on Sasha was driving her totally insane with lust.

Suzette felt her own nipples aching in sympathy as she watched Mr. Aldridge fitting Sasha's hard nipple between the teeth of the binder clip. He let go, and Sasha let out a wild, wailing moan of agony as the teeth of the binder clip closed on her nipple, taking hold of it and gripping. Sasha squirmed, whimpering pathetically, but despite her discomfort, Mr. Aldridge didn't hesitate

The Office

in taking hold of her other nipple and fitting it between the teeth of the next binder clip.

"Oh, no…no no no…oh, no, not the other one too…oh, please, Master…please no, Master…don't make me take it—oh! OH! OH!"

Hearing Sasha beg for mercy was incredibly erotic for Suzette, especially with the beautiful Mrs. Aldridge holding her still for her husband to torment. Sasha almost crumpled as the intense sensations flowed through her breasts. She slumped against Mrs. Aldridge and wriggled her ass against her. But to Suzette's surprise, the torture of Sasha's breasts wasn't over yet.

"Now, now, Sasha. You know as well as I do that there are a dozen of these things to the box. And I don't intend to waste a single one.…"

Sasha whimpered as Mr. Aldridge took his time applying the clips to the soft flesh of her breast, gathering it up in his thumb and forefinger and clamping it down. Each clip brought a new shudder and a wail of discomfort from Sasha, making Suzette more and more excited. Soon Sasha's breasts looked like some sort of modern art sculpture, with binder clips jutting out at every angle. Mr. Aldridge took his time testing the sensitivity of her flesh, tweaking the clips with his hands, gently brushing them and listening to Sasha's moans of agony as he tugged at them.

"God…please, Master…please stop…please don't make me take this.…"

"There's lots more where that came from," snarled Mrs. Aldridge from behind Sasha. "Or perhaps you'd prefer to tell us how wet you are!"

"I...I don't know, Mistress..."

"A slut like you? I know that a little two-bit whore like yourself must know about her cunt every minute of every day! I'm sure you've known all day that your pussy is as wet as it gets—just being around that little slut you want to fuck! Isn't it?"

"Mistress...oh, please..."

Mr. Aldridge reached for another packet of binder clips.

"Isn't it?"

"Y—yes...Mistress...I'm incredibly wet... I've been thinking about her all day..."

A moment of silence passed, marked only by Sasha's heavy breathing.

"And you want to fuck her, don't you?" Mrs. Aldridge's voice now had a tender, soothing sound to it.

Tears shimmering in her eyes, Sasha nodded. "Yes, Mistress. I want to fuck her."

"Now what did I tell you?" growled Mrs. Aldridge. "What did I tell you about that little slut?"

Sasha squirmed in Mrs. Aldridge's grasp, and Mr. Aldridge picked up the second box of binder clips.

"You told me..."

"Yes? Speak up, you whore. Tell me what I said."

The Office

"You told me she's off-limits. To me."

"That's right. And so why are you showing yourself off to her like that?"

"I—I don't know, Mistress…" Sasha was beginning to relax in Mrs. Aldridge's arms, perhaps sensing that her torment was drawing to a close.

"I think you do," said Mrs. Aldridge cruelly, and nodded to her husband.

"No…no…no…" whimpered Sasha as Mr. Aldridge reached down and lifted her skirt. He put his hands underneath and quickly pulled Sasha's panties down her thighs—Suzette saw that this was just a skimpy, barely-there thong. Sasha squirmed as Mr. Aldridge took the thong off over her ankles and tossed it on the copier.

"Always copy me on all relevant correspondence," snarled Mrs. Aldridge, hitting the COPY button so that Sasha's lacy thong was bathed in light and copied on 11 x 17 for future reference.

"Spread your legs a little," hissed Mrs. Aldridge, as Sasha begged them to stop. Sasha didn't obey at first, pressing her thighs together tightly as Mr. Aldridge yanked her short, tight skirt up to her waist. Mrs. Aldridge reached down and pulled it up from behind, tucking the tight skirt up until Sasha's whole gorgeous ass was exposed. Suzette now got her first glimpse of those perfect hemispheres. She had certainly noticed how attractive Sasha's ass was, displayed as it was in the tight skirts and—occasionally—skintight pantsuits she wore. But now, she got her first opportunity to admire those beautiful cheeks unencumbered by clothing. Mrs. Aldridge pushed Sasha down again, bending her over at the waist, so that the girl was forced to lean on the copier, her breasts—with their full array of tormenting binder clips—pressed firmly against the glass. Mrs. Aldridge made a few more copies as she rammed her knee up between Sasha's slightly spread thighs. A moan escaped Sasha's lips.

"Spread them wider," Mrs. Aldridge said firmly. Sasha snuggled her ass back against Mrs. Aldridge as she spread her thighs further, leaning more heavily against the copier. This forced her tits more fully against the glass, changing the perspective, no doubt, so Mrs. Aldridge quickly got a few more copies for posterity.

"Ooooh," cooed Mrs. Aldridge as Mr. Aldridge went down on his knees behind Sasha. "Such a wet little pussy. And shaved. How nice that you keep it shaved... or is it that you can't fit into those tight little skirts of yours if you don't shave it?"

Mrs. Aldridge's hand slowly rose and fell between Sasha's spread thighs, stroking the secretary's exposed pussy. Suzette was struck immediately by how much the scene made her think of her fantasy where Mrs. Aldridge felt her up from behind—except this was happening for real! Suzette could hardly believe it.

Sasha's butt wriggled as first one, then two of Mrs. Aldridge's fingers disappeared inside her. Sasha let out a tormented moan, one which told Suzette that the secretary was mounting toward orgasm more than she let on.

"So wet," said Mrs. Aldridge. "So delicious and wet. You must be positively *dripping* all day long, working so close to Suzette like that. Isn't that right?"

"Y-yes, Mistress," whimpered Sasha, wiggling her ass as Mrs. Aldridge explored her with her fingers. "I get very wet being so close to her."

Hearing that excited Suzette, and her own quick finger-fucking picked up speed as she watched and listened.

Now Mr. Aldridge was all the way down on his knees, his face right behind Sasha's exposed cunt. He would have been in a perfect position to rim her or maybe even eat her out from behind. But in his hand he held a box of binder clips, and Suzette knew that nothing so banal was about to be done to Sasha's helpless, willing body. Suzette shuddered as she thought about what was to come—she wondered if Sasha was anticipating it, or was merely expecting to be fucked.

Mr. Aldridge gently teased apart Sasha's cuntlips, exposing the ripe bud of her clit. He took one of her smooth lips between thumb and forefinger and delicately placed a binder clip on it, near the entrance.

Sasha's body spasmed and her tits pressed harder to

the glass as the first binder clip went on. A low, pathetic moan escaped her lips, followed by a whimper that Suzette could only interpret as pleasure.

Sasha *must* be enjoying this, thought Suzette. She *must* be. I bet this is all her idea.

God knows I would enjoy it, she thought. *I would really enjoy it.*

Suzette watched Sasha spasming and writhing as Mr. Aldridge put the full twelve binder clips around her pussylips, crowding them very close together and putting them at strange angles to make them fit. By the time he had them all on, Mrs. Aldridge had pulled Sasha up a little bit, and now the two women were kissing deeply, their tongues entwining as Mr. Aldridge tormented Sasha's cunt.

"You little bitch," Mrs. Aldridge said when their mouths pulled apart. "You know I just do this because I love you."

"Yes, Mistress," breathed Sasha, and then moaned as Mr. Aldridge teased her tormented cuntlips further open, exposing her tight little hole.

He had done quite an admirable job. From what Suzette could see, the binder clips radiated outward in a perfect pattern, looking not unlike a whirlpool or funnel drawing energy into Sasha's exposed pussy. Suzette felt a surge of jealousy, wishing she could be the one with her pussy all done up like that. The thought of the commensurate pain only brought more desire into Suzette's hungry body.

Now Mr. Aldridge was reaching down with one hand to hike Sasha's skirt up further, exposing those delicate globes of her ass more fully. His other hand appeared holding a thick metal ruler, and Sasha whimpered when she saw it. Mrs. Aldridge held Sasha tightly, kissing her hungrily, nipping at her bottom lip with her teeth, as Mr. Aldridge tested the weight of the ruler. After a few exploratory slaps, Mr. Aldridge lifted the rule and Sasha let out a wailing moan of desperate fear as she anticipated what was coming. The muscles of that gorgeous ass tightened just as Mr. Aldridge brought the ruler down with a loud SLAP! Sasha squirmed as he lifted the ruler again and brought it down, harder this time. Suzette watched, horrified and fascinated, and very turned on, as Sasha's ass wriggled back and forth under the merciless spanking. Her cheeks reddened under the rapid blows, until her milk-white ass was striped with red. Sasha looked up at Mrs. Aldridge and desperately moaned, "Mercy…."

Suzette was surprised and pleased to find that that only made Mr. Aldridge bring the ruler down harder on Sasha's bare ass. Sasha pressed her ass back, as if presenting it for Mr. Aldridge, and she suffered the beating as it grew faster and faster. Then, with sudden finality, it stopped.

Mr. Aldridge reached down between Sasha's legs with the tip of the ruler and teased the binder clips that kept her pussylips so enticingly open. Sasha gave a little whimper of shock as he did.

"I think we've tormented this little bitch enough for one night, don't you?" he asked his wife.

"I suppose so," said Mrs. Aldridge. "I think it would be giving her exactly what she wants to take those clips off right now and fuck her until she screams. Isn't that right, Sasha? Isn't that exactly what you want?"

"Y-yes," whimpered Sasha. "That is exactly what I want, Mistress. I want Mr. Aldridge to fuck me."

"Then let's send her home," said Mrs. Aldridge. "Sasha, I want you to wear these clips on your pussy all the way home. When you get there, I want you to lie down and take them off one at a time. Only *then* can you have an orgasm, either by getting yourself off or letting someone else fuck you like the slut you are. Either way, it makes no difference to me. Of course, needless to say, I expect you here on time tomorrow morning."

"Yes, Mistress," said Sasha obediently as Mrs. Aldridge helped her to stand up.

"Oh, yes," said Mrs. Aldridge. "We still need to lighten her load a little bit. She'll never be able to get home on the bus wearing these things on her tits.

Mr. and Mrs. Aldridge took the binder clips off Sasha's tits one at a time, each time massaging the blood back

The Office

into her tortured flesh. Sasha let out a wailing moan with each clip that was removed, and Suzette remembered reading something about that in a little blurb in the catalog. The nipple clips hurt worse when you take them off than when you put them on. Would the same be true for the clips on Sasha's pussylips? Suzette was sure that it would. At least, she certainly hoped so. The image of Sasha lying there taking the binder clips off her pussy, moaning, was enough to make Suzette want to follow her home.

Finally, all the binder clips were off of Sasha's breasts. Suzette watched as Mrs. Aldridge untied Sasha's wrists, and then Sasha shrugged her little demi-bra back on and pulled down her blouse. Sasha had some difficulty getting her skirt down, since of course she could by no means close her thighs. She stood awkwardly, her thighs forced to remain apart by the cruel clips on her pussy. Every time she moved her legs even a little bit, she gasped and whimpered in pain.

"Enjoy yourself on the way home," snickered Mrs. Aldridge viciously. "That commute is really long, isn't it? I hope this teaches you a lesson."

"Yes, Mistress," said Sasha obediently as she put on her coat. She had one of those long, thin, shimmery raincoats that isn't really made for the rain. Luckily for Sasha, that would conceal most of the awkward position of her legs as she rode the bus home.

Suzette realized that she had stayed too long—now, without the distraction of Sasha's torment to keep their attention, Mr. and Mrs. Aldridge would surely see her if she made a dash to the door! Suzette looked around for an escape route, and the best she could do was to shrink into the shadows behind the shelving. She tried to remain very still and not to make any noise at all.

Mrs. Aldridge took a moment to kiss Sasha hungrily. Then Sasha walked very slowly to the door—but not without dignity.

Suzette looked after her desperately, wondering if she was going to be trapped in here all night. But the second Sasha was out of the office, Mrs. Aldridge turned to Mr. Aldridge and embraced him.

"You were magnificent, darling," he sighed as he kissed her. "You're never as gorgeous as when you're disciplining some young slut."

"Thank you, my dear," said Mrs. Aldridge, lifting one leg to wrap it around Mr. Aldridge's body and pull him close. She arched her back, pressing her full breasts against Mr. Aldridge's chest.

"Do you think she'll learn her lesson?" asked Mr. Aldridge as he began to unbutton Mrs. Aldridge's blouse, revealing her large, enticing tits.

"Of course not," said Mrs. Aldridge. "The little slut is incapable of sexual restraint. She'll bed Suzette yet—but so much the better, then we get to punish both of them."

THE OFFICE

Suzette felt a surge go through her body, her nipples stiffening as she heard that. Mrs. Aldridge was planning to punish her. There were terrifying things in store for Suzette—and knowing they were on their way excited her immeasurably!

"Surely she won't try to bed Suzette on company time," said Mr. Aldridge. "Not now that you've confronted her on it."

"Just you wait," sighed Mrs. Aldridge, reaching down and slipping her hand inside Mr. Aldridge's pants, stroking his cock. "I fully expect to come back from lunch one day soon and find the two of them fucking on the reception desk."

"Please take Polaroids," said Mr. Aldridge as Mrs. Aldridge dropped to her knees, swiftly opening his pants and taking his long, hard cock out. Suzette watched, enraptured, as Mr. Aldridge's cock came into view. It was huge, even larger than Rob's—which was saying a lot. And Mrs. Aldridge dove onto it with obvious relish, hungrily swallowing as much of the erect pole as she could. Mr. Aldridge moaned in pleasure and rocked his hips forward as he ran his hands through his wife's hair. She pumped his cock into her mouth, undoing her blouse and bra, freeing those large, delicious tits. She let her husband's cock slip out of her mouth, then moved up just enough to slide his meat between her tits, pressing them together and embracing his shaft with her cleavage. Mr. Aldridge's hips moved in a slow circle, fucking his wife's enticing tits while her tongue slipped out to lick around the head of his cock.

Next, Mrs. Aldridge stood up and bent over the counter, hiking her skirt up to expose her ass. Suzette saw that Mrs. Aldridge wasn't wearing conventional panties—just a tiny little G-string framed by her white garters. Suzette had a perfect view from where she was hiding, and despite her terror of being discovered—much worse now that Sasha was no longer here—she watched hungrily as Mr. Aldridge came up from behind her and eased the string out of the way, fitting his cockhead into his wife's accepting channel and pushing forward, driving it home.

"Oh, God," she moaned as he penetrated her. "I'm so wet, I'm so hot, I'm going to come right away! God, shove it into me!"

"That's a good thing," groaned Mr. Aldridge. "After seeing that little slut's ass wiggle back and forth while I spanked her, I'm ready to come myself!"

"God! Fuck me!" Mrs. Aldridge was pumping her ass up and down, shoving it back against her husband's body, pushing herself onto his cock. He fucked her faster, and the two of them started moaning wildly as their mutual pleasure neared.

Suzette realized with disappointment that this was her chance. With all the noise the couple was making, there was no way they would notice the door closing. And if she didn't go now, there was no telling whether they might find her as soon as they didn't have their raging lusts to distract them.

But Suzette desperately wanted to see the couple fuck! In fact, it was making her so excited seeing Mr. Aldridge fuck his wife from behind, that Suzette was quite sure she could come with just a minimum of effort.

No! She had to go.

"FUCK ME! OH GOD FUCK ME FUCK ME HARDER! FUCK—FUCK! FUCK!"

Mrs. Aldridge was thrashing about on the counter, pumping her ass against her husband, impaling herself rhythmically on his prick. Suzette managed to tiptoe out from her hiding place, then quickly dart for the front door. She heard the couple's moans rising in volume as she opened the office door as silently as she could, then slipped out and closed it.

Once in the hall, Suzette realized that she was soaked in sweat—and, worst of all, she realized she had left her panties back there in the shadows behind the supply shelves, where she'd been hiding! God damn it! She couldn't go back and get them now...but what if they were discovered?

The moans of the happy couple were penetrating into the hallway, so that anyone on this whole floor could hear them. Luckily for everyone, it was almost eleven o'clock, and there was no one on the floor. Suzette would have been horribly embarrassed to run into a cleaning person as she was coming out of an office with that kind of caterwauling going on.

Suzette tried to collect herself. No one would notice the panties before morning. They were back in the corner, in the darkness. She would just go in a little early and pick them up first thing. It would be okay.

Besides, she thought as a moan echoed through the halls, *Neither of them is going to be paying attention to what's on the floor behind the shelves tonight.*

Of course, then there was the added problem that she had to go home on the bus without any panties at all. And she was wearing one of her tighter skirts, a little bit shorter than usual. Oh, well, nothing could be done about that. But standing there as the elevator accelerated, Suzette found herself acutely aware of the fact that she wasn't wearing anything under the skirt. It was perversely exciting to her—there was just something very rebellious and dangerous to it. Alone in the elevator, she lifted her skirt and slipped her hand between her legs, checking to see whether she was wet. She certainly was, so wet that her upper thighs were slick with sweat and with the juices of her cunt. Suzette laughed a little as she tugged her skirt down. It was going to be a long bus ride home—and damn it, she hadn't even remembered to get her bus pass from her desk!

Chapter 6

Suzette had already reached the bus stop when she recognized the woman standing there—it was Sasha.

Suzette's heart almost stopped. She stood there dumbfounded, staring at Sasha while Sasha looked back with casual surprise.

"Suzette," said Sasha. "What are you doing down here so late? You left work hours ago."

"Sasha...hi there...I...um...I was having dinner with a friend just a few blocks away from here," Suzette lied quickly. "At...Panache, that new restaurant, have you heard of it?"

"Yes," said Sasha, casually. "I think I've heard of it. Good?"

"Yes, yes, very good. Great food. You're not just leaving work now, I hope?"

"Well, almost," said Sasha, her eyes flickering over Suzette's body. Suzette noticed the evident discomfort with which Sasha was standing, and remembered the binder clips on her cunt. God, they must really be hurting by now. "I left twenty minutes ago, but I'm still waiting for the bus."

"Yeah," said Suzette. "That sucks." Then, nervously, "Where do you live?" she blurted out, too quickly and eagerly.

"Up near Seventeenth Street and Second Ave, up the hill," said Sasha, her face reddening as she shifted her body a bit. Suzette took special notice of the way Sasha moved her hips and legs—she was obviously keeping her thighs just far enough apart to keep the clips apart. "I really need to get home soon," she said. "Really soon. Really soon." Sasha's voice sounded strained.

"I...I live up there," lied Suzette. "Want to share a cab?"

Sasha looked puzzled, but only for a second. She jumped at the opportunity. "Yes," she said. "I would like that very much."

In the cab, Suzette kept looking at the uncomfortable way Sasha was sitting, thinking about those clips sprouting off her pussylips, threatening to turn them black and blue if she didn't get them off quickly. The clips had to be torturing Sasha's most private place, tormenting her full and swollen cuntlips. All because Sasha was hot for Suzette. All because Mrs. Aldridge wanted to punish her for the way she had been flirting. God, that was hot. Suzette could smell the tang of Sasha's sweat mixed with the diluted scent of her musky perfume. She thought about Sasha's cunt being all tormented by those clips under her skirt. She looked up into Sasha's face, noticing again how attractive she was, and how nice the swell of her breasts looked under that revealing blouse.

"How long have you lived in the neighborhood?" asked Sasha, giving Suzette a somewhat knowing glance through the discomfort on her face.

That was a difficult question—Suzette didn't live in the neighborhood at all, she lived quite the other direction. She didn't know why she had blurted out that she lived in Sasha's neighborhood—except that the idea of sharing a cab with Sasha while she was experiencing such painful genital torture had excited her so.

"Oh…about two months," said Suzette.

"You live alone?" Sasha asked provocatively. Sasha's eyes were roving over Suzette, the way they usually did. Except now, at eleven o'clock at night, in a cab on the way to Sasha's house, and with the scene Suzette had just witnessed, the heavy flirtation vibe that Sasha always gave off had quite a new emphasis to it.

"I...I have a roommate."

"Just a roommate?"

"Yes," said Suzette, smiling. She could tell that Sasha was definitely flirting with her, despite the extreme discomfort she must have been feeling. Suzette was in quite a bit of discomfort herself, not having been able to get off while she was watching the scene in the office, for fear of making noise and being discovered. That meant that the ache of unreleased lust filled her whole lower body, making her even a little bit sick to her stomach. She imagined that Sasha might be feeling a little bit the same way—after all, Mr. and Mrs. Aldridge hadn't let Sasha get off before banishing her to this torturous ride home.

"It's up here on the left," said Sasha, and the cab pulled over in front of a big white apartment building.

Sasha looked at Suzette for a long, silent moment, while Suzette stared nervously back at her.

"Would you like to come up for a cup of tea? Maybe a glass of wine?"

Sasha's eyes sparkled as she said it, and Suzette knew if she accepted she would find herself in bed with Sasha before the night was out.

"Oh, it's so late," said Suzette. "I really should be getting home. I don't want...I don't want to keep you up. I don't want to inconvenience you."

"It's no inconvenience at all, and I won't sleep for a

few hours anyway," said Sasha, and her eyes locked on Suzette's. Suzette knew very well that she was being seduced, and the fact that it was being done by a woman with such extreme yet temporary genital distress at the hands of the divine Mrs. Aldridge was enough to make her go mad with desire. She knew quite well that she was about to go to bed with another woman, to make love with Sasha. The idea was painfully arousing to her.

"Please come up," said Sasha. "Just for one cup of tea. Just one."

"All right," said Suzette. She fumbled for money to pay the cab, but Sasha had already gotten it. They got out of the cab and Suzette followed Sasha up three flights of stairs, noticing with each step how awkwardly Sasha moved. Suzette's nipples were very hard under her blouse. God, Sasha had a gorgeous body. Suzette wondered if she liked men as well as women—well, she had let Mr. Aldridge take part in punishing her.

Sasha's apartment was a surprisingly large one-bedroom, with a beautiful view of the city through a large set of bay windows. There was a big, fluffy white couch in front of the bay windows, and a number of expensive prints on the walls. Suzette was slightly embarrassed to note that they were all erotic drawings or black-and-white photographs of naked women. But she supposed that shouldn't have embarrassed her, given what she and Sasha were about to do.

"If you'll excuse me," said Sasha in a slightly strained voice, "there's something I have to do. I won't be long. Please make yourself at home."

Sasha disappeared into the single bedroom and closed the door.

Suzette felt her knees going weak as she thought about what Sasha was going to do. She was going in there to lift her skirt, spread her legs…and slowly take off the clips on her pussy, one by one. God, the pain she must be feeling. God, the humiliation of being made to go home wearing them. *Oh, my…*

Suzette suddenly sank into the couch, finding it delightfully soft and fluffy. She was getting incredibly turned on thinking about Sasha's torment, but she didn't dare touch herself. This was all on top of the already painful arousal surging through her body. God, she was helpless. She would do anything for sexual release. She knew she was at Sasha's mercy, that she would spend the rest of the night making love with Sasha, experiencing her first taste of sex with another woman. Suzette whimpered in anticipation.

From the other room, Suzette heard a low moan, then a gasp. Even Sasha couldn't suppress her moans of pain as the circulation flowed back into her tortured pussylips.

Suzette imagined what Sasha was doing. Perhaps she had lifted her skirt and lay down on the bed, spreading her legs wide. Then, slowly, she had plucked the first clip from her pussy, the pain exploding through her as the blood flowed back into her tortured lips. She arched her back and thrashed in pain, moaning. God, Suzette could come right now if she could just rub her legs together a little.

Afraid to be caught touching herself with her hand—Suzette didn't even know if Sasha had roommates who might walk in any minute—Suzette pressed her thighs firmly together and felt the pressure against her clit, swollen and awakened as it was. She felt so slutty not wearing panties to go to Sasha's apartment. Well, soon they wouldn't be wearing anything. Suzette was sure of it. She felt a wave of fear and wondered if she shouldn't get up and leave. But then she would have to go home all by herself...and if she stayed, she would get to spend the rest of the night touching Sasha's beautiful body.

Another moan came from the bedroom. Suzette shuddered as her arousal mounted. She felt totally helpless. She belonged completely to Sasha.

She remembered what she had heard back at the office. She was off-limits to Sasha. That meant if Mrs. Aldridge found out that the two of them had gone home together, then Sasha would be deliciously punished again. Perhaps even more cruelly punished this time.

Sasha's moans died off, and a few minutes later she came out of the bedroom wearing a long white silk robe.

Suzette looked at Sasha and felt an immediate hunger; Sasha looked gorgeous in that robe. The robe plunged at the perfect angle to accentuate her large breasts, and the material clung to her curves perfectly. Suzette watched as Sasha sauntered into the kitchen and heard the sound of a cork popping.

After a few minutes, Sasha came back out, holding two goblets of red wine.

"I decided we should have wine, instead of tea," said Sasha. "I hope you like red."

"I love it," said Suzette breathlessly, accepting the goblet of wine Sasha handed to her. She sipped it and found it excellent though she probably would have found anything excellent at that point.

Sasha sat down on the couch, just a trifle closer to Suzette than would usually be considered appropriate. Suzette's body responded immediately. She felt as if her erect nipples were showing quite obviously through her blouse, and she didn't doubt that they probably were. And that Sasha had probably noticed as she leaned a little closer to Suzette, her arm propped up on the back of the couch.

"Do you live alone?" Suzette asked nervously.

"No," said Sasha. "I have a boyfriend. He lives here with me."

"Is he..."

"He's out of town," said Sasha smoothly. "He's a

photographer, and he does a lot of traveling. I'm alone here quite a bit."

"Oh," said Suzette with some difficulty. "I see."

A long silence passed. "Does he know...what you do?"

Sasha smiled provocatively. "What do I do?"

"I mean...about Bondage..."

"Yes, he knows. He's one of their photographers."

"You mean..."

"That's right," said Sasha. "He takes bondage photos. I'm even in some of them."

"Oh, my." Suzette's pussy was aching something awful, and the scent of Sasha's body so close to her was more than she could stand. She gulped her wine and turned to face Sasha.

"Does he know...um...about your...personal interests?"

"Personal interests? What personal interests do I have?" Sasha was looking into Suzette's eyes, and Suzette felt Sasha's hand gently brushing against her arm.

"You know...I mean...are you interested in bondage and stuff...as a lifestyle, I mean? Do you do it in real life?"

"What do you think?" asked Sasha flirtatiously.

"I...I don't know, we've never talked about it. Do you?"

Sasha leaned very close. "Do you?"

"I...I think it's very interesting...the images are very sexy, of course, and I like the ideas..." Suzette was very nervous now, not making much sense. Sasha leaned still closer. Her lips parted slightly.

"John loves to tie me up and fuck me," said Sasha. "And I love it when he ties my breasts up. You've seen the pictures of breast bondage in the catalog? Like that. It turns me on so much I come just from the slightest pressure on my clit, when I've got my tits all trussed up like that. Does that shock you?"

Sasha's eyes were locked on Suzette's, and Suzette slowly shook her head. In fact, it turned her on incredibly.

Sasha leaned forward and kissed Suzette hungrily. Suzette let out a little whimper and relaxed into Sasha's arms. Sasha held her close, pressing their bodies together, as they continued kissing. Sasha crawled slowly on top of Suzette, the clasp of the white robe coming undone. The rope opened up and Suzette felt the delicious texture of Sasha's naked body against her hands. Unable to stop herself, or unwilling, Suzette let her hands creep over Sasha's beautiful breasts, feeling the slightly raised places where the clips had been applied. Suzette felt Sasha's knee creeping up between her legs, then felt Sasha deftly lifting her skirt.

"No underwear," said Sasha. "You little slut."

Sasha began kissing Suzette again, while Suzette

played with Sasha's delightful breasts. Her nipples were extremely hard, and very sensitive, judging from the little moaning sounds she made as Suzette teased her nipples. Sasha went to work on Suzette's blouse, quickly unbuttoning it and exposing Suzette's breasts to her subtle caresses.

"You have such lovely tits," said Sasha. "I've been admiring them ever since you came to that interview."

Suzette was about to respond in kind, but Sasha firmly pinched her nipples, making a surge of pleasure on the very edge of pain go through Suzette's body. Her back arched as she pressed up against Sasha, and she writhed with pleasure as Sasha teased and pinched her nipples.

Sasha eased back just long enough to stare seductively into Suzette's eyes. "Would you like to...go into the bedroom?"

Suzette nodded, her breath coming short. It was about to happen: she was about to go to bed with Sasha.

Sasha stood, holding Suzette's hand, and led her into the bedroom.

Suzette stood there while Sasha slowly undressed her, helping her off with the blouse, bra, and skirt, then shrugging off her own robe so the two of them stood naked together. Sasha inched up to Suzette's body until her hard nipples just brushed Suzette's; she put her arms around Suzette and the two of them began to kiss as they moved slowly toward the bed.

Once on the bed, Suzette moaned softly as Sasha climbed on top of her, bringing her knee up between her slightly-parted thighs. Suzette closed her thighs tightly around Sasha's knee, rocking rhythmically against her and writhing in pleasure as she felt the pressure of Sasha's knee against her clit. Suzette was almost in ecstasy, tottering on the brink of her orgasm, feeling the climax well up inside of her from the hours and hours of arousal she'd suffered. She lay there tangled in the sheets as Sasha ran her hands over her body, kissing and sucking as she explored Suzette's naked form. Suzette dimly felt Sasha taking hold of her wrists, then pinning them over her head, against the headboard. Suzette hardly knew what was happening as Sasha quickly bound her wrists together over her head and then lashed them to the headboard. Suzette didn't care what Sasha was going to do to her—she only knew that Sasha was taking complete control, and Suzette could give herself over to Sasha's total possession. Suzette lay with her wrists tied on the bed as Sasha retrieved more rope from the nightstand and pinned Suzette's right ankle to the bed, lashing it with rope and then tying it to the post of the four-poster bed. As Sasha went to work on Suzette's right ankle, restraining that as well, Suzette began to realize just what was happening—she was being tied to the bed by a woman she barely knew. But this was a woman who was so enticing, so intriguing to Suzette that she was prepared to go to bed with her even after witnessing the hopelessly perverse scene at the office.

Suzette struggled a little against the bonds and found that she was expertly tied to the bed. She panicked, looking up helplessly at Sasha as Sasha glared down at her coldly. Sasha's naked, beautiful body towered over Suzette, and Suzette knew that she was going to be put to the brutal test. This would not be the gentle lovemaking she had anticipated—rather, Suzette was going to be put through her paces as Mr. and Mrs. Aldridge had put Sasha through hers.

Suzette could not mistake the look of total domination on Sasha's face as she towered over the bound and helpless Suzette. Suzette squirmed on the bed, pulling harder against her bonds and finding that she was securely tied. Slowly, Sasha lowered herself on top of Suzette's bound, naked, writhing body.

"You can't tell me you haven't been fantasizing about this," growled Sasha roughly. "You can't tell me you haven't been wanting this ever since you walked in the door. I see the way you look at me. You've wanted to do this ever since you first laid eyes on me."

Suzette didn't know how to answer; Sasha gripped Suzette's hair and breathed warmly into her ear.

"You little slut, you've been waiting to get up to my

apartment. Your pussy was all wet just thinking about it. You even waited for me after work so you could get back to my place and throw yourself at me. Didn't you, you little slut?"

Suzette whimpered, feeling the pressure of Sasha's naked body bearing her down. Her cunt ached in painful arousal, and she was sure she was incredibly wet.

"You're wet right now, aren't you? You're incredibly wet."

"Ohhh...no...no...," Suzette murmured her protestations more because it turned her on to do so than because she wasn't wet or didn't want Sasha to be doing this to her. In fact, Suzette was incredibly wet, and hearing Sasha call her a slut was making her wetter with every word. Sasha leaned heavily on Suzette, grasping her hair and pulling her head to the side so she could growl into Suzette's ear.

"You didn't even wear any underwear. You waited for me after work so you could follow me home and throw yourself at me. Isn't that right, you little slut?"

Suzette was mad with arousal, the painful throb of her cunt just begging for attention. But in this position, bound spread-eagled on Sasha's bed, Suzette couldn't even rub her thighs together, let alone get herself off. Suzette was wholly and totally at Sasha's mercy. And Sasha was relishing the power she had over the very soundly trussed Suzette.

The Office

"Have you ever been with a woman before?" growled Sasha, ramming her knee up into Suzette's spread and exposed crotch. Suzette's back arched and she moaned softly as she felt the pressure against her vulnerable cunt.

"Tell me!"

"No," said Suzette breathlessly, grinding her hips to press her cunt up against Sasha's knee. Sasha's hand moved down under Suzette's pert ass and gripped it hard, pulling Suzette against her so the firmness of Sasha's knee pressed harder into Suzette's cunt. "I've never been with a woman," she whispered.

"Mmmm…a virgin…," sighed Sasha. "I hope I'm not going too fast for you, you little slut. After all, if this is your first time…"

Suzette's eyes went wide as she looked up at Sasha. "No," she said, her mouth slack with rapture. "Please don't stop. Make me yours. I want to be completely owned by you. I want you to be rough with me. You can do anything. Do whatever you want to me."

Suzette couldn't believe she was saying those things. She was completely intoxicated by lust and by the delicious feeling of having Sasha's body pressed against hers. She squirmed under Sasha, pressing up against her as Sasha smiled down at her.

"Anything…whatever I want?" Sasha was plainly aroused by the concept. "Anything I want with this juicy virgin body of yours…" In the hour since she had left the office, Sasha had turned from a whimpering submissive into a powerful dominant, completely taking over Suzette's body. "I own you. You are mine. I'm going to take everything I want from your body and you're going to give it to me whether you want to or not." Sasha rammed her knee more firmly against Suzette's cunt, and Suzette strained up against her, on the very brink of her climax. She began to pant rhythmically, hovering at the edge of her come, and as Sasha realized how close Suzette was, she laughed.

"Not until I come, Suzette. Don't you always know, the mistress always comes first? You're the one tied up, you're going to have to do what *I* want. And I want to come. You've been teasing me for weeks with that juicy little body of yours. Now let's see if you can put it to some good use and make me come."

"Yes…," panted Suzette. "Please…"

"If you've never been with a woman, then you've never eaten pussy before," said Sasha harshly. "You've never had that pretty mouth of yours on a woman's cunt."

Suzette shook her head. "I haven't. I've never eaten pussy," she said breathlessly.

Sasha chuckled. "But you know what you like to have done to you," she said. "Well, you're eating pussy tonight. That pretty mouth of yours is going to work like the dickens until I get off, you little slut. Understand?"

Suzette was overwhelmed with lust, totally beside herself with hunger for Sasha's pussy. She wanted to eat Sasha out—but the fact that she was tied up and unable to say "no" made her ten times more desperate to do it. Sasha didn't wait for Suzette to respond before she climbed on top of her, repositioning her body until her legs were spread around Suzette's face. Suzette's arms were still stretched out over her head, bound to the headboard. That gave Sasha the perfect opportunity to tuck a pillow under Suzette's head and place her mouth at exactly the right angle to service her sexually. "You'd better learn how to do this well," she said roughly. Sasha's cunt was bright red, tortured from the earlier application of the clips. Suzette remembered how beautiful her pussy had looked all stretched out and displayed with the clips around it like the petals of a flower. The memory made a surge of thirst for Sasha's pussy take Suzette over, and she parted her lips, her eyes rolling back in her head as she descended into rapture. Sasha reached down and gently parted the lips of her pussy with two fingers, exposing the juicy, drizzling center and the ripe bud of her clit. She settled down on Suzette's face, wriggling her ass as she did.

Sasha moaned as she felt Suzette's tongue pressing up into her, teasing her clit and the lips of her sex.

Suzette's first taste was of the overwhelming tang and musk of Sasha's pussy. She forced her tongue up against the soft, yielding flesh, then licked her way up to the clit and teased that with the tip of her tongue. She heard Sasha moaning uncontrollably, so she must have been doing the right things. She remembered what she liked having done to her when Rob was going down on her—which he did often—and what she had thought about doing for years in her fantasies about women. Suzette had never really thought she would end up in bed with a woman—certainly not tied up like this for her first time!—but she had spent long, lush hours fantasizing about what it would be like to lick another woman's pussy, with its delicious tangy musk and all its crevasses of pleasure.

Now she explored it firsthand, slipping her tongue up between the lips of Sasha's sex, teasing her erect clit, slipping the tip of her tongue into Sasha's entrance. Sasha moaned especially when she did that; she must have had a very sensitive vagina. But mostly Suzette focused on the clit, and that produced the most rhythmic noises from Sasha's eager mouth, as if she was going to come. Suzette pulled at the bonds and struggled, imagining that she was being forced to service Sasha against her will. In reality, nothing could have been further from the truth— Suzette was so delirious with pleasure at having sex with Sasha that she was beside herself. But thinking about being forced, about being Sasha's unwilling slave, made Suzette that much more excited and made her eager tongue-thrusts that much more enthusiastic. Sasha was moaning, rocking her hips in perfect rhythm. Suzette's mouth was filled with the sharp taste of Sasha's pussy, and she desperately wanted Sasha to come on her mouth. Would she be able to feel the contractions of Sasha's pussy muscles when she came? She hoped so. She licked rapidly, spending a lot of time caressing Sasha's clit as she strove upward to pleasure the dominant woman.

Sasha, meanwhile, was enjoying herself immensely, loving the sight of Suzette bound to the bed, servicing her eagerly. She knelt over Suzette's face, rocking her body up and down. Each hand pinched and rolled a nipple as she worked her breasts around in large circles. She was going to come any minute, she knew, but there was no reason to rush it—she wanted to make Suzette work as hard as possible. After all, the little bitch had gotten so much enjoyment out of spying on her, it was only proper that she give something back now.

Sasha threw her head back, her red hair streaming down her naked back. She ground her hips down, forcing her pussy roughly onto Suzette's eagerly seeking mouth. Suzette's tongue worked its wonders inside

Sasha's sex, and Sasha's lips parted wide in a moan of unspeakable ecstasy. Then Sasha was coming, writhing and pumping her hips back and forth as she rode Suzette's face, climaxing with every cell of her body.

Suzette licked more eagerly as she heard Sasha coming—it gave her incredible pleasure to be bringing Sasha off like this. When Sasha had finished, she settled down on Suzette's face for long minutes, savoring the afterglow and the feel of Suzette's warm mouth against her pussy. Then she lifted herself off Suzette and crouched over her, looking down at Suzette's face, which glistened with the juices of Sasha's pussy.

"Not bad for a beginner," said Sasha uncharitably. "You need a few pointers, but I'll give those to you later. When it's my turn. For now...I want to know how much you saw."

"Wh—what are you talking about?"

"You know what I'm talking about," growled Sasha, pinching Suzette's nipples so she gasped and squirmed. "Now confess."

Suzette whimpered in fear. "I...I saw Mr. and Mrs. Aldridge punishing you."

"Yes. What did you see?" Sasha tormented Suzette's nipples, and her knee came to rest between Suzette's thighs, pressing against her cunt, sending waves of pleasure through Suzette's body, rocking up and down as Suzette spoke.

"They started by...by pressing your tits against... against the copier."

"Yes," whispered Sasha, remembering fondly. "Go on."

"The glass must have gotten very hot..."

"Oh, it did. *Very* hot. Tomorrow when Mrs. Aldridge goes to lunch, I'll show you just *how* hot."

"Oh, God..." Suzette's cunt surged at the thought. Sasha pinched her nipples harder.

"Continue!" she said harshly.

"Then—then Mr. Aldridge put clips all over your breasts..."

"Mmmm...," sighed Sasha rapturously, stroking Suzette's breasts. "Keep going."

"And....all over your cunt."

"Yessss...," hissed Sasha, rubbing her body against Suzette's. "So you know I had the clips on the whole way home."

"Aaaah!" Suzette's back arched. Sasha, sensing the imminence of Suzette's climax, rammed her knee against Suzette's cunt and began thrusting hard. Suzette came with a shuddering moan, her whole body twitching and spasming in ecstasy as she gave herself over to the climax.

"Then you know what Mrs. Aldridge has in mind for you," sighed Sasha, kissing Suzette's spittle-flecked lips as Suzette finished coming. "You know that she's going to seduce you, and make you her slave. I think that she never would have hired you if she didn't know that's what you wanted from the first moment you saw her."

"Oh, God...," panted Suzette, her mind awash with mixed emotions. "Is she really going to do that?"

"She is really going to do that," sighed Sasha. "She's going to seduce you, and you're going to give yourself willingly. Once she's had you, she's going to make you her slave, make you wholly owned by her. Like she's done with me. I have John, but Mrs. Aldridge is the one who really owns me. I started out an employee just like you. But that didn't last long. When Mrs. Aldridge understood that I wanted to be hers, she seduced me. And soon I belonged to her. I do whatever she says."

"But...but...you're making love to me even though she told you not to," said Suzette, puzzled.

A look of fear crossed Sasha's face. "I know. I'm being bad. Please...please don't tell her. You can't tell her. No matter what she does. You have to keep it a secret. Please? I'll be in horrible trouble if she finds out we slept together."

"All right," promised Suzette. "I won't tell her. Are you really that afraid of her authority?"

Sasha shuddered. "Yes. She owns me completely. If she finds out I disobeyed her, she'll punish me horribly. Why do you think I call her Mrs. Aldridge? It's a term of respect, showing that I am her inferior. When you said you wanted to call her by that formal title...she—

and I—both knew that you were destined to end up on your knees before her."

Suzette's body was aching with desire just hearing about this. Sasha easily slipped two fingers into Suzette's cunt, and began to finger-fuck her as she went on talking.

"She's going to own you totally. Soon you'll be on your knees, servicing her and her husband. I know you'll like that."

"H—how does it happen?" panted Suzette. Part of her was horrified at what she was hearing, but she knew that it was what she had wanted all along. She had sensed that Mrs. Aldridge would own her, and now she knew it was going to happen. It was only a matter of time.

"Oh, she'll call you into her office…upbraid you for some imagined offense…then she'll start the discipline. If you're the type she thinks you are, then you'll come up with the punishments yourself. Maybe it will start with spanking, then with exhibition…soon she'll expect you to service her as a regular duty. Orally, I mean. Like you just did for me. Soon she'll take you home with her, or on some business trip with her and her husband. By the end of the weekend you won't be able to walk straight, you will have been fucked so many times. And you'll be totally owned by the Aldridges. Assuming that's what you want, of course."

"Oh, God, yes...," panted Suzette, not even really aware of what she was saying. She arched her back, pushing her hips up so that Sasha could finger-fuck her harder and faster. She was almost ready to come, but listening to Sasha's description of what must be her ultimate submission to Mrs. Aldridge was turning her on so much Suzette didn't want Sasha to stop.

"She'll start instructing you in what to wear to the office...those tight clothes I wear, they were all purchased on her credit card, on her orders. And I've been conservative because you've been around. Believe me, when she's really training you, really showing you how you belong to her, you'll know it from what she has you wear. Tight, short skirts without any panties... thin tops without any bras. Sometimes she'll like to send you out on your lunch hour and tell you to find someone you don't know to have a sexual experience with, then come back and tell her about it. She's done that to me a dozen times."

Suzette panted in time with Sasha's finger-thrusts into her pussy. "And...and...did you—did you do it?"

"Oh, yes, every time," said Sasha. "It was difficult at first, but I knew if I didn't do it I would displease Mrs. Aldridge. And I wouldn't want to do that. The first time I just found a businessman down at the bus station... well, we did it in the rest room. I certainly can't say I didn't enjoy it, and Mrs. Aldridge was very proud of me. We spent all afternoon in her office after that one. The next few times were women…then men…I like to alternate, it makes Mrs. Aldridge happy. She likes to see me being a perfect slut with both sexes…"

As Sasha pronounced that word "slut," a wave of pleasure went through Suzette's body, and she began arching her back, thrusting her hips back and forth, heaving herself forward to push herself onto Sasha's fingers. Sasha now had three fingers in Suzette, thrusting them quickly. Suzette was moaning and thrashing wildly, but she could hear Sasha perfectly as she went on.

"Other times, Mr. Aldridge will come by…and you'll have to have sex with him in front of Mrs. Aldridge. Does that bother you?"

"Aaaah— Oh, God—no—no—no—I want it—" moaned Suzette as Sasha's fingers pistoned inside her. Suzette's mind was filled with images of having sex with Mr. Aldridge as Mrs. Aldridge watched.

"All of this assumes your absolute submission, of course…if you would prefer not to be Mrs. Aldridge's slave, you can certainly keep your job, and I'll even stop flirting with you—"

"No, no, no, no—n-n-no no no!" Suzette panted and moaned as Sasha finger-fucked her rapidly, holding her on the brink of climax.

Sasha smiled, only slightly winded from the vigorous finger-fucking she was giving Suzette. "All right, then. Then you know what's going to happen." She picked up speed, pounding her fingers into Suzette's willing, receptive cunt. "You will give yourself totally to Mrs. Aldridge, and you'll be soundly made her slave—soon to be on your knees before her, eating her sweet pussy—oh, yes—come, you little bitch—come—come—"

And Suzette came, straining against the ropes, thrashing on the bed, pumping her hips to receive the powerful thrusts of Sasha's fingers as they penetrated her again and again and again.

Chapter 7

Suzette felt an almost painful anticipation. Now that Sasha had told her all of Mrs. Aldridge's secrets, she was more frightened of Mrs. Aldridge —and eager to impress her—than she had been before. And she felt, deep inside, that a stern punishment from her employer was in her immediate future.

But just *how* would her punishment happen? That was the source of Suzette's greatest anxiety. Would she be called in to Mrs. Aldridge's office and then ordered to lift her skirt for a spanking? Would she be taken out on a business dinner and then made to fuck Mr. Aldridge in the bathroom of some expensive French restaurant? Or would she be left in torment, made to suffer endless weeks of painful arousal as Mrs. Aldridge toyed with her, never giving Suzette the punishment she so acutely craved?

Suzette arrived at the office five minutes late. That was something she had never done—she had always been early or exactly on time, and she usually stayed late. But she had been so slow to get started this morning, after the exquisitely trying night she'd endured at Sasha's hands.

Suzette's face turned deep pink as she walked through the office door. Mrs. Aldridge had already arrived.

Mrs. Aldridge was looking through some files near the front door of the office. She was bent over gracefully, her ass stretched beautifully against the conservative gray wool of her business suit. Her hair, which was not pulled back as usual, streamed down invitingly over her face. From the angle at which Mrs. Aldridge was bent over, Suzette could just barely see down her blouse. Mrs. Aldridge was wearing a tight, low-cut camisole, that allowed Suzette an unimpeded view of the woman's luscious cleavage. Suzette felt her blood pressure rising as she walked past Mrs. Aldridge.

"Good morning," Suzette murmured uncomfortably.

Mrs. Aldridge quickly looked up, just catching Suzette's unintentional leer as she looked down the older woman's blouse. Did she know what Suzette was looking at? Suzette felt hot all of a sudden, and as she began to speak, her voice caught in her throat.

"S-sorry I'm late," she mumbled nervously, feeling the heat flood through her body from the stern look Mrs. Aldridge gave her.

Mrs. Aldridge looked down again, without the slightest acknowledgment of either the "Good morning" or the "Sorry I'm late." Her clear annoyance sent an electric charge through Suzette's body, and she became painfully aware of the fact that the skirt she was wearing was two sizes too small.

Suzette sat down at her desk, acutely feeling the tightness of her skirt, and wished she'd run home to change. God, she was incredibly turned on already. She felt humiliated by having walked in late in front of Mrs. Aldridge—should she apologize again, and tell her it wouldn't happen again? Thinking about doing that sent a new warmth through Suzette's body, as she contemplated the ritual humbling of employee before employer. Suzette was beginning to get wet.

There was a thick envelope on her desk with her full name on it.

Quickly, Suzette stood up and walked over to where Mrs. Aldridge was bent over the files. She cleared her throat and stood near her.

"M-M-Mrs. Aldridge?" Suzette began, then blurted out: "I just want to say I'm very sorry that I was late this morning. I want you to know that I don't intend to make a habit of it. It won't happen again."

Mrs. Aldridge slowly stood, the file she'd been seeking clutched firmly in her hand. She looked Suzette up and down cruelly, obviously exploring the curves of the younger woman's body. Then Mrs. Aldridge tossed her hair imperiously and, without a word, stalked past Suzette and into her office.

Suzette felt a shudder go through her. She had been put so soundly in her place by Mrs. Aldridge's profound disregard for her that a new flood of arousal had gone through her body. Maybe she shouldn't have said anything. But Suzette had been powerless to stop her ritual supplication before Mrs. Aldridge, as powerless as she had been to stop herself from touching her pussy and rubbing herself to near orgasm while she watched the scene last night.

Suzette's nipples were very hard, showing plainly through her blouse. She could feel that she was already quite wet, having melted under Mrs. Aldridge's steely gaze. Mrs. Aldridge's rudeness at not even acknowledging Suzette's apology was something she didn't expect. But it had served to place Suzette, figuratively speaking, low on her knees before her employer.

Suzette's body shivered as she thought to herself how much she would like to be there quite literally. To literally lower herself to her knees before Mrs. Aldridge.

The Office

The door opened and Sasha came in, shattering Suzette's erotic daydreaming. Nervously, Suzette hurried over to her own desk and sat down, as Sasha breezed by with a half-hearted, "Good morning, Suzette." She barely even acknowledged Suzette's existence. Sasha was putting on a very good act.

But then, as Sasha moved behind Suzette's desk to get to the counter which held the coffee pot, she casually brushed against Suzette, her breasts with their rockhard nipples rubbing against Suzette's back. Sasha hesitated just a moment too soon, and Suzette felt the acute ache of her arousal beginning anew. After all, that sort of blatant tease was typical for Sasha—she'd been doing it regularly to Suzette for weeks now. But now that they'd been to bed together, it was more than just a casual flirtation. It was a promise of potential delights to come.

Suzette had an intense memory of being tied naked to Sasha's bed, Sasha's fingers thrust rhythmically into her cunt as Sasha whispered dirty words to her about what a whore Suzette was, what a little slut she had proven herself to be, what a juicy little bitch she was, and how she was going to find herself bound and gagged on her knees....

Suzette was *definitely* getting wet now.

The coffee pot was on the counter just behind Suzette's desk. So it wasn't really unthinkable that Sasha would need to bend forward so far to get the coffee out of the bottom drawer…to bend over so far, pressing her ass in that tight wool miniskirt against Suzette's shoulder…bringing a faint quickening to Suzette's breathing…

Then again, it seemed that Sasha was definitely leaning back further than she really needed to.

"Sasha," came Mrs. Aldridge's voice. "I would like to see you in my office, please."

Quickly, Sasha stood upright, turned and gave Suzette a conspiratorial look, and walked over to Mrs. Aldridge's office. Suzette briefly noticed how attractive her legs and ass looked perched on those unnecessarily-high heels.

"Close the door," said Mrs. Aldridge as Sasha entered the office.

Sasha turned to give Suzette another conspiratorial look as she closed the door. Then the thick soundproof door was shut, and Suzette was left with only her imagination to tell her what might be going on in that richly-furnished office.

Suzette finally managed to wrench her attention away from her memories of the previous night and the attractiveness of her new bed partner. She lifted the large lumpy envelope on her desk, and reached for her letter opener. She quickly slit the envelope.

Suzette gasped, and immediately her eyes widened in horror. The envelope contained a pair of black panties—

The Office

the pair that Suzette had left last night in the office, in the darkness behind the shelves. Also in the envelope were several of the photocopies Mrs. Aldridge had made while tormenting Sasha's breasts with the heat of the photocopier glass. The photocopies showed a crisp, if distorted, black-and-white image of Sasha's large and enticing breasts, with the dark circles of her nipples prominently displayed. Her breasts were clearly flattened firmly against the glass, and it made Suzette wince in pain to remember how Sasha had wailed as the photocopier glass had heated up with repeated imaging.

Finally, the envelope held a formal memorandum from Mrs. Aldridge to Suzette.

```
            Memorandum

From: B. Aldridge
To: Suzette Sullivan
Date: August 14, 19--
Re: Interim Review

Please report to my office at 10:00 A.M.
today for a brief discussion of your
performance in your current position.

Please bring your files from last night.
```

Suzette's heart pounded. Her breath came in short gasps. Distantly, she heard a faint *thwack!* through the door to Mrs. Aldridge's office.

She quickly closed the envelope, clutching it to her chest.

A few moments later, the door to Mrs. Aldridge's office opened and Sasha came out, walking a little more awkwardly than before, her face completely composed but quickly reddening. She left the office door open. Sasha's skirt was slightly wrinkled as if it had recently been pulled up to her waist.

"Coffee?" said Sasha absently.

It was 9:45 A.M. Suzette shuddered.

Suzette had been up until four in the morning, bound naked and spread-eagled to Sasha's bed. Sasha had fucked Suzette over and over again with her incredibly skillful hands, teasing orgasm upon orgasm out of Suzette's helpless but eager and willing body. Suzette had felt Sasha's gifted fingertips tease her clit in ways she never would have thought possible. The intricate magic Sasha wrought inside Suzette's open pussy brought fireworks of overwhelming pleasure to her vulnerable body. She had felt Sasha stimulate every inch of her pussy, teasing new sensations out of Suzette's well-fucked opening. By the time Sasha had finally curled up on top of Suzette and gone to sleep, Suzette had lost count of the number of times she had climaxed on Sasha's fingers, had lost count of how often she had begged Sasha not to stop fucking her. She was well aware that her pussy was getting red and raw from the fervent finger-fucking she was receiving—but it never entered her mind to ask Sasha to slow down or stop, for even the pain couldn't diminish Suzette's extreme pleasure.

But, of course, Sasha had taken her time to extract her own pleasure from Suzette's eager and available mouth. With each taste she was granted of Sasha's delicious pussy, her hunger grew for more. Each time Sasha spread her legs around Suzette's face and firmly settled her pussy onto Suzette's mouth, growling, "Eat me, you slut," Suzette's mouth would eagerly do its job on Sasha's pussy. Suzette eagerly offered her services to Sasha, finding that her eagerness to lick pussy didn't diminish as her night of servitude wore on. In fact, with each stroke of Suzette's tongue on Sasha's pussy, Sasha's lust for Suzette seemed to grow, and soon Sasha was even more insatiable than before, devouring Suzette's body with hungry mouth and hungry hands. One pleasure that Sasha didn't allow herself, however, was the pleasure of eating Suzette's sweet, virgin pussy. Suzette's cunt had never been eaten by another woman, Sasha knew, and that excited her too much to let her devour it in a hurry. Instead, Sasha pressed home the feeling of her power over Suzette, making Suzette service her over and over again until she was completely satisfied, and fucking Suzette silly with her hands between her sessions of sitting on Suzette's face. Sasha knew she would eat Suzette's cunt soon enough, but now Suzette was the one who would offer oral service.

And Suzette had no reason to complain, totally delirious as she was with the pleasure of making cruel, violent love with Sasha.

She had never imagined that such pleasures could be hers.

Clearly the pleasure of having Sasha's delicious body rubbing against her, of feeling Sasha's firm breasts pressed against her thighs as they fucked, of the weight of Sasha's body pressing down on her face while she serviced her, was a fantastic excitement to Suzette. And Sasha's incredible skill at fucking her was a great part of the ecstasy Suzette felt—Sasha had never been finger-fucked like that by any of her lovers! But the most intense newfound and erotic experience for Suzette was to be bound, helpless, spread-eagled, and fully exposed for sexual use by another woman. She had lost any tentativeness as she gave herself to Sasha again and again, offering up her body for complete use by this enticing woman.

When Sasha had finally dropped off to sleep atop Suzette, Suzette knew she had been an adequate lover. She still felt the ache in her pussy that told her she wanted more, but she was as satisfied as she could hope to be. She relaxed into the feeling of being bound, caressed by the softness of Sasha's bed and the warmth of Sasha's naked body on top of her, protecting her.

†††

When Suzette awakened, she was no longer bound, though she had no memory of being untied. Sasha was asleep, stretched out next to her. She pressed her body up against Sasha's, entwining her limbs with those of her lover, feeling the heat of Sasha's flesh, the curve of her ass and back. Suzette reached down and found herself still wet. Very wet.

She had been much too horny to get back to sleep. She already had fantasies of her eventual submission to Mrs. Aldridge flowing through her mind. And feeling Sasha's naked body against her was enough to set her off again. Savoring the feeling of Sasha's body, Suzette had reached down between her legs and slowly, sensuously, rubbed herself—trying not to wake Sasha. When Suzette felt her orgasm coming, she couldn't help but whimper a little and whisper, "Oh, God," as the pleasure exploded through her. Sasha had rolled over and given a cruel little chuckle, as if to let her know that, in fact, Sasha had been awake through the whole thing, and knew damn well that Suzette had just gotten herself off again. Suzette reddened, but then she pressed against Sasha's body and the two of them embraced, dropping off to a sensuous, exhausted slumber.

Suzette almost cried when the alarm went off. Sasha was already up and showered, having put on her white garter belt and suntan stockings. Sasha's breasts hung free, and Sasha took a long time easing them into the front-clasp bra she had selected—well aware that Suzette was watching. Sasha took the time to caress her breasts, tease her nipples, slide the smooth lace over the mounds of her tits, and finally clasp them in their bondage with her cleavage spilling over invitingly, enticing Suzette to call in sick and give herself to Sasha all day long. But Suzette would never dream of doing that—the very thought sent a shudder through her body. She couldn't disappoint Mrs. Aldridge.

She realized with horror that the only clothes she had were the ones she'd worn to work yesterday—and she didn't even have any panties, she'd left those in the office toward the end!

What was she going to do?

"You can borrow a skirt of mine," Sasha told Suzette. "But you'll never fit one of my blouses." Sasha gave a little smile and ran her hands down over her own impressive tits. That was for sure—Suzette's tits were much smaller than Sasha's.

"Maybe you can borrow one from Sabrina," said Sasha thoughtfully.

"Sabrina? Who's Sabrina?"

Suzette laughed a little. "She's a girl who sometimes shares the apartment with me. And John."

Suzette's excitement mounted as she wondered what kind of relationship this "Sabrina" might have with

Sasha and John. Then again, maybe she didn't want to know. Oh, yes, she did.

Sasha went over to a side closet and brought out a fetching white blouse, somewhat businesslike but a little slutty. A little more formal than would be expected for the office. But very low-cut.

"This should do," said Sasha, laying the blouse out on the bed. "And this bra should fit you—it's a B-cup."

"I wear a C," said Suzette.

"Then you'll just have to squeeze," said Sasha, smiling devilishly. "How does this skirt look?" She held up a slender, straight skirt that was not quite knee-length.

"It might fit," said Suzette. "It seems like it would be a little tight, maybe."

"Good," said Sasha. "That's the way Mrs. Aldridge would like it. You can wear your panties from last night, can't you?"

Suzette reddened, wrapping the sheet more tightly around her naked body.

"What's that?"

"I wasn't wearing any," she said nervously, suppressing a giggle. When Sasha looked blankly at her, Suzette said, "I wasn't wearing any panties!" a little irritably.

"Oh, that's right," said Sasha, who had obviously known—but just wanted to hear Suzette say it. She held her gaze on Suzette a little longer than was necessary.

"Then you shouldn't wear any today, I suppose," said

Sasha, as she tossed the skirt on the bed and went off to put on her own blouse.

"Sasha!" murmured Suzette, scandalized but a little excited by having her new lover dictate what she was going to wear to the office. She felt her nipples stiffening, wondered if Sasha could see them through the thin white sheet. She clutched it a little closer.

"It's not like you need them," said Sasha. "I mean, maybe with your pussy dripping all day long they'd be a good idea. But Mrs. Aldridge..."

"What?"

"Forget it," said Sasha, buttoning up her low-cut blouse. "You better get in the shower if you're going to make it on time.

Suzette took a quick shower, realizing just how sore her pussy was from the sound fucking Sasha had given it last night. She felt as though she could hardly walk! She soaped up her naked body, admiring the faint marks the ropes had left on her wrists and ankles. She wondered if she could borrow a couple of bracelets from Sasha so the marks wouldn't be noticeable at work. As Suzette showered, Sasha came in to the bathroom and finished her makeup—it excited Suzette to be showering behind the frosted glass, naked before Sasha's gaze. She began to get a little turned on again—no, there wasn't time for that!

When Suzette came out of the shower, there was a

THE OFFICE

garter belt and a pair of stockings laid on top of her skirt. She guessed that Sasha was making a firm little suggestion about what she should wear—as firm as the insistence that she not wear any panties. Suzette could have slipped her hand into Sasha's top drawer and borrowed a pair—but it somehow excited her to have her wardrobe dictated by Sasha and her unbending will. Suzette wondered what Sasha might have her wear as their weeks of working together wore on. *If* Sasha wanted to let this happen again.

Suzette got into the garter belt and stockings, then had to struggle to get the B-cup bra clasped around her C-cup breasts. The bra was low cut to begin with—not at all what you would wear to the office most of the time—damn Sasha, anyway! But Suzette wouldn't think of protesting; each little tease that Sasha made her endure excited her more. Once she had succeeded in getting her tits bound into the bra, with her cleavage spilling over invitingly, she borrowed some of Sasha's makeup—foundation, blush, lipstick, mascara, and a little eyeshadow. Suzette squirmed into the skirt, which she also found to be a little too tight. Quite a bit too tight, actually. With the garters and the fact that she wasn't wearing any panties, it made Suzette feel like a perfect slut. Luckily, the skirt wasn't all that short, or it would have been completely indecent walking down the street. Suzette felt a surge going through her as she thought about that.

Suzette realized that her shoes from yesterday—red pumps—wouldn't go at all with this black-and-white outfit. But Sasha had thoughtfully set out a pair of shoes she could borrow—just about the right size. But with four-inch heels. Suzette actually thought for a moment of protesting that choice...but the excitement of her submission to Sasha was too intense. She pulled the shoes on and tottered uncomfortably, looking at herself in the mirror. God, she looked like more of a slut than usual. But not *too* obvious. Suzette would have changed if she hadn't known that seeing her like this would please Sasha.

And maybe please Mrs. Aldridge?

That was too much for Suzette to think about just yet. It sent a flood of excitement to her fucked-raw pussy, and she wasn't ready to start thinking about her employer just yet this morning—or she would never make it in to the office.

Sasha had made coffee and toast, and the two of them enjoyed a little breakfast as they sat at the small breakfast table in the kitchen. Suzette was famished, having skipped dinner the night before, despite what she'd originally told Sasha. Sasha seemed to be doing OK, considering that she had hardly had time for dinner herself!

Sasha leaned forward, perhaps a little more than was necessary, as she poured Suzette's coffee. This made her bare knee rub against Suzette's, and slide gently between Suzette's legs—just a little. Suzette's breathing quickened.

"We can get a cab together," Sasha was saying, "but we can't walk in together, or she'll guess what's been going on between us. So let's walk in to work five minutes or so apart. We don't want Mrs. Aldridge to suspect that we've been sleeping together." Sasha gave a little shudder. "The punishment would be extreme. *Will* be extreme, if she finds out." Sasha gave Suzette a hungry glance, and put her hand on Suzette's knee, her fingers easing up under Suzette's skirt—just a little. Suzette knew, without doubt, that Sasha planned to make sure that Mrs. Aldridge *did* find out *exactly* what had gone on last night, if only to experience that succulent punishment that Mrs. Aldridge would then mete out. And Suzette didn't doubt that the punishment wouldn't be limited to Sasha once Mrs. Aldridge found out what a perfect slut Suzette had been.

Thinking of that, Suzette shivered.

And now, it looked like that very punishment was awaiting Suzette, if for somewhat different reasons. Suzette could tell from the awkward way that Sasha moved her body that she'd gotten quite a spanking in Mrs. Aldridge's office. And Suzette knew that that same punishment—or worse—waited for her in Mrs. Aldridge's office.

It was 10:00.

She rose, still clutching the envelope—"the files from last night"—to her breasts. She could feel how tight her skirt was, how tightly the B-cup bra fit her breasts. How naked she felt without any panties on at all.

Nervously, Suzette walked in to Mrs. Aldridge's office.

Mrs. Aldridge was wearing her glasses, bent over her desk reading a document of some sort. She did not look up as Suzette entered.

"Should I close the door?" Suzette asked nervously, as she clutched the envelope to her chest. She realized how obvious that must look, how obvious it must make her nervousness in the face of what she had done. Suzette let the envelope drop to her side, trying to hold it casually with one hand.

"Please," said Mrs. Aldridge, without looking up.

Suzette closed the door, but not before Sasha had given her a smoldering glance of lust.

Suzette just stood there, afraid to sit down without being invited. Mrs. Aldridge took her time finishing with the document she was inspecting. Suzette acutely felt the power imbalance between them, and felt her nipples stiffening under her blouse. As they did, she felt them poking out over the lace of the too-tight bra, jutting out uncomfortably and visibly through the sheer blouse. Suzette shifted nervously, but of course she couldn't reach up and tuck her nipples back into

The Office

her bra with Mrs. Aldridge standing there! And she didn't dare ask to be excused to go to the rest room! But as she stood there uncomfortably, feeling the embarrassment of being made to stand and wait for Mrs. Aldridge to finish, Suzette did not feel her nipples softening, but only felt them poking more firmly out over the top of her low-cut bra. Her breathing quickened.

Mrs. Aldridge looked up at Suzette and smiled tightly. Her gaze flickered up and down Suzette's body, and Suzette felt the intensity of her judgment against her. Suzette could feel her excitement mounting as her fear did the same.

"May I sit down?" blurted Suzette nervously.

Mrs. Aldridge nodded, even as she stood up.

Suzette feared she may have gone too far, but she obeyed, taking the chair in front of Mrs. Aldridge's desk. Suzette still clutched the envelope in one hand, knowing full well that both of them knew exactly what was in there. And that it was a promise of retribution to come. Suzette pressed her thighs together nervously.

Mrs. Aldridge came around the desk and sat on the edge of it, looking Suzette up and down again, this time more slowly, as if inspecting every inch of her attire, her posture, her body. Suzette shifted nervously under Mrs. Aldridge's gaze, feeling its heat undress her.

"You were late this morning," said Mrs. Aldridge, firmly.

"Yes, Mrs. Aldridge," said Suzette. "I'm very sorry. It won't happen again."

"Did we speak about this when you interviewed with me?" Mrs. Aldridge's gaze enveloped Suzette, who could not look up to meet it.

"Yes, Mrs. Aldridge. We did."

"What exactly did we speak about?"

Suzette could feel Mrs. Aldridge's stare, could feel herself being undressed with those stern eyes. Could feel her blouse being unbuttoned, her skirt being lifted. Or was that just her imagination?

"You said...that you expected your employees to be on time."

"That's right," said Mrs. Aldridge. She leaned a little closer to Suzette and said firmly, "No matter *what* they may have been doing the night before."

Suzette felt a shudder go through her body, as she crumbled under Mrs. Aldridge's will. She strove to remain calm even as her heart pounded inside her body.

"Yes, Mrs. Aldridge," she said hoarsely.

"Suzette...and I hope you don't mind my asking... what were *you* doing last night? That led to your being late this morning?"

Suzette's nipples were now fully hard, almost painfully so, jutting over the top of the lacy bra, and Suzette was quite sure that they were visible through the thin blouse Sasha had selected for her. She wished she could cross her arms—but that would just call attention to it, she was sure. But, oh, how embarrassed she felt with her nipples so plainly evident beneath the blouse. Especially as she was being questioned like this—

"Suzette? I asked you a question. That is, if you don't mind my inquiring about your personal life. Insofar as it seems to have an impact on your job. I wouldn't ask, you understand, if it didn't seem to affect your performance." Mrs. Aldridge leaned closer, and Suzette could smell the faint scent of her expensive perfume. "Suzette? *What* is it you were doing last night? That led to your being so late?"

Suzette knew intellectually this was ridiculous—she was only five minutes late, for God's sake! But the completeness of her humiliation before Mrs. Aldridge made her accept totally the woman's authority. Suzette knew that even this tiny infraction was enough to place her firmly in Mrs. Aldridge's merciless hands. And despite her fear, despite her nervousness, she wanted nothing more than to be punished and humiliated horribly for being late.

But—she *couldn't* tell Mrs. Aldridge what she had been doing last night!

"I...I'm sorry, Mrs. Aldridge. It won't happen again."

"Won't it? But I don't believe you've answered my question. Do you mind my asking this question? I think it's very relevant to your job performance, don't you? Don't you?" Suzette nodded nervously. "Then what is it that you were doing? That led to your being late this morning?"

They had already wasted more than five minutes talking about it, but Suzette didn't question Mrs. Aldridge's right to interrogate her in this fashion. Rather, she accepted it completely. Suzette kept her eyes lowered, unable to look up at Mrs. Aldridge.

"I was having dinner with a friend," she lied.

"A friend. A platonic friend? Or someone you're romantic with?"

Suzette had fallen completely under her employer's spell. She knew she would answer all her questions, no matter how personal they got.

"S—someone I'm romantic with."

"Really," said Mrs. Aldridge without expression. "It's good to be romantic, Suzette, especially at your age."

Suzette nodded. "Thank you, Mrs. Aldridge." She didn't know why she said that, but it was the only thing she could come up with to say.

"This... this romantic friend. Are you sometimes... sexual with this person as well?"

Suzette hesitated, acutely feeling the pain of her own arousal. She felt sure Mrs. Aldridge could see how much she was sweating, how deeply she was blushing.

"Suzette? Are you sexual with this friend of yours? This romantic friend of yours?"

Suzette finally nodded. "Yes," she mumbled.

The Office

"And were you sexual last night with this person?"

Suzette felt Mrs. Aldridge's gaze, all heat and power, lazing over the outline of her firm body. Suzette finally managed to look up into Mrs. Aldridge's gaze, as if to confront her, as if to tell her that she'd gone too far. But as she met Mrs. Aldridge's gaze, Suzette suddenly felt the full flush of her humiliation, her submission to Mrs. Aldridge, and she looked quickly down again, overwhelmed by how beautiful the older woman was.

"Yes," said Suzette. "I was sexual with this person last night."

"That is to say, you slept with this person last night. You had sex."

Suzette, no longer able to resist the interrogation, nodded quickly. "Uh-huh," she said, still looking down, knowing that she would never again meet Mrs. Aldridge's gaze with even a hint of defiance.

Long, painful moments of silence passed. Suzette kept her eyes lowered as Mrs. Aldridge stood and walked slowly around, gradually circling Suzette as she spoke.

"So you slept with this person. You went to bed with someone last night, and that's why you were late. Is that correct?"

Suzette nodded quickly. "Yes," she panted.

"And was this the first time you had been sexual with this person? The first time you had gone to bed with this person?"

More slowly, feeling the acute nature of her confession, Suzette nodded. "Uh-huh," she mumbled.

"So I imagine you were up late, then," said Mrs. Aldridge, now standing behind Suzette, who could, even so, feel the power of her presence.

"Uh-huh," whimpered Suzette. "Very late."

"How late?"

Suzette took a long time before she answered, "Three in the morning."

That was a lie—she had glanced at the clock just before she closed her eyes, and it was just after four. But Suzette somehow found herself editing—perhaps to lessen the severity of her transgression, or maybe because she *wanted* to be caught in a lie, as Mrs. Aldridge had done when Suzette had claimed to have had dinner with a friend.

"My, that is late. I guess the sex with this person was fairly successful. If it kept you up that late."

"Yes," breathed Suzette, feeling Mrs. Aldridge standing very, very close to her, towering over her shoulder.

"Did you climax?"

Suzette didn't hesitate this time, fully aware that Mrs. Aldridge had taken possession of her, and would now learn *all* of Suzette's secrets—most of them before lunch.

"Yes," whimpered Suzette.

Mrs. Aldridge leaned forward slightly, so that Suzette

could just feel the brush of Mrs. Aldridge's jacket on her shoulder. "How many times?"

Suzette's mind raced, thinking back on all the times she'd twisted in her bonds, climaxing on Sasha's skillfully-thrusting fingers....

"I...I don't know," she whispered.

"You don't know how many times you climaxed?"

"I—I lost count," Suzette said softly.

"Ten? Twelve?"

There was a long moment of silence. "At least," Suzette said at last.

"You think it might be more than that? More than twelve times that you climaxed?"

Suzette nodded. "More," she whimpered.

"Goodness," said Mrs. Aldridge. "That is quite a lot. I guess you enjoyed yourself, then."

Suzette nodded quickly. "Yes," she panted. "I enjoyed myself a lot."

"It's very good to enjoy yourself," said Mrs. Aldridge. "Except when it interferes with your work."

"Yes, Mrs. Aldridge. It won't happen again."

"Perhaps it won't, Suzette. Tell me...was there bondage involved in last night's lovemaking?"

Suzette closed her eyes, knowing she couldn't deny Mrs. Aldridge any detail of last night's tryst—except who it had been with. She couldn't confess that she had been with Sasha.

"Yes," Suzette breathed as she nodded. "There was bondage involved."

"Really. Were you the one tied up, or did you tie her up? Or both?"

"Just me," said Suzette. "She tied me up."

"She tied your wrists? Your ankles? Standing up?"

"She tied me to the bed," said Suzette. "My wrists and ankles."

"She tied you...spread out, then? Spread-eagled?"

"Uh-huh."

"Like the blonde woman on page sixty-one of last fall's catalog?"

"Yes," whimpered Suzette, remembering the photograph. "Exactly like her."

Suzette's nipples were painful in their arousal, as they strained against the top of the lace bra. What's more, she was quite sure that at the angle Mrs. Aldridge was standing over her, she could see down Suzette's blouse quite easily, which meant she could see how bare her breasts were, sticking out over the tops of the tight bra cups like that. Knowing that Mrs. Aldridge could see her so well, Suzette's arousal mounted. Her pussy, still aching from last night's fucking, felt wet and slick between her tightly-pressed thighs. She had to fight to keep still.

"Suzette," began Mrs. Aldridge after a long pause. "I'm going to ask you something, and I want you to know that you should not feel obligated to answer. But

The Office

if you do answer, please know that your answer will be kept in the strictest of confidence. I do not believe in any kind of sexual discrimination or prejudice of any kind. I want to make that perfectly clear."

"Yes, Mrs. Aldridge," said Suzette, nodding slightly. Mrs. Aldridge bent forward.

"Suzette," said Mrs. Aldridge. "Was this a man or a woman that you spent last night with?"

Suzette felt a shudder go through her. She wanted to lower herself to her knees and lift her skirt, offering her ass for the succulent punishment of Mrs. Aldridge, the punishment Sasha had received. Suzette felt her jealousy rising—Sasha had gotten a sound whipping, why shouldn't she?

"Suzette? Was it a man or a woman who made love to you last night?"

"It was a woman," Suzette finally whispered, feeling her arousal increase with each confession Mrs. Aldridge demanded of her.

"A woman. And was she...someone you already knew? You said that it was the first time she had made love to you. But was she someone with whom you were acquainted already? Or someone you just sort of... picked up?"

Suzette's tongue felt tied. She couldn't confess how she knew the woman she'd been with—that would mean telling Mrs. Aldridge that she'd gone to bed with Sasha! Then Sasha would be in for a stern punishment....

"You didn't really have dinner with this woman, did you?"

Slowly, Suzette shook her head.

"You didn't have dinner at all last night, did you?"

Suzette shook her head. "No," she said.

"This woman didn't take you out on a date before taking you home to have sex with you?"

Suzette shook her head quickly. "No," she whispered. "She didn't." Suzette acutely felt Mrs. Aldridge's hot gaze, feeling as if it were undressing her, stripping her naked.

"Suzette," said Mrs. Aldridge. "Clearly you read this morning's memorandum. Or else you wouldn't be here."

Suzette's body stiffened. She was about to receive her scolding for what she'd done last night.

"With the memorandum's—*attachments?* I assume? Suzette?"

Suzette nodded. "Yes, Mrs. Aldridge. I...I read them."

Not knowing what to do, she quickly opened the interoffice envelope and took out the pair of panties and the photocopies of Sasha's breasts. She clutched the panties in her lap, wishing she could put them on—maybe then she wouldn't be so acutely aware of her moistening pussy.

"That's right," said Mrs. Aldridge. "Those are the attachments I was referring to. Now...you must remember not to forget your things around the office. Can you promise me to remember that, Suzette?"

The Office

"I'll try," she mumbled nervously. She looked down at the panties and remembered how soaked they'd been when she slipped them off last night. Suzette shivered in mounting arousal.

"Suzette?" said Mrs. Aldridge.

"Yes," breathed Suzette nervously.

"Your bra is one cup size too small," said Mrs. Aldridge, leaning forward to look more fully down Suzette's blouse. "Your breasts are spilling out over the top. Especially when the nipples get hard like that. They show through the blouse."

Suzette's body seemed to spasm with excitement to hear Mrs. Aldridge talking like that. "Thank you, Mrs. Aldridge," Suzette said breathlessly as she nervously slipped her hands down her blouse and tugged the too-tight bra cups—somewhat unsuccessfully—back up, tucking her nipples inside them as best she could.

"Much better?" asked Mrs. Aldridge, still able to see down Suzette's blouse from overhead.

"Yes," breathed Suzette, more comfortable but quite aware that as her arousal increased, or if her body shifted even a little bit, those nipples were going to spill right back out again.

Mrs. Aldridge leaned close. Suzette could feel the woman's warm breath on her ear.

"Suzette?" she asked. "This woman you slept with."

"Yes?" Suzette nodded.

"Was this someone you knew already? Or was it a woman you simply picked up?"

Suzette breathed heavily.

"It was someone I knew," she said.

Mrs. Aldridge let Suzette feel the warmth of her breath for a moment longer before asking, "How did you know her?"

Suzette answered, too quickly, "She was someone I knew from college."

Mrs. Aldridge seemed to lean ever-so-slightly closer to Suzette. "Someone you knew from college."

"Yes," said Suzette nervously.

"What was her name?"

Suzette was silent, her tongue swollen in her mouth. The guilt from having lied to Mrs. Aldridge washed over her as she squirmed in her chair, knowing that she could not continue the lie.

"I'm sorry," she whimpered, on the verge of tears. "It wasn't really someone I knew from college."

Mrs. Aldridge's voice was not yet harsh, but Suzette felt tears forming in her eyes. She had promised. She had promised Sasha she wouldn't tell. She couldn't...

But she couldn't deny Mrs. Aldridge.

"Suzette," said Mrs. Aldridge firmly. "You're going to tell me the truth now. What was the woman's name? The woman you spent last night with?"

Suzette felt the tears rolling down her cheeks.

"Sasha," she said.

"Sasha. And how did you know her?"

Suzette choked back a small sob.

"From here. From the office."

"Sasha. My Sasha? Our receptionist?"

Suzette nodded, her sobs choking her. She couldn't believe she'd confessed after promising Sasha she wouldn't. Now she'd probably screwed up the new relationship she had with Sasha—the first time she'd ever gone to bed with a woman.

"You and Sasha made love last night."

"Yes," said Suzette, looking down as her tears rolled down her cheeks and splashed across the blouse Sasha had loaned her.

"And she tied you up. Tied you to the bed, spread out. While she made love to you. While she fucked you."

Suzette nodded, unable to speak.

"And did you service her? With your mouth? Did you go down on Sasha? Did you…pleasure her orally?"

Suzette nodded, but couldn't answer except in a pathetic whimper as her sobs filled her throat. She wept openly and buried her face in her hands.

Mrs. Aldridge produced a handkerchief and handed it to Suzette.

"Well, Suzette. This has been a most instructive review. I do hope you'll be on time from now on." Mrs. Aldridge rounded the desk and sat behind it. "Do leave the door open when you go."

Suzette hesitated, but she didn't dare disobey Mrs. Aldridge. Quickly, she got up and left the office, still weeping into the handkerchief, which smelled deliciously of Mrs. Aldridge.

Chapter 8

Suzette, still choking back sobs and dabbing tears from her cheeks, went out into the office and discovered Sasha bent over the file cabinet, offering a flawless view of her gorgeous ass in that tight skirt. That just made a new wave of remorse flood through Suzette's body, and the guilt at having confessed the tryst with Sasha to Mrs. Aldridge—even though Sasha had asked her not to—overcame her. Sobbing momentarily, she sat down at her desk to try to compose herself.

Sasha looked back at her, smoothing the skirt down over her hips. She offered Suzette a faint smile, then a little look of concern. Sasha, looking as sexy as ever, walked over to Suzette's desk and leaned forward, putting her arms around Suzette's shoulders. Suzette could just smell the inviting scent of Sasha's perfume, and she felt herself beginning to react. After the intense sexual torment Mrs. Aldridge had forced on her, she was almost helpless in her desire. She was as wet as can be, and desperately horny, despite the fact that she was sobbing uncontrollably at having been forced to confess to Mrs. Aldridge. And as Sasha sat down on the edge of Suzette's chair and put her arms around Suzette more firmly, Suzette's tears evaporated into the heat of lust, as she remembered all the times she'd climaxed under Sasha's thrusting body.

Suzette realized that they were in full view of Mrs. Aldridge's office—but then again, this could simply be the supportive hug of a fellow office worker. Not that Mrs. Aldridge wouldn't know the truth—after all, Suzette had just told her everything....

"There, there," sighed Sasha, patting Suzette's hair as platonically as she could manage—just in case Mrs. Aldridge was watching. "Everything will be all right."

Then, to Suzette's horror, in a furtive whisper, Sasha asked, "Did you tell her?"

What could Suzette do? She had just about described their whole night's sex-play to Mrs. Aldridge, against Sasha's explicit instructions! What was she going to do now? She couldn't lie to Sasha? But then, she couldn't very well tell Sasha what she'd done....

Suzette reacted almost automatically, biting back her

tears and looking into Sasha's eyes as she shook her head, "No."

"Oh, thank God," sighed Sasha, embracing Suzette and kissing the top of her head. She rose quickly, giving Suzette the pleasure of Sasha's breasts brushing against her face as she pulled away.

"Just wait until lunch," smirked Sasha cruelly. "I'll show you just how hot that photocopier can get."

Despite her intense guilt—or, more likely, because of it—hearing Sasha talk like that made Suzette as wet as could be, and her nipples ached longingly for the forced attention of the photocopier.

Through the morning, Suzette's guilt at having confessed to Mrs. Aldridge lessened. Perhaps Mrs. Aldridge would take no action, and Sasha wouldn't find out that Suzette had told her the whole thing. Perhaps things could continue without Sasha finding out that Suzette was a liar and a stool pigeon.

Suzette hoped with all her heart that things could continue. She had so enjoyed being taken like that by Sasha, tied to the bed and ravished by those fierce hands and that insistent mouth, being made to service that insatiable pussy with her lips and tongue. Her night of heated lovemaking with Sasha had been the most intense fuck she'd ever had. Now she would do almost anything for Sasha.

But despite this, her most powerful allegiance was to Mrs. Aldridge. In fact, Suzette would almost place her life on the line for the pleasure of Mrs. Aldridge. Suzette couldn't say why—she had never experienced such an intense desire to submit, and certainly not to another woman! But something about Mrs. Aldridge compelled her, commanded her—made her want to give herself, wholly, to Mrs. Aldridge—and her husband, whose attentions would make Suzette feel that much more a plaything. No matter how much she loved Sasha and deeply desired to be dominated by her, Suzette was bound to follow Mrs. Aldridge's will no matter what complicated and humiliating submissions her employer demanded of her.

Suzette's arousal mounted through the morning. It was a particularly hot day, and the air conditioning was malfunctioning—by noon, it felt as though it must have been eighty in the small, airless office. The sweat sheened Suzette's body and made her blouse and skirt cling to her voluptuous curves. She was acutely aware all morning that she was wearing no panties.

Then when she heard Mrs. Aldridge leaving, her heart pounded. At that moment, Suzette was standing over the photocopier. For almost half an hour, she had, on Mrs. Aldridge's orders, been photocopying page after page of bondage equipment from a competitor's catalog.

The Office

The photocopier had been going full speed for many long minutes, and Suzette could feel the heat of the glass rising up ominously.

What's more, Suzette had sneaked a look at Mrs. Aldridge's schedule in the appointment book Sasha kept at her desk. It was one of Sasha's main duties to schedule all of Mrs. Aldridge's meetings.

So when she heard Mrs. Aldridge leaving, she knew it would be a long lunch.

Sasha crept up behind Suzette and suddenly pressed her body to Suzette's back, grabbing Suzette's hair and pushing her against the copier.

Sasha's knee came up between Suzette's legs. Sasha rammed it into Suzette's vulnerable, unprotected cunt, just hard enough to make her gasp and to make a moan of pleasure come from Suzette's mouth. Sasha pushed her forward, sweeping the competitor's catalog away quickly so that Suzette's breasts pressed hard against the intensely hot glass, through the material of her thin blouse. The heat—painful against her breasts—made Suzette squirm in discomfort.

Sasha bent forward and put her lips very close to Suzette's.

"She's taking a two-hour lunch," growled Sasha. "Plenty of time for me to show you a thing or two around the office. Understand?"

Suzette nodded, squirming at the increasing heat on

her breasts. She whimpered as Sasha ground her knee harder into her pussy.

"Start by pulling up this skirt," Sasha said. "Show me what you're wearing underneath."

Suzette was in heaven, completely subjected to Sasha's cruel will. She wanted Sasha to punish her, torture her, to make her pay for having spilled the beans to Mrs. Aldridge. Even if Sasha didn't know it, Suzette hoped that a particularly vicious thrashing and fucking over the lunch hour would purge her of her wrongdoing.

Feeling the humiliation flowing through her, Suzette slowly lifted her skirt, exposing her upper thighs, then her pussy, and finally her luscious, rounded ass. Sasha rammed her knee harder into Suzette's naked crotch, grinding her knee against the increasing wetness of Suzette's pussy.

"That's right," growled Sasha. "Nothing on underneath. I forgot what a slut you are."

Suzette whimpered, her cunt aching with intense pleasure. She was already mounting toward climax from the many hours of arousal in Mrs. Aldridge's office and afterward.

"You remember what we do to sluts around here, don't you?"

Groaning, Suzette shook her head. "No," she whispered. "Please don't."

"You saw it last night. You saw what they do to sluts around here."

The Office

Suzette nodded slowly, her pussy almost ready to explode in climax. Sasha shoved her knee rhythmically against Suzette's cunt, wedging it deeper between her slightly-spread thighs. She shoved so hard that several times Suzette's ass was raised up and her feet actually left the ground by a few inches. She was amazed at how strong Sasha was. It made her feel that much more vulnerable, that much more completely under Sasha's control.

"You saw what they do," she growled. "You saw them doing it to me. Do you remember?"

Suzette did. How could she forget the scene that had made her explode with desire? She had wanted it to be her, tits exposed before Mr. and Mrs. Aldridge, being subjected to their tortures. Now, she was. Her breasts were reddened and felt swollen under the thin blouse. Her nipples were fully erect and pressed even harder against the scalding glass. Her tits had started to spill out of the B-cups again, and her nipples were dangerously exposed. If her breasts pressed naked against that glass, Suzette knew the pain would be overwhelming. Slowly, Suzette nodded. "Yes," she gasped. "I remember."

"Then open your shirt," snarled Sasha contemptuously. "You little slut."

Suzette moaned as she straightened her back just enough to unbutton her blouse. Sasha grabbed the blouse and pulled it up and off, dragging Suzette's arms up. Now her breasts were only encased ineffectually in the tight, too-small bra. But Sasha was having no mercy.

"That, too," she growled as she tossed the blouse away. "Take off the bra."

Suzette was almost ready to come. The rhythmic thrusting of Sasha's knee against her cunt was going to push her over the edge. Her entire body ached for release at Sasha's merciless hands, and almost her whole body was exposed for her. Suzette bent over the copier with her skirt pulled up to her waist, her legs spread, giving all of herself to Sasha's control. At her new lover's orders, she reached between her breasts and opened the front-clasp of the bra.

The tortured garment sprang open, Suzette's firm breasts exposed for Sasha's abuse.

"Slip it off," ordered Sasha. "All the way."

Whimpering in fear and anticipation, Suzette slipped the bra off and let it fall to the floor.

Suzette barely knew what was happening. From somewhere, Sasha produced a pair of handcuffs. She had them on Suzette's wrists, cuffing her hands behind her back, before Suzette could even whisper a squeal of protest. Her whole body filled with fear as she realized that she was totally and utterly in Sasha's power. Nothing had ever been more erotic to her.

Sasha grasped Suzette's hair firmly and laughed.

"Now," she snarled. "This is what they do to sluts around *this* office—a *well-run* office!"

The Office

With that, Sasha threw her whole weight on Suzette's back, forcing her down onto the copier, forcing her firm, naked, exposed breasts hard against the scalding-hot glass of the photocopier.

The pain was excruciating. Suzette wailed and moaned as her naked breasts were scalded by the smooth, slippery glass. Sasha held her against it, her fist holding Suzette's hair and her other hand pulling up on Suzette's cuffed wrists, forcing Suzette's tits against the smooth, flaming-hot glass. Suzette squirmed desperately, the extreme heat of the copier glass lighting her breasts on fire. Squirming back against Sasha's rhythmically-thrusting body, and feeling the pressure of Sasha's knee in her crotch, she knew she was going to come, and she knew there was nothing she could do to stop herself from coming as her breasts throbbed and exploded with the intense pain. She was going to climax whether she liked it or not.

Suzette lifted her head just enough to utter a piercing, desperate scream of agony and ecstasy, before the orgasm shuddered through her and her whole body spasmed in pleasure. The climax flowed through her body mercilessly, mixing pain with delight as her tortured breasts pressed against the scalding glass. Sasha laughed maniacally, ramming her knee forcibly into Suzette's crotch again and again and again, until Suzette feared that her cunt would be damaged—though she didn't care at all, she just wanted to feel the firm thrust of Sasha's body against her, wanted to be taken by the violent blow of Sasha's knee in her cunt. Then she was coming even harder, the rhythmic slam of Sasha's knee bringing her off again and again, her orgasms stringing together until she had lost count, until she wasn't sure if she was having a dozen tiny orgasms or one enormous one. Either way, Suzette was completely overcome with the most intense pleasure of her life, and she was completely and totally in Sasha's control. Her screams dwindled to wails and her wails lessened to pathetic whimpers as her pleasure dwindled and her orgasms echoed away inside her ravished body. Suzette's tits were still pressed against the hot glass, but her flesh had become acclimated to it, and the glass had begun to cool.

Suzette could just see Sasha over her shoulder. Sasha was a vision of beauty. Her office clothes were askew, her face sheened with sweat so that her mascara was running. Her own blouse had come undone, so her large breasts pressed against her own miniature push-up bra, the nipples evident and quite erect as they rubbed against Suzette's back. Her own skirt was hiked up high from lifting her knee up against Suzette's pussy, and Sasha's own moist panties were visible under the hem of the lifted skirt. And, most attractive of all (to Suzette at least), Sasha was breathing very

The Office

hard from the exertion of fucking Suzette to orgasm, even as she chuckled in deeply pleasured satisfaction.

"How do you like that, you little slut?" she asked Suzette with more than a little affection in her voice.

Suddenly the door opened, and Sasha gasped—but didn't have time to release Suzette and move back before Mrs. Aldridge stood there looking at them.

Sasha jumped back, standing awkwardly with her tits exposed and her skirt pulled up. She blushed a deep red as she desperately pulled her skirt down.

"Mrs. Aldridge. I'm quite sorry. I was just showing Suzette some of the advanced features of the photocopier!" Sasha began to button her blouse quickly, her nipples still showing through the thin fabric.

Suzette was unable to move. She still bent over the photocopier, her skirt lifted up and her wet pussy exposed between her slightly-spread legs, her tits pressed mercilessly against the cooling glass of the photocopier. But the most unquestionably incriminating sight was the handcuffs on Suzette's wrists. She moaned uncontrollably as she leaned hard on the photocopier. She was so overcome with bliss, she hardly even knew that Mrs. Aldridge had walked in on them.

"Sasha," said Mrs. Aldridge without emotion. "Note in my calendar, Mr. Bensington had to cancel our lunch date at the last minute; reschedule for next Thursday at noon."

Without further comment, Mrs. Aldridge turned and walked into her office.

"And Suzette?"

Suzette heard Mrs. Aldridge dimly through the thick fog of her own sexual excitement. She finally managed an answer.

"Y-yes, Mrs. Aldridge?" Suzette called hoarsely.

"My husband and I have some work we need to do tonight."

Suzette managed to focus her mind, to listen to what Mrs. Aldridge was saying.

"Some copying work."

Suzette felt the warmth of the copier flooding through her tits. She managed to stand, and looked down to see her breasts deeply reddened and sensitized from the heat of the glass.

"Yes, Mrs. Aldridge?"

"And we'll be needing your help. Could you possibly stay a few extra hours?"

Sasha was moving quickly to unlock Suzette's handcuffs. She gave Suzette a dirty look, jealous and angry.

"Suzette? A few extra hours? Certainly no later than nine."

"Yes, Mrs. Aldridge," Suzette whimpered as Sasha began to pull her skirt down. "I would be glad to."

"Very well."

Sasha and Suzette looked at each other.

The Office

"You little bitch," snarled Sasha bitterly, and stalked over to her desk.

"And Sasha?" Mrs. Aldridge had appeared in the doorway, her body held at a provocative angle. Suzette could see the swell of Mrs. Aldridge's breasts pressing through her blouse. She had taken off her suit jacket, and it was quite evident that her nipples were hard.

"Yes, Mrs. Aldridge?" said Sasha nervously.

"We'll be needing your help with the copying, as well."

Suzette numbly fumbled to get her blouse on. In her excitement and post-orgasmic splendor, she forgot all about her bra.

Sasha flashed Suzette a nasty look, but this time it was a conspiratorial, seductive nastiness, telling her that Sasha would enjoy watching Suzette's suffering at the hands of Mr. and Mrs. Aldridge—perhaps even more than Suzette would enjoy it.

"I would be happy to stay," said Sasha as she looked hungrily at Suzette. Sasha let her hands drift absently down the front of her sweat-soaked shirt, just barely brushing the evidently firm buds of her own erect nipples.

"Great," said Mrs. Aldridge. "We'll send out for sushi." She slammed the door to her office.

Sasha's eyes met Suzette's, and Suzette saw in them a smoldering kind of excitement.

"Well," said Sasha. "It looks like we'll both be working late."

Then, coolly, Sasha began to arrange some papers on her desk.

The evening, both Sasha and Suzette knew, would be even hotter than the afternoon. And each of them would pay for what she had done.

MASQUERADE

AMERICA'S FASTEST GROWING EROTIC MAGAZINE

SPECIAL OFFER

RECEIVE THE NEXT TWO ISSUES FOR ONLY $5.00—A 50% SAVINGS!

A bimonthly magazine packed with the very best the world of erotica has to offer. Each issue of *Masquerade* contains today's most provocative, cutting-edge fiction, sizzling pictorials from the masters of modern fetish photography, scintillating and illuminating exposés of the worldwide sex-biz written by longtime industry insiders, and probing reviews of the many books and videos that cater specifically to your lifestyle.

Masquerade presents radical sex uncensored—from homegrown American kink to the fantastical fashions of Europe. Never before have the many permutations of the erotic imagination been represented in one publication.

THE ONLY MAGAZINE THAT CATERS TO YOUR LIFESTYLE

Masquerade/Direct • 801 Second Avenue • New York, NY 10017 • FAX: 212.986.7355
E-Mail: MasqBks @aol.com • MC/VISA orders can be placed by calling our toll-free number: 800.375.2356

☐ 2 ISSUES ~~$10~~ *SPECIAL* $5!

☐ 6 ISSUES (1 YEAR) FOR ~~$30~~ *SPECIAL* $15!

☐ 12 ISSUES (2 YEARS) FOR ~~$60~~ *SPECIAL* $25!

NAME _____

ADDRESS _____

CITY _____ STATE _____ ZIP _____

E-MAIL _____

PAYMENT: ☐ CHECK ☐ MONEY ORDER ☐ VISA ☐ MC

CARD # _____ EXP. DATE _____

No C.O.D. orders. Please make all checks payable to Masquerade/Direct. Payable in U.S. currency only.

MASQUERADE BOOKS

MASQUERADE

CLAIRE THOMPSON
SARAH'S SURRENDER
$6.95/620-0
Lovely Sarah denies her true desires for many years, hoping to find happiness with the pallid men who court her. Unable to hide her true feelings anymore, Sarah explores the SM scene—and tastes fulfillment for the first time. Gradually, her desires lead her to Lawrence, a discriminating man whose course of erotic training bring Sarah to a fuller realization of her submissive nature—and a deeper love—than she had ever imagined possible....

S. CRABB
CHATS ON OLD PEWTER
$6.95/611-1
A compendium of tales dedicated to dominant women. From domineering check-out girls to merciless flirts on the prowl, these women know what men like—and are highly skilled at reducing men to putty in their hands.

PAT CALIFIA
SENSUOUS MAGIC
$7.95/610-3
"*Sensuous Magic* is clear, succinct and engaging.... Califia is the Dr. Ruth of the alternative sexuality set..."
—*Lambda Book Report*

Erotic pioneer Pat Califia provides this unpretentious peek behind the mask of dominant/submissive sexuality. With her trademark wit and insight, Califia demystifies "the scene" for the novice, explaining the terms and techniques behind many misunderstood sexual practices.

ANAÏS NIN AND FRIENDS
WHITE STAINS
$6.95/609-X
A lost classic of 1940s erotica returns! Written by Anaïs Nin, Virginia Admiral, Caresse Crosby, and others for a dollar per page, this breathtakingly sensual volume was printed privately and soon became an underground legend. After more than fifty years, this priceless collection of explicit but sophisticated musings is back in print.

DENISE HALL
JUDGMENT
$6.95/590-5
Judgment—a forbidding edifice where unfortunate young women find themselves degraded and abandoned to the wiles of their cruel masters. Callie MacGuire descends into the depths of this prison, discovering a capacity for sensuality she never dreamed existed.

CLAIRE WILLOWS
PRESENTED IN LEATHER
$6.95/576-X
At the age of nineteen, Flora Price is whisked to the south of France, where she is imprisoned in Villa Close, an institution devoted to the ways of the lash—not to mention the paddle, the strap, the rod...

ALISON TYLER & DANTE DAVIDSON
BONDAGE ON A BUDGET
$6.95/570-0
Filled with delicious scenarios requiring no more than simple household items and a little imagination, this guide to DIY S&M will explode the myth that adventurous sex requires a dungeonful of expensive custom-made paraphernalia.

JEAN SADDLER
THE FASCINATING TYRANT
$6.95/569-7
A reprint of a classic tale from the 1930s. Jean Saddler's most famous novel, *The Fascinating Tyrant* is a riveting glimpse of sexual extravagance in which a young man discovers his penchant for flagellation and sadomasochism.

ROBERT SEWALL
THE DEVIL'S ADVOCATE
$6.95/553-0
Clara Reeves appeals to Conrad Garnett, a New York district attorney, for help in tracking down her missing sister, Rita. Clara soon finds herself being "persuaded" to accompany Conrad on his descent into a modern-day hell, where unspeakable pleasures await....

LUCY TAYLOR
UNNATURAL ACTS
$7.95/552-2
"A topnotch collection" —*Science Fiction Chronicle*

Unnatural Acts plunges deep into the dark side of the psyche and brings to life a disturbing vision of erotic horror. Unrelenting angels and hungry gods play with souls and bodies in Taylor's murky cosmos: where heaven and hell are merely differences of perspective.

J. A. GUERRA, ED.
COME QUICKLY: For Couples on the Go
$6.50/461-5
The increasing pace of daily life is no reason to forgo a little carnal pleasure whenever the mood strikes. Here are over sixty of the hottest fantasies around—all designed especially for modern couples on a hectic schedule.

MASQUERADE BOOKS

OLIVIA M. RAVENSWORTH
DOMESTIC SERVICE
$6.95/615-4
Though married for twenty-five years, Alan and Janet still manage to find sensual excitement in each other's arms. Sexy magazines fan the flames of their desire—so much so that Janet yearns to bring her own most private fantasy to life. Janet persuades Alan to hire live-in domestic help—and their home soon becomes the neighborhood's most infamous household!

THE DESIRES OF REBECCA
$6.50/532-8
Rebecca follows her passions from the simple love of the girl next door to the lechery of London's most notorious brothel, hoping for the ultimate thrill. She casts her lot with a crew of sapphic buccaneers, each of whom is more than capable of matching Rebecca's lust.

THE MISTRESS OF CASTLE ROHMENSTADT
$5.95/372-4
Lovely Katherine inherits a secluded European castle from a mysterious relative. Upon arrival she discovers, much to her delight, that the castle is a haven of sexual perversion. Before long, Katherine is truly Mistress of the house!

GERALD GREY
LONDON GIRLS
$6.50/531-X
In 1875, Samuel Brown arrives in London, determined to take the glorious city by storm. Samuel quickly distinguishes himself as one of the city's most notorious rakehells. Young Mr. Brown knows well the many ways of making a lady weak at the knees—and uses them not only to his delight, but to his enormous profit!

ATAULLAH MARDAAN
KAMA HOURI/DEVA DASI
$7.95/512-3
"Mardaan excels in crowding her pages with the sights and smells of India, and her erotic descriptions are convincingly realistic."
—Michael Perkins,
The Secret Record: Modern Erotic Literature

Kama Houri details the life of a sheltered Western woman who finds herself living within the confines of a harem. *Deva Dasi* is a tale dedicated to the sacred women of India who devoted their lives to the fulfillment of the senses.

ERICA BRONTE
LUST, INC.
$6.50/467-4
Explore the extremes of passion that lurk beneath even the most businesslike exteriors. Join in the sexy escapades of a group of professionals whose idea of office decorum is like nothing you've ever encountered!

VISCOUNT LADYWOOD
GYNECOCRACY
$9.95/511-5
Julian is sent to a private school, and discovers that his program of study has been devised by stern Mademoiselle de Chambonnard. In no time, Julian is learning the many ways of pleasure and pain—under the firm hand of this beautifully demanding headmistress.

N. T. MORLEY
THE OFFICE
$6.95/616-2
Lovely Suzette interviews for a desirable new position on the staff of a bondage magazine. Once hired, she discovers that her new employer's interest in dominance and submission extends beyond the printed page. Before long, Suzette and her fellow staffers are putting in long hours—and benefitting from some very specialized on-the-job training!

THE CONTRACT
$6.95/575-1
Meet Carlton and Sarah, two true connoisseurs of discipline. Sarah is experiencing some difficulty in training her current submissive. Carlton proposes an unusual wager: if Carlton is unsuccessful in bringing Tina to a full appreciation of Sarah's domination, Carlton himself will become Sarah's devoted slave....

THE LIMOUSINE
$6.95/555-7
Brenda was enthralled with her roommate Kristi's illicit sex life: a never ending parade of men who satisfied Kristi's desire to be dominated. Brenda decides to embark on a trip into submission, beginning in the long, white limousine where Kristi first met the Master.

THE CASTLE
$6.95/530-1
Tess Roberts is held captive by a crew of disciplinarians intent on making all her dreams come true—even those she'd never admitted to herself. While anyone can arrange for a stay at the Castle, Tess proves herself one of the most gifted applicants yet....

BUY ANY 4 BOOKS & CHOOSE 1 ADDITIONAL BOOK, OF EQUAL OR LESSER VALUE, AS YOUR FREE GIFT

MASQUERADE BOOKS

THE PARLOR
$6.50/496-8
The mysterious John and Sarah ask Kathryn to be their slave—an idea that turns her on so much that she can't refuse! Little by little, Kathryn not only learns to serve, but comes to know the inner secrets of her keepers.

VANESSA DURIES
THE TIES THAT BIND
$6.50/510-7
This best-selling account of real-life dominance and submission will keep you gasping with its vivid depictions of sensual abandon. At the hand of Masters Georges, Patrick, Pierre and others, this submissive seductress experiences pleasures she never knew existed....

M. S. VALENTINE
THE GOVERNESS
$6.95/562-X
Lovely Miss Hunnicut eagerly embarks upon a career as a governess, hoping to escape the memories of her broken engagement. Little does she know that Crawleigh Manor is far from the upstanding household it appears. Mr. Crawleigh, in particular, devotes himself to Miss Hunnicut's thorough defiling.

AMANDA WARE
BOUND TO THE PAST
$6.50/452-6
Doing research in an old Tudor mansion, Anne finds herself aroused by James, a descendant of the property's owners. Together they uncover the perverse desires of the mansion's long-dead master—desires that bind Anne inexorably to the past—not to mention the bedpost!

SACHI MIZUNO
SHINJUKU NIGHTS
$6.50/493-3
Using Tokyo's infamous red light district as his backdrop, Sachi Mizuno weaves an intricate web of sensual desire, wherein many characters are ensnared by the demands of their carnal natures.

PASSION IN TOKYO
$6.50/454-2
Tokyo—one of Asia's most historic and seductive cities. Come behind the closed doors of its citizens, and witness the many pleasures that await intrepid explorers. Men and women from every stratum of society free themselves of all inhibitions in this thrilling tour through the libidinous East.

MARTINE GLOWINSKI
POINT OF VIEW
$6.50/433-X
The story of one woman's extraordinary erotic awakening. With the assistance of her new, unexpectedly kinky lover, she discovers and explores her exhibitionist tendencies—until there is virtually nothing she won't do before the horny audiences her man arranges. Soon she is infamous for her unabashed sexual performances!

RICHARD McGOWAN
A HARLOT OF VENUS
$6.50/425-9
A highly fanciful, epic tale of lust on Mars! Cavortia—the most famous and sought-after courtesan in the cosmopolitan city of Venus—finds love and much more during her adventures with some cosmic characters. A sexy, sci-fi fairytale.

M. ORLANDO
THE SLEEPING PALACE
$6.95/582-4
Another thrilling volume of erotic reveries from the author of *The Architecture of Desire*. *Maison Bizarre* is the scene of unspeakable erotic cruelty; the *Lust Akademie* holds captive only the most luscious students of the sensual arts; *Baden-Eros* is the luxurious retreat of one's nastiest dreams.

CHET ROTHWELL
KISS ME, KATHERINE
$5.95/410-0
Beautiful Katherine can hardly believe her luck. Not only is she married to the charming Nelson, she's free to live out all her erotic fantasies with other men. Katherine's desires are more than any one man can handle—and plenty of men wait to fulfill her extraordinary needs!

MARCO VASSI
THE STONED APOCALYPSE
$5.95/401-1/Mass market
"Marco Vassi is our champion sexual energist." —VLS

During his lifetime, Marco Vassi's reputation as a champion of sexual experimentation was worldwide. Funded by his groundbreaking erotic writing, *The Stoned Apocalypse* is Vassi's autobiography; chronicling a cross-country trip on America's erotic byways, it offers a rare an stimulating glimpse of a generation's sexual imagination.

MASQUERADE BOOKS

THE SALINE SOLUTION
$6.95/568-9/Mass market

"I've always read Marco's work with interest and I have the highest opinion not only of his talent but his intellectual boldness."
—Norman Mailer

During the Sexual Revolution, Vassi established himself as an explorer of an uncharted sexual landscape. Through this story of one couple's brief affair and the events that lead them to desperately reassess their lives, Vassi examines the dangers of intimacy in an age of extraordinary freedom.

ROBIN WILDE
TABITHA'S TEASE
$6.95/597-2
When poor Robin arrives at The Valentine Academy, he finds himself subject to the torturous teasing of Tabitha—the Academy's most notoriously domineering co-ed. Adding to Robin's delicious suffering is the fact that Tabitha is pledge-mistress of a secret sorority dedicated to enslaving young men. Robin finds himself the and wildly excited captive of Tabitha & Company's weird desires!

TABITHA'S TICKLE
$6.50/468-2
Tabitha's back! Once again, men fall under the spell of scrumptious co-eds and find themselves enslaved to demands and desires they never dreamed existed. Think it's a man's world? Guess again. With Tabitha around, no man gets what he wants until she's completely satisfied....

CHARLES G. WOOD
HELLFIRE
$5.95/358-9
A vicious murderer is running amok in New York's sexual underground—and Nick O'Shay, a virile detective with the NYPD, plunges deep into the case. He soon becomes embroiled in the Big Apples notorious nightworld of dungeons and sex clubs, hunting a madman seeking to purge America with fire and blood sacrifices.

CHARISSE VAN DER LYN
SEX ON THE NET
$5.95/399-6
Electrifying erotica from one of the Internet's hottest authors. Encounters of all kinds—straight, lesbian, dominant/submissive and all sorts of extreme passions—are explored in thrilling detail.

STANLEY CARTEN
NAUGHTY MESSAGE
$5.95/333-3
Wesley Arthur discovers a lascivious message on his answering machine. Aroused beyond his wildest dreams by the acts described, he becomes obsessed with tracking down the woman behind the seductive voice. His search takes him through strip clubs, sex parlors and no-tell motels—before finally leading him to his randy reward....

CAROLE REMY
FANTASY IMPROMPTU
$6.50/513-1
Kidnapped to a remote island retreat, Chantal finds herself catering to every sexual whim of the mysterious Bran. Bran is determined to bring Chantal to a full embracing of her sensual nature, even while revealing himself to be something far more than human....

BEAUTY OF THE BEAST
$5.95/332-5
A shocking tell-all, written from the point-of-view of a prize-winning reporter. All the licentious secrets of an uninhibited life are revealed.

ANONYMOUS
DANIELLE: DIARY OF A SLAVE GIRL
$6.95/591-3
At the age of 19, Danielle Appleton vanishes. The frantic efforts of her family notwithstanding, she is never seen by them again. After her disappearance, Danielle finds herself doomed to a life of sexual slavery, obliged to become the ultimate instrument of pleasure to the man—or men—who own her and dictate her every move and desire.

ROMANCE OF LUST
$9.95/604-9
"Truly remarkable...all the pleasure of fine historical fiction combined with the most intimate descriptions of explicit love-making."
—The Times

One of the most famous erotic novels of the century! First issued between 1873 and 1876, this titillating collaborative work of sexual awakening in Victorian England was repeatedly been banned for its "immorality"—and much sought after for its vivid portrayals of sodomy, sexual initiation, and flagellation. *Romance of Lust* not only offers the reader a linguistic tour de force, but also delivers a long look at the many possibilities of sexual love.

BUY ANY 4 BOOKS & CHOOSE 1 ADDITIONAL BOOK, OF EQUAL OR LESSER VALUE, AS YOUR FREE GIFT

MASQUERADE BOOKS

SUBURBAN SOULS
$9.95/563-8
One of American erotica's first classics. Focusing on the May-December sexual relationship of nubile Lillian and the more experienced Jack, all three volumes of *Suburban Souls* now appear in one special edition—guaranteed to enrapture modern readers with its lurid detail.

THE MISFORTUNES OF COLETTE
$7.95/564-6
The tale of one woman's erotic suffering at the hands of the sadistic man and woman who take her in hand. Beautiful Colette is the victim of an obscene plot guaranteed to keep her in erotic servitude—first to her punishing guardian, then to the man who takes her as his wife. Passed from one lustful tormentor to another, Colette wonders whether she is destined to find her greatest pleasures in punishment!

LOVE'S ILLUSION
$6.95/549-2
Elizabeth Renard yearned for the body of rich and successful Dan Harrington. Then she discovered Harrington's secret weakness: a need to be humiliated and punished. She makes him her slave, and together they commence a thrilling journey into depravity that leaves nothing to the imagination!

NADIA
$5.95/267-1
Follow the delicious but neglected Nadia as she works to wring every drop of pleasure out of life—despite an unhappy marriage. With the help of some very eager men, Nadia soon experiences the erotic pleasures she had always dreamed of…. A classic title providing a peek into the sexual lives of another time and place.

TITIAN BERESFORD
CHIDEWELL HOUSE AND OTHER STORIES
$6.95/554-9
What keeps Cecil a virtual, if willing, prisoner of Chidewell House? One man has been sent to investigate the sexy situation—and reports back with tales of such depravity that no expense is spared in attempting Cecil's rescue. But what man would possibly desire release from the breathtakingly corrupt Elizabeth?

CINDERELLA
$6.50/500-X
Beresford triumphs again with this intoxicating tale, filled with castle dungeons and tightly corseted ladies-in-waiting, naughty viscounts and impossibly cruel masturbatrixes—nearly every conceivable method of erotic torture is explored and described in lush, vivid detail.

JUDITH BOSTON
$6.50/525-5
A bestselling chronicle of female domination. Edward would have been lucky to get the stodgy companion he thought his parents had hired for him. But an exquisite woman arrives at his door, and Edward finds—to his increasing delight—that his lewd behavior never goes unpunished by the unflinchingly severe Judith Boston! An underground classic—from the Victorian mold.

AKBAR DEL PIOMBO
THE FETISH CROWD
$6.95/556-5
An infamous trilogy presented in one volume guaranteed to appeal to the modern sophisticate. Separately, *Paula the Piquôse*, the infamous *Duke Cosimo*, and *The Double-Bellied Companion* are rightly considered individual masterpieces—together they make for an unforgettably lusty volume.

TINY ALICE
THE GEEK
$5.95/341-4
An offbeat classic of modern erotica, *The Geek* is told from the point of view of, well, a chicken who reports on the various perversities he witnesses as part of a traveling carnival. When a gang of renegade lesbians kidnaps Chicken and his geek, all hell breaks loose. A strange but highly arousing tale, filled with outrageous erotic oddities, that finally returns to print after years of infamy.

LYN DAVENPORT
THE GUARDIAN II
$6.50/505-0
The tale of submissive Felicia Brookes continues. No sooner has Felicia come to love Rodney than she discovers that she has been sold—and must now accustom herself to the guardianship of the debauched Duke of Smithton. Surely Rodney will rescue her from the domination of this depraved stranger. *Won't he?*

GWYNETH JAMES
DREAM CRUISE
$4.95/3045-8
Angelia has it all—exciting career and breathtaking beauty. But she longs to kick up her high heels and have some fun, so she takes an island vacation and vows to leave her inhibitions behind. From the moment her plane takes off, she finds herself in one steamy encounter after another—and wishes her horny holiday would never end!

MASQUERADE BOOKS

LIZBETH DUSSEAU

THE BEST OF LIZBETH DUSSEAU
$6.95/630-8

A special collection of this popular writer's best work. *Member of the Club*, *Spanish Holiday*, *Caroline's Contract* and *The Applicant* have made Lizbeth Dusseau a favorite with fans of contemporary erotica. This volume is full of heroines who are unafraid to put everything on the line in order to experience pleasure at the hands of a virile man…

MEMBER OF THE CLUB
$6.95/608-1

A restless woman yearns to realize her most secret, licentious desires. There is a club that exists for the fulfillment of such fantasies—a club devoted to the pleasures of the flesh, and the gratification of every hunger. When its members call she is compelled to answer—and serve each in an endless quest for satisfaction….

SPANISH HOLIDAY
$4.95/185-3

Lauren didn't mean to fall in love with the enigmatic Sam, but a once-in-a-lifetime European vacation gives her all the evidence she needs that this hot, insatiable man might be the one for her….Soon, both lovers are exploring the furthest reaches of their desires.

JOCELYN JOYCE

PRIVATE LIVES
$4.95/309-0

The dirty habits of the illustrious make for a sizzling tale of French erotic life. A widow has a craving for a young busboy; he's sleeping with a rich businessman's wife; her husband is minding his sex business elsewhere!

SABINE
$4.95/3046-6

There is no one who can refuse her once she casts her spell; no lover can do anything less than give up his whole life for her. Great men and empires fall at her feet; but she is haughty, distracted, impervious. It is the eve of WW II, and Sabine must find a new lover equal to her talents and her tastes.

SARA H. FRENCH

MASTER OF TIMBERLAND
$6.95/595-6

A tale of sexual slavery at the ultimate paradise resort—where sizzling submissives serve their masters without question. One of our bestselling titles, this trek to Timberland has ignited passions the world over.

MARY LOVE

ANGELA
$6.95/545-X

Angela's game is "look but don't touch," and she drives everyone mad with desire, dancing for their pleasure but never allowing a single caress. Soon her sensual spell is cast, and she's the only one who can break it!

MASTERING MARY SUE
$5.95/351-1

Mary Sue is a rich nymphomaniac whose husband is determined to declare her mentally incompetent and gain control of her fortune. He brings her to a castle where, to Mary Sue's delight, she is unleashed for a veritable sex-fest! No one could have predicted the depth of Mary Sue's hungers.

AMARANTHA KNIGHT

THE DARKER PASSIONS: FRANKENSTEIN
$6.95/617-0

The mistress of erotic horror sets her sights on Mary Shelley's darkest creation. What if you could create a living, breathing human? What shocking acts could it be taught to perform, to desire, to love? Find out what pleasures await those who play God in another breathtaking journey through the Darker Passions.

The Darker Passions: CARMILLA
$6.95/578-6

Captivated by the portrait of a beautiful woman, a young man finds himself becoming obsessed with her remarkable story. Little by little, he uncovers the many blasphemies and debaucheries with which the beauteous Laura filled her hours—even as an otherworldly presence began feasting upon her….

The Darker Passions: THE PICTURE OF DORIAN GRAY
$6.50/342-2

One woman finds her most secret desires laid bare by a portrait far more revealing than she could have imagined. Soon she benefits from a skillful masquerade, indulging her previously hidden and unusual whims.

The Darker Passions: DR. JEKYLL AND MR. HYDE
$4.95/227-2

It is a sexy story of incredible transformations. Explore the steamy possibilities of a tale where no one is quite who—or what—they seem. Victorian bedrooms explode with hidden demons!

BUY ANY 4 BOOKS & CHOOSE 1 ADDITIONAL BOOK, OF EQUAL OR LESSER VALUE, AS YOUR FREE GIFT

MASQUERADE BOOKS

THE DARKER PASSIONS READER
$6.50/432-1
Here are the most eerily erotic passages from the acclaimed sexual reworkings of *Dracula*, *Frankenstein*, *Dr. Jekyll & Mr. Hyde* and *The Fall of the House of Usher*.

THE PAUL LITTLE LIBRARY

SLAVE ISLAND
$6.95/655-3
A tale of ultimate sexual license from this modern master. A leisure cruise is waylaid by Lord Henry Philbrock, a sadistic genius. The ship's passengers are kidnapped and spirited to his island prison, where the women are trained to accommodate the most bizarre sexual cravings of the rich and perverted.

DOUBLE NOVEL
$7.95/647-2
Two best-selling novels of illicit desire combined into one spell-binding volume! Paul Little's *The Metamorphosis of Lisette Joyaux* tells the story of an innocent young woman seduced by a group of beautiful and experienced lesbians. *The Story of Monique* explores an underground society's clandestine rituals and scandalous encounters.

TEARS OF THE INQUISITION
$6.95/612-X
"There was a tickling inside her as her nervous system reminded her she was ready for sex. But before her was…the Inquisitor!" Titillating accusations ring through the chambers of the Inquisitor as men and women confess their every desire....

CHINESE JUSTICE
$6.95/596-4
The notorious Paul Little indulges his penchant for discipline in these wild tales. *Chinese Justice* is already a classic—the story of the excruciating pleasures and delicious punishments inflicted on foreigners under the tyrannical leaders of the Boxer Rebellion.

FIT FOR A KING/BEGINNER'S LUST
$8.95/571-9/Trade paperback
Two complete novels. Voluptuous and exquisite, she is a woman *Fit for a King*—but could she withstand the fantastic force of her carnality? *Beginner's Lust* pays off handsomely for a novice in the many ways of sensuality.

SENTENCED TO SERVITUDE
$8.95/565-4/Trade paperback
A haughty young aristocrat learns what becomes of excessive pride when she is abducted and forced to submit to ordeals of sensual torment. Trained to accept her submissive state, the icy young woman soon melts under the heat of her owners, discovering a talent for love she never knew existed....

ROOMMATE'S SECRET
$8.95/557-3/Trade paperback
A woman is forced to make ends meet by the most ancient of methods. From the misery of early impoverishment to the delight of ill-gotten gains, Elda learns to rely on her considerable sensual talents.

TUTORED IN LUST
$6.95/547-6
This tale of the initiation and instruction of a carnal college co-ed and her fellow students unlocks the sex secrets of the classroom.

**LOVE SLAVE/
PECULIAR PASSIONS OF MEG**
$8.95/529-8/Trade paperback
What does it take to acquire a willing *Love Slave* of one's own? What are the appetites that lurk within *Meg*? The notoriously depraved Paul Little spares no lascivious detail in these two relentless tales!

CELESTE
$6.95/544-1
It's definitely all in the family for this female duo of sexual dynamics. While traveling through Europe, these two try everything and everyone on their horny holiday.

ALL THE WAY
$6.95/509-3
Two hot Little tales in one big volume! *Going All the Way* features an unhappy man who tries to purge himself of the memory of his lover with a series of quirky and uninhibited vixens. *Pushover* tells the story of a serial spanker and his celebrated exploits.

THE END OF INNOCENCE
$6.95/546-8
The early days of Women's Emancipation are the setting for this story of very independent ladies. These women were willing to go to any lengths to fight for their sexual freedom, and willing to endure any punishment in their desire for total liberation.

THE BEST OF PAUL LITTLE
$6.50/469-0
Known for his fantastic portrayals of punishment and pleasure, Little never fails to push readers over the edge of sensual excitement. His best scenes are here collected for the enjoyment of all erotic connoisseurs.

CAPTIVE MAIDENS
$5.95/440-2
The scandalously sexy story of three independent and beautiful young women who find themselves powerless against the debauched landowners of 1824 England. The unlucky lovelies find themselves banished to a sex colony, where they are subjected to unspeakable perversions.

MASQUERADE BOOKS

THE PRISONER
$5.95/330-9
Judge Black has built a secret room below a penitentiary, where he sentences his female prisoners to hours of exhibition while his friends watch. Judge Black's justice keeps his captives on the brink of utter pleasure!

DOUBLE NOVEL
$6.95/86-6
The Metamorphosis of Lisette Joyaux tells the story of a young woman initiated into an incredible world of lesbian lusts. *The Story of Monique* reveals the twisted sexual rituals that beckon the willing Monique.

ALIZARIN LAKE
MISS HIGH HEELS
$6.95/632-4
Forced by his wicked sisters to dress and behave like a proper lady, Dennis Beryl finds he enjoys life as Denise much more! Petticoats and punishments make for one kinky romp!

CLARA
$6.95/548-4
The mysterious death of a beautiful woman leads her old boyfriend on a harrowing journey of discovery. His search uncovers an unimaginably sensuous woman embarked on a quest for deeper and more unusual sensations, each more shocking than the one before!

SEX ON DOCTOR'S ORDERS
$5.95/402-X
Naughty nurse Beth uses her considerable skills to further medical science by offering insatiable assistance in the gathering of specimens. Soon she's involved everyone in her horny work—and no one leaves without surrendering what Beth wants!

THE EROTIC ADVENTURES OF HARRY TEMPLE
$4.95/127-6
Harry Temple's memoirs chronicle his incredibly amorous adventures—from his initiation at the hands of insatiable sirens, through his stay at a house of hot repute, to his encounters with a chastity-belted nympho, and much more!

LUSCIDIA WALLACE
THE ICE MAIDEN
$6.95/613-8
Edward Canton has everything he wants in life, with one exception: Rebecca Esterbrook. He whisks her away to his remote island compound, where she learns to shed her inhibitions. Fully aroused for the first time in her life, she becomes a slave to desire!

JOHN NORMAN
HUNTERS OF GOR
$6.95/592-1
Tarl Cabot ventures into the wilderness of Gor, pitting his skill against brutal outlaws and sly warriors. His life on Gor been complicated by three beautiful, very different women: Talena, Tarl's one-time queen; Elizabeth, his fearless comrade; and Verna, chief of the feral panther women. In this installment of Norman's million-selling sci-fi phenomenon, the fates of these uncommon women are finally revealed....

CAPTIVE OF GOR
$6.95/581-6
On Earth, Elinor Brinton was accustomed to having it all—wealth, beauty, and a host of men wrapped around her little finger. But Elinor's spoiled existence is a thing of the past. She is now a pleasure slave of Gor—a world whose society insists on her subservience to any man who calls her his own. And despite her headstrong past, Elinor finds herself succumbing—with pleasure—to her powerful Master.

RAIDERS OF GOR
$6.95/558-1
Tarl Cabot descends into the depths of Port Kar—the most degenerate port city of the Counter-Earth. There Cabot learns the ways of Kar, whose residents are renowned for the grip in which they hold their voluptuous slaves....

ASSASSIN OF GOR
$6.95/538-7
The chronicles of Counter-Earth continue with this examination of Gorean society. Here is the caste system of Gor: from the Assassin Kuurus, on a mission of vengeance, to Pleasure Slaves, trained in the ways of personal ecstasy.

NOMADS OF GOR
$6.95/527-1
Cabot finds his way across Gor, pledged to serve the Priest-Kings. Unfortunately for Cabot, his mission leads him to the savage Wagon People—nomads who may very well kill before surrendering any secrets....

PRIEST-KINGS OF GOR
$6.95/488-7
Tarl Cabot searches for his lovely wife Talena. Does she live, or was she destroyed by the all-powerful Priest-Kings? Cabot is determined to find out—though no one who has approached the mountain stronghold of the Priest-Kings has ever returned alive....

BUY ANY 4 BOOKS & CHOOSE 1 ADDITIONAL BOOK, OF EQUAL OR LESSER VALUE, AS YOUR FREE GIFT

MASQUERADE BOOKS

OUTLAW OF GOR
$6.95/487-9

Tarl Cabot returns to Gor. Upon arriving, he discovers that his name, his city and the names of those he loves have become unspeakable. Once a respected Tarnsman, Cabot has become an outlaw, and must discover his new purpose on this strange planet, where even simple answers have their price....

TARNSMAN OF GOR
$6.95/486-0

This controversial series returns! Tarl Cabot is transported to Gor. He must quickly accustom himself to the ways of this world, including the caste system which exalts some as Warriors, and debases others as slaves.

SYDNEY ST. JAMES
RIVE GAUCHE
$5.95/317-1

The Latin Quarter, Paris, circa 1920. Expatriate bohemians couple wildly—before eventually abandoning their ambitions amidst the temptations waiting to be indulged in every bedroom.

DON WINSLOW
THE BEST OF DON WINSLOW
$6.95/607-3

Internationally best-selling fetish author Don Winslow personally selected his hottest passages for this special collection. Sizzling excerpts from *Claire's Girls*, *Gloria's Indiscretion*, *Katerina in Charge*, *The Insatiable Mistress of Rosedale*, and others are artfully woven together to make this an extraordinarily powerful overview of Winslow's greatest hits.

SLAVE GIRLS OF ROME
$6.95/577-8

Never were women so relentlessly used as were ancient Rome's voluptuous slaves! With no choice but to serve their lustful masters, these captive beauties learn to perform their duties with the passion of Venus herself.

PRIVATE PLEASURES
$6.50/504-2

Frantic voyeurs and licentious exhibitionists are here displayed in all their wanton glory—laid bare by the perverse and probing eye of Don Winslow.

THE INSATIABLE MISTRESS OF ROSEDALE
$6.50/494-1

Edward and Lady Penelope reside in Rosedale manor. While Edward is a connoisseur of sexual perversion, it is Lady Penelope whose mastery of complete sensual pleasure makes their home infamous. Indulging one another's bizarre whims is a way of life for this wicked couple....

N. WHALLEN
THE EDUCATION OF SITA MANSOOR
$6.95/567-0

On the eve of her wedding, Sita Mansoor is left without a bridegroom. Sita travels to America, where she hopes to become educated in the ways of a permissive society. She could never have imagined the wide variety of tutors—both male and female—who would be waiting to take on so beautiful a pupil. The ultimate in Sex Ed!

THE CLASSIC COLLECTION
THE ENGLISH GOVERNESS
$6.95/622-7

When Lord Lovell's son was expelled from his prep school for masturbation, he hired a very proper governess to tutor the boy—giving her strict instructions not to spare the rod to break him of his bad habits. Upon her arrival in Lord Lovell's home, governess Harriet Marwood reveals herself a force to be reckoned with—particularly by her randy charge. In no time, Master Lovell's onanism is under control—as are all other aspects of his life. Governess Harriet Marwood gives the Lovell family a lesson they'll never forget!

MAN WITH A MAID
$4.95/307-4

The adventures of Jack and Alice have delighted readers for eight decades! A classic of its genre, *Man with a Maid* tells a tale of desire, revenge, and submission. Join Jack in the Snuggery, where many lovely women learn the ways of pleasure.

MASQUERADE READERS
THE 50 BEST PLAYGIRL FANTASIES
$7.95/648-0

A steamy selection of women's fantasies straight from the pages of PLAYGIRL—the leading magazine of sexy entertainment for women. Contemporary heroines pursue thrilling liaisons with horny men from every walk of life in these tales of modern lust. Specially selected by no less an authority than Charlotte Rose, author of such best-selling classics of women's erotica as *Women at Work* and *The Doctor is In*—these wicked delights are sure to set your pulse racing.

INTIMATE PLEASURES
$4.95/38-6

Indulge your most private penchants with this specially chosen selection of Masquerade's hottest moments. Try a tempting morsel of *The Prodigal Virgin* and *Eveline*, the bizarre public displays of carnality in *The Gilded Lily* or the relentless and shocking carnality of *The Story of Monique*.

MASQUERADE BOOKS

RHINOCEROS

M. CHRISTIAN, ED.
EROS EX MACHINA
$7.95/593-X
As the millennium approaches, technology is not only an inevitable, but a deeply desirable addition to daily life. *Eros Ex Machina* explores the thrill and danger of machines—our literal and literary love of technology. Join over 25 of today's hottest writers as they explore erotic relationships with all kinds of gizmos, gadgets, and devices.

LEOPOLD VON SACHER-MASOCH
VENUS IN FURS
$7.95/589-1
The alliance of Severin and Wanda epitomizes Sacher-Masoch's obsession with a cruel goddess and the urges that drive the man held in her thrall. Exclusive to this edition are letters exchanged between Sacher-Masoch and Emilie Mataja—an aspiring writer he sought as the avatar of his desires.

JOHN NORMAN
IMAGINATIVE SEX
$7.95/561-1
The author of the Gor novels outlines his philosophy on relations between the sexes, and presents fifty-three scenarios designed to reintroduce fantasy to the bedroom.

KATHLEEN K.
SWEET TALKERS
$6.95/516-6
"If you enjoy eavesdropping on explicit conversations about sex... this book is for you." —*Spectator*

A explicit look at the burgeoning phenomenon of phone sex. Kathleen K. ran a phone-sex company in the late 80s, and she opens up her diary for a peek at the life of a phone-sex operator. Transcripts of actual conversations are included.
Trade /$12.95/192-6

THOMAS S. ROCHE
NOIROTICA 2: Pulp Friction (Ed.)
$7.95/584-0
Another volume of criminally seductive stories set in the murky terrain of the erotic and noir genres. Thomas Roche has gathered the darkest jewels from today's edgiest writers to create this provocative collection. A must for all fans of contemporary erotica.

NOIROTICA: An Anthology of Erotic Crime Stories (Ed.)
$6.95/390-2
A collection of darkly sexy tales, taking place at the crossroads of the crime and erotic genres. Here are some of today's finest writers, all of whom explore the extraordinary and arousing terrain where desire runs irrevocably afoul of the law.

DARK MATTER
$6.95/484-4
"*Dark Matter* is sure to please gender outlaws, bodymod junkies, goth vampires, boys who wish they were dykes, and anybody who's not to sure where the fine line should be drawn between pleasure and pain. It's a handful."—Pat Califia

"Here is the erotica of the cumming millennium.... You will be deliciously disturbed, but never disappointed."
—Poppy Z. Brite

DAVID MELTZER
UNDER
$6.95/290-6
The story of a 21st century sex professional living at the bottom of the social heap. After surgeries designed to increase his physical allure, corrupt government forces drive the cyber-gigolo underground, where even more bizarre cultures await.... A thrilling, disturbing look at the future.

LAURA ANTONIOU, ED.
SOME WOMEN
$7.95/573-5
Introduction by Pat Califia
"Makes the reader think about the wide range of SM experiences, beyond the glamour of fiction and fantasy, or the clever-clever prose of the perverati." —*SKIN TWO*

Over forty essays written by women actively involved in consensual dominance and submission. Professional mistresses, lifestyle leatherdykes, whipmakers, titleholders—women from every conceivable walk of life lay bare their true feelings about issues as explosive as feminism, abuse, pleasure and public image. A bestselling title and valuable resource for anyone interested in sexuality.

NO OTHER TRIBUTE
$7.95/603-0
A volume sure to challenge Political Correctness. Tales of women kept in bondage to their lovers by their deepest passions. Love pushes these women beyond acceptable limits, rendering them helpless to deny anything to the men and women they adore.

BUY ANY 4 BOOKS & CHOOSE 1 ADDITIONAL BOOK, OF EQUAL OR LESSER VALUE, AS YOUR FREE GIFT

MASQUERADE BOOKS

BY HER SUBDUED
$6.95/281-7
These tales all involve women in control—of their lives and their lovers. So much in control that they can remorselessly break rules to become powerful goddesses of those who sacrifice all to worship at their feet.

AMELIA G, ED.
BACKSTAGE PASSES: Rock n' Roll Erotica from the Pages of *Blue Blood* Magazine
$6.95/438-0
Amelia G, editor of the goth-sex journal *Blue Blood*, has brought together some of today's most irreverent writers, each of whom has outdone themselves with an edgy, antic tale of modern lust.

ROMY ROSEN
SPUNK
$6.95/492-5
Casey, a lovely model poised upon the verge of super-celebrity, falls for an insatiable young rock singer—not suspecting that his sexual appetite has led him to experiment with a dangerous new aphrodisiac. Soon, Casey becomes addicted to the drug, and her craving plunges her into a strange underworld....

MOLLY WEATHERFIELD
CARRIE'S STORY
$6.95/485-2
"I was stunned by how well it was written and how intensely foreign I found its sexual world.... And, since this is a world I don't frequent... I thoroughly enjoyed the National Geo tour."
—bOING bOING

"Hilarious and harrowing... just when you think things can't get any wilder, they do." —*Black Sheets*

Weatherfield's bestselling examination of dominance and submission. "I had been Jonathan's slave for about a year when he told me he wanted to sell me at an auction...." A rare piece of erotica, both thoughtful and hot!

CYBERSEX CONSORTIUM
CYBERSEX: The Perv's Guide to Finding Sex on the Internet
$6.95/471-2
You've heard the objections: cyberspace is soaked with sex, mired in immorality. Okay—so where is it!? Tracking down the good stuff—the real good stuff—can waste an awful lot of expensive time, and frequently leave you high and dry. The Cybersex Consortium presents an easy-to-use guide for those intrepid adults who know what they want.

LAURA ANTONIOU ("Sara Adamson")

"Ms. Adamson creates a wonderfully diverse world of lesbian, gay, straight, bi and transgendered characters, all mixing delightfully in the melting pot of sadomasochism and planting the genre more firmly in the culture at large. I for one am cheering her on!" —Kate Bornstein

THE MARKETPLACE
$7.95/602-2
The first title in Antoniou's thrilling Marketplace Trilogy, following the lives an lusts of those who have been deemed worthy to participate in the ultimate BD/SM arena.

THE SLAVE
$7.95/601-4
The Slave covers the experience of one talented submissive who longs to join the ranks of those who have proven themselves worthy of entry into the Marketplace. But the price, while delicious, is staggeringly high....

THE TRAINER
$6.95/249-3
The Marketplace Trilogy concludes with the story of the trainers, and the desires and paths that led them to become the ultimate figures of authority.

THE CATALYST
$6.95/621-9
A kinky art movie inspires the audience members—het and queer—to try some SM play of their own. Different from a lot of SM smut in that it depicts actual consensual SM scenes between just plain folks rather than wild impossible fantasies, *The Catalyst* is both sweet-natured and nastily perverse. The "why don't we give this kinky stuff a try" tone is a true delight.
—*Blowfish*

After viewing an explicitly kinky film full of images of bondage and submission, several audience members find themselves deeply moved by the erotic suggestions they've seen on the screen. Bondage, discipline, and unimaginable sexual perversity are explored as long-denied urges explode with new intensity. The first of this author's best-selling BD/SM titles.

TAMMY JO ECKHART
AMAZONS: Erotic Explorations of Ancient Myths
$7.95/534-4
The Amazon—the fierce woman warrior—appears in the traditions of many cultures, but never before has the erotic potential of this archetype been explored with such energy and imagination. Powerful pleasures await anyone lucky enough to encounter Eckhart's legendary spitfires.

MASQUERADE BOOKS

PUNISHMENT FOR THE CRIME
$6.95/427-5

Stories that explore dominance and submission. From an encounter between two of society's most despised individuals, to the explorations of longtime friends, these tales take you where few others have ever dared....

GERI NETTICK WITH BETH ELLIOT
MIRRORS: Portrait of a Lesbian Transsexual
$6.95/435-6

Born a male, Geri Nettick knew something just didn't fit. Even after coming to terms with her own gender dysphoria she still fought to be accepted by the lesbian feminist community to which she felt she belonged. A remarkable and inspiring true story of self-discover and acceptance.

TRISTAN TAORMINO & DAVID AARON CLARK, EDS.
RITUAL SEX
$6.95/391-0

The contributors to *Ritual Sex* know that body and soul share more common ground than society feels comfortable acknowledging. From memoirs of ecstatic revelation, to quests to reconcile sex and spirit, *Ritual Sex* provides an unprecedented look at private life.

AMARANTHA KNIGHT, ED.
DEMON SEX
$7.95/594-8

Examining the dark forces of humankind's oldest stories, the contributors to *Demon Sex* reveal the strange symbiosis of dread and desire. Stories include a streetwalker's deal with the devil; a visit with the stripper from Hell; the secrets behind an aging rocker's timeless appeal; and many more guaranteed to shatter preconceptions about modern lust.

SEDUCTIVE SPECTRES
$6.95/464-X

Tours through the erotic supernatural via the imaginations of today's best writers. Never have ghostly encounters been so alluring, thanks to otherworldly characters well-acquainted with the pleasures of the flesh.

SEX MACABRE
$6.95/392-9

Horror tales designed for dark and sexy nights—sure to make your skin crawl, and heart beat faster.

FLESH FANTASTIC
$6.95/352-X

Humans have long toyed with the idea of "playing God": creating life from nothingness, bringing life to the inanimate. Now Amarantha Knight collects stories exploring not only the act of Creation, but the lust that follows.

GARY BOWEN
DIARY OF A VAMPIRE
$6.95/331-7

"Gifted with a darkly sensual vision and a fresh voice, [Bowen] is a writer to watch out for."
—Cecilia Tan

Rafael, a red-blooded male with an insatiable hunger for the same, is the perfect antidote to the effete malcontents haunting bookstores today. The emergence of a bold and brilliant vision, rooted in past and present.

GRANT ANTREWS
LEGACIES
$7.95/605-7

Kathi Lawton discovers that she has inherited the troubling secret of her late mother's scandalous sexuality. In an effort to understand what motivated her mother's desires, Kathi embarks on an exploration of SM that leads her into the arms of Horace Moore, a mysterious man who seems to see into her very soul. As she begins falling for her new master, Kathi finds herself wondering just how far she'll go to prove her love.... Another moving exploration of adult love and desire from the author of *My Darling Dominatrix*.

SUBMISSIONS
$7.95/618-9

Antrews portrays the very special elements of the dominant/submissive relationship with restraint—this time with the story of a lonely man, a winning lottery ticket, and a demanding dominatrix. Suddenly finding himself a millionaire, Kevin Donovan thinks his worries are over—until his restless soul tires of the high life. He turns to the icy Maitresse Genevieve, hoping that her ministrations will guide him to some deeper peace....

ROGUES GALLERY
$6.95/522-0

A stirring evocation of dominant/submissive love. Two doctors meet and slowly fall in love. Once lovely Beth reveals her hidden, kinky desires to Jim, the two explore the forbidden acts that will come to define their distinctly exotic affair.

BUY ANY 4 BOOKS & CHOOSE 1 ADDITIONAL BOOK, OF EQUAL OR LESSER VALUE, AS YOUR FREE GIFT

MASQUERADE BOOKS

MY DARLING DOMINATRIX
$7.95/566-2
When a man and a woman fall in love, it's supposed to be simple, uncomplicated, easy—unless that woman happens to be a dominatrix. This highly praised and unpretentious love story captures the richness and depth of this very special kind of love without leering or smirking.

JEAN STINE
THRILL CITY
$6.95/411-9
Thrill City is the seat of the world's increasing depravity, and this classic novel transports you there with a vivid style you'd be hard pressed to ignore. No writer is better suited to describe the extremes of this modern Babylon.

JOHN WARREN
THE TORQUEMADA KILLER
$6.95/367-8
Detective Eva Hernandez gets her first "big case": a string of murders taking place within New York's SM community. Eva assembles the evidence, revealing a picture of a world misunderstood and under attack—and gradually comes to face her own hidden longings.

THE LOVING DOMINANT
$7.95/600-6
Everything you need to know about an infamous sexual variation, and an unspoken type of love. Warren, a scene veteran, guides readers through this rarely seen world, and offers clear-eyed advice guaranteed to enlighten any erotic explorer.

DAVID AARON CLARK
SISTER RADIANCE
$6.95/215-9
A meditation on love, sex, and death. The vicissitudes of lust and romance are examined against a backdrop of urban decay in this testament to the allure—and inevitability of the forbidden.

THE WET FOREVER
$6.95/117-9
The story of Janus and Madchen—a small-time hood and a beautiful sex worker on the run—examines themes of loyalty, sacrifice, redemption and obsession amidst Manhattan's sex parlors and underground S/M clubs.

MICHAEL PERKINS
EVIL COMPANIONS
$6.95/3067-9
Evil Companions has been hailed as "a frightening classic." A young couple explores the nether reaches of the erotic unconscious in a confrontation with the extremes of passion.

THE SECRET RECORD:
Modern Erotic Literature
$6.95/3039-3
Michael Perkins surveys the field with authority and unique insight. Updated and revised to include the latest trends, tastes, and developments in this misunderstood genre.

AN ANTHOLOGY OF CLASSIC ANONYMOUS EROTIC WRITING
$6.95/140-3
Michael Perkins has collected the best passages from the world's erotic writing. "Anonymous" is one of the most infamous bylines in publishing history—and these excerpts show why!

HELEN HENLEY
ENTER WITH TRUMPETS
$6.95/197-7
Helen Henley was told that women just don't write about sex. So Henley did it alone, flying in the face of "tradition" by writing this touching tale of arousal and devotion in one couple's kinky relationship.

ALICE JOANOU
THE BEST OF ALICE JOANOU
$7.95/623-5
"Joanou has created a series of sumptuous, brooding, dark visions of sexual obsession and is undoubtedly a name to look out for in the future." —*Redeemer*

"Outstanding erotic fiction." —*Susie Bright*

A major name in the renaissance of American erotica, Joanou is responsible for some of the decade's most unforgettable images. This volume includes excerpts from *Cannibal Flower*, *Tourniquet* and *Black Tongue*—the titles that announced her talent to the world.

BLACK TONGUE
$6.95/258-2
"Joanou has created a series of sumptuous, brooding, dark visions of sexual obsession, and is undoubtedly a name to look out for in the future." —*Redeemer*

Exploring lust at its most florid and unsparing, *Black Tongue* is redolent of forbidden passions.

PHILIP JOSÉ FARMER
A FEAST UNKNOWN
$6.95/276-0
"Sprawling, brawling, shocking, suspenseful, hilarious..." —*Theodore Sturgeon*

Lord Grandrith—armed with the belief that he is the son of Jack the Ripper—tells the story of his remarkable life. His story progresses to encompass the furthest extremes of human behavior.

MASQUERADE BOOKS

FLESH
$6.95/303-1
Stagg explored the galaxies for 800 years. Upon his return, the hero Stagg is made the centerpiece of an incredible public ritual—one that will take him to the heights of ecstasy, and drag him toward the depths of hell.

SAMUEL R. DELANY
THE MAD MAN
$8.99/408-9/Mass market
"Delany develops an insightful dichotomy between [his protagonist]'s two worlds: the one of cerebral philosophy and dry academia, the other of heedless, 'impersonal' obsessive sexual extremism. When these worlds finally collide...the novel achieves a surprisingly satisfying resolution...."
—Publishers Weekly

Graduate student John Marr researches the life of Timothy Hasler: a philosopher whose career was cut tragically short over a decade earlier. Marr begins to find himself increasingly drawn toward shocking sexual encounters with the homeless men, until it begins to seem that Hasler's death might hold some key to his own life as a gay man in the age of AIDS. Surely this legendary writer's most mind-blowing novel.

TUPPY OWENS
SENSATIONS
$6.95/3081-4
Tuppy Owens takes a rare peek behind the scenes of *Sensations*—the first big-budget sex flick. Originally commissioned to appear in book form after the release of the film in 1975, *Sensations* is finally available.

DANIEL VIAN
ILLUSIONS
$6.95/3074-1
Two tales of danger and desire in Berlin on the eve of WWII. From private homes to lurid cafés, passion is exposed in stark contrast to the brutal violence of the time, as desperate people explore their darkest sexual desires.

PERSUASIONS
$4.95/183-7
"The stockings are drawn tight by the suspender belt, tight enough to be stretched to the limit just above the middle part of her thighs, tight enough so that her calves glow through the sheer silk..." A double novel, including the classics *Adagio* and *Gabriela and the General*, this volume traces lust around the globe.

LIESEL KULIG
LOVE IN WARTIME
$6.95/3044-X
Madeleine knew that the handsome SS officer was dangerous, but she was just a cabaret singer in Nazi-occupied Paris, trying to survive in a perilous time. When Josef fell in love with her, he discovered that a beautiful woman can be as dangerous as any warrior.

SOPHIE GALLEYMORE BIRD
MANEATER
$6.95/103-9
Through a bizarre act of creation, a man attains the "perfect" lover—by all appearances a beautiful, sensuous woman, but in reality something far darker. Once brought to life she will accept no mate, seeking instead the prey that will sate her hunger.

BADBOY

DAVID MAY
MADRUGADA
$6.95/574-3
Set in San Francisco's gay leather community, *Madrugada* follows the lives of a group of friends—and their many acquaintances—as they tangle with the thorny issues of love and lust. Uncompromising, mysterious, and arousing, David May weaves a complex web of relationships in this unique story cycle.

PETER HEISTER
ISLANDS OF DESIRE
$6.95/480-1
Red-blooded lust on the wine-dark seas of classical Greece. Anacraeon yearns to leave his small, isolated island and find adventure in one of the overseas kingdoms. Accompanied by some randy friends, Anacraeon makes his dream come true—and discovers pleasures he never dreamed of!

KITTY TSUI WRITING AS "ERIC NORTON"
SPARKS FLY
$6.95/551-4
The highest highs—and most wretched depths—of life as Eric Norton, a beautiful wanton living San Francisco's high life. *Sparks Fly* traces Norton's rise, fall, and resurrection, vividly marking the way with the personal affairs that give life meaning.

BUY ANY 4 BOOKS & CHOOSE 1 ADDITIONAL BOOK, OF EQUAL OR LESSER VALUE, AS YOUR FREE GIFT

MASQUERADE BOOKS

BARRY ALEXANDER
ALL THE RIGHT PLACES
$6.95/482-8
Stories filled with hot studs in lust and love. From modern masters and slaves to medieval royals and their subjects, Alexander explores the mating rituals men have engaged in for centuries—all in the name of desire...

MICHAEL FORD, ED.
BUTCHBOYS:
Stories For Men Who Need It Bad
$6.50/523-9
A big volume of tales dedicated to the rough-and-tumble type who can make a man weak at the knees. Some of today's best erotic writers explore the many possible variations on the age-old fantasy of the thoroughly dominating man.

WILLIAM J. MANN, ED.
GRAVE PASSIONS:
Gay Tales of the Supernatural
$6.50/405-4
A collection of the most chilling tales of passion currently being penned by today's most provocative gay writers. Unnatural transformations, otherworldly encounters, and deathless desires would make for a collection sure to keep readers up late at night.

J. A. GUERRA, ED.
COME QUICKLY:
For Boys on the Go
$6.50/413-5
Here are more than sixty of the hottest fantasies around—all designed to get you going in less time than it takes to dial 976. Julian. Anthony Guerra has put together this volume especially for you—a busy man on a modern schedule, who still appreciates a little old-fashioned action.

JOHN PRESTON
HUSTLING: A Gentleman's Guide to the Fine Art of Homosexual Prostitution
$6.50/517-4
"Fun and highly literary. What more could you expect form such an accomplished activist, author and editor?"—*Drummer*

John Preston solicited the advice and opinions of "working boys" from across the country in his effort to produce the ultimate guide to the hustler's world. *Hustling* covers every practical aspect of the business, from clientele and payment to "specialties," and drawbacks. A must for men on either side of the transaction.
Trade $12.95/137-3

MR. BENSON
$4.95/3041-5
Jamie is an aimless young man lucky enough to encounter Mr. Benson. He is soon learns to accept this man as his master. Jamie's incredible adventures never fail to excite—especially when the going gets rough!

TALES FROM THE DARK LORD
$5.95/323-6
Twelve stunning works from the man *Lambda Book Report* called "the Dark Lord of gay erotica." The ritual of lust and surrender is explored in all its manifestations in this heart-stopping triumph of authority and vision.

TALES FROM THE DARK LORD II
$4.95/176-4

THE ARENA
$4.95/3083-0
Preston's take on the ultimate sex club–where men go to abolish all personal limits. Only the author of *Mr. Benson* could have imagined so perfect an institution for the satisfaction of male desire.

THE HEIR•THE KING
$4.95/3048-2
The Heir, written in the lyric voice of the ancient myths, tells the story of a world where slaves and masters create a new sexual society. *The King* tells the story of a soldier who discovers his monarch's most secret desires.

THE MISSION OF ALEX KANE
GOLDEN YEARS
$4.95/3069-5
When evil threatens the plans of a group of older gay men, Kane's got the muscle to take it head on. Along the way, he wins the support—and very specialized attentions—of a cowboy plucked right out of the Old West.

DEADLY LIES
$4.95/3076-8
Politics is a dirty business and the dirt becomes deadly when a smear campaign targets gay men. Who better to clean things up than Alex Kane!

STOLEN MOMENTS
$4.95/3098-9
Houston's evolving gay community is victimized by a malicious newspaper editor who is more than willing to boost circulation by printing homophobic slander. He never counted on Alex Kane, fearless defender of gay dreams and desires.

SECRET DANGER
$4.95/111-X
Alex Kane and the faithful Danny are called to a small European country, where a group of gay tourists is being held hostage by brutal terrorists.

MASQUERADE BOOKS

LETHAL SILENCE
$4.95/125-X
Chicago becomes the scene of the right-wing's most noxious plan—facilitated by unholy political alliances. Alex and Danny head to the Windy City to battle the mercenaries who would squash gay men underfoot.

MATT TOWNSEND
SOLIDLY BUILT
$6.50/416-X
The tale of the relationship between Jeff, a young photographer, and Mark, the butch electrician hired to wire Jeff's new home. For Jeff, it's love at first sight; Mark, however, has more than a few hang-ups.

JAY SHAFFER
ANIMAL HANDLERS
$4.95/264-7
In Shaffer's world, every man finally succumbs to the animal urges deep inside. And if there's any creature that promises a wild time, it's a beast who's been caged for far too long.

FULL SERVICE
$4.95/150-0
One of today's best chroniclers of masculine passion. No-nonsense guys bear down hard on each other as they work their way toward release in this finely detailed assortment of fantasies.

D. V. SADERO
IN THE ALLEY
$4.95/144-6
Hardworking men bring their special skills and impressive tools to the most satisfying job of all: capturing and breaking the male animal.

SCOTT O'HARA
DO-IT-YOURSELF PISTON POLISHING
$6.50/489-5
Longtime sex-pro Scott O'Hara draws upon his acute powers of seduction to lure you into a world of hard, horny men long overdue for a tune-up.

SUTTER POWELL
EXECUTIVE PRIVILEGES
$6.50/383-X
No matter how serious or sexy a predicament his characters find themselves in, Powell conveys the sheer exuberance of their encounters with a warm humor rarely seen in contemporary gay erotica.

GARY BOWEN
WESTERN TRAILS
$6.50/477-1
Some of gay literature's brightest stars tell the sexy truth about the many ways a rugged stud found to satisfy himself—and his buddy—in the Very Wild West.

MAN HUNGRY
$5.95/374-0
A riveting collection of stories from one of gay erotica's new stars. Dipping into a variety of genres, Bowen crafts tales of lust unlike anything being published today.

ROBERT BAHR
SEX SHOW
$4.95/225-6
Luscious dancing boys. Brazen, explicit acts. Take a seat, and get very comfortable, because the curtain's going up on a very special show no discriminating appetite can afford to miss.

KYLE STONE
THE HIDDEN SLAVE
$6.95/580-8
"This perceptive and finely-crafted work is a joy to discover. Kyle Stone's fiction belongs on the shelf of every serious fan of gay literature."
—Pat Califia

A young man searches for the perfect master. An electrifying tale of erotic discovery.

HOT BAUDS 2
$6.50/479-8
Stone conducted another heated search through the world's randiest gay bulletin boards, resulting in one of the most scalding follow-ups ever published.

HOT BAUDS
$5.95/285-X
Stone combed cyberspace for the hottest fantasies of the world's horniest hackers. Sexy, shameless, and eminently user-friendly.

FIRE & ICE
$5.95/297-3
A collection of stories from the author of the adventures of PB 500. Stone's characters always promise one thing: enough hot action to burn away your desire for anyone else....

FANTASY BOARD
$4.95/212-4
Explore the future—through the intertwined lives of a collection of randy computer hackers. On the Lambda Gate BBS, every horny male is in search of virtual satisfaction!

BUY ANY 4 BOOKS & CHOOSE 1 ADDITIONAL BOOK, OF EQUAL OR LESSER VALUE, AS YOUR FREE GIFT

MASQUERADE BOOKS

THE CITADEL
$4.95/198-5
The sequel to *PB 500*. Micah faces new challenges after entering the Citadel. Only his master knows what awaits....

THE INITIATION OF PB 500
$4.95/141-3
He is a stranger on their planet, unschooled in their language, and ignorant of their customs. But Micah will soon be trained in every detail of erotic service. When his training is complete, he must prove himself worthy of the master who has chosen him....

RITUALS
$4.95/168-3
Via a computer bulletin board, a young man finds himself drawn into sexual rites that transform him into the willing slave of a mysterious stranger. His former life is thrown off, and he learns to live for his Master's touch....

JASON FURY
THE ROPE ABOVE, THE BED BELOW
$4.95/269-8
A vicious murderer is preying upon New York's go-go boys. In order to solve this mystery and save lives, each studly suspect must lay bare his soul—and more!

ERIC'S BODY
$4.95/151-9
Follow the irresistible Jason through sexual adventures unlike any you have ever read—touching on the raunchy, the romantic, and a number of highly sensitive areas in between....

---

1 900 745-HUNG

THE connection for hot handfuls of eager guys! No credit card needed—so call now for access to the hottest party line available. Spill it all to bad boys from across the country! (Must be over 18.) Pick one up now.... $3.98 per min.

LARS EIGHNER
WANK: THE TAPES
$6.95/588-3
Lars Eighner gets back to basics with this look at every guy's favorite pastime. Horny studs bare it all and work up a healthy sweat during these provocative discussions about masturbation.

WHISPERED IN THE DARK
$5.95/286-8
A volume demonstrating Eighner's unique combination of strengths: poetic descriptive power, an unfailing ear for dialogue, and a finely tuned feeling for the nuances of male passion. An extraordinary collection of this influential writer's work.

AMERICAN PRELUDE
$4.95/170-5
Eighner is one of gay erotica's true masters, producing wonderfully written tales of all-American lust, peopled with red-blooded, oversexed studs.

DAVID LAURENTS, ED.
SOUTHERN COMFORT
$6.50/466-6
Editor David Laurents now unleashes a collection of tales focusing on the American South—stories reflecting not only the Southern literary tradition, but the many sexy contributions the region has made to the iconography of the American Male.

WANDERLUST: Homoerotic Tales of Travel
$5.95/395-3
A volume dedicated to the special pleasures of faraway places—and the horny men who lie in wait for intrepid tourists. Celebrate the freedom of the open road, and the allure of men who stray from the beaten path....

THE BADBOY BOOK OF EROTIC POETRY
$5.95/382-1
Erotic poetry has long been the problem child of the literary world—highly creative and provocative, but somehow too frank to be "art." *The Badboy Book of Erotic Poetry* restores eros to its place of honor in gay writing.

AARON TRAVIS
BIG SHOTS
$5.95/448-8
Two fierce tales in one electrifying volume. In *Beirut*, Travis tells the story of ultimate military power and erotic subjugation; *Kip*, Travis' hypersexed and sinister take on *film noir*, appears in unexpurgated form for the first time.

EXPOSED
$4.95/126-8
Cops, college jocks, ancient Romans—even Sherlock Holmes and his loyal Watson—cruise these pages, fresh from the pen of one of our hottest authors.

IN THE BLOOD
$5.95/283-3
Early tales from this master of the genre. Includes "In the Blood"—a heart-pounding descent into sexual vampirism.

THE FLESH FABLES
$4.95/243-4
One of Travis' best collections. Includes "Blue Light," as well as other masterpieces that established him as one of gay erotica's master storytellers.

MASQUERADE BOOKS

BOB VICKERY
SKIN DEEP
$4.95/265-5
So many varied beauties no one will go away unsatisfied. No tantalizing morsel of manflesh is overlooked—or left unexplored!

JR
FRENCH QUARTER NIGHTS
$5.95/337-6
Sensual snapshots of the many places where men get down and dirty—from the steamy French Quarter to the steam room at the old Everard baths.

TOM BACCHUS
RAHM
$5.95/315-5
Tom Bacchus brings to life an extraordinary assortment of characters, from the Father of Us All to the cowpoke next door, the early gay literati to rude, queercore mosh rats.

BONE
$4.95/177-2
Queer musings from the pen of one of today's hottest young talents. Tom Bacchus maps out the tricking ground of a new generation.

KEY LINCOLN
SUBMISSION HOLDS
$4.95/266-3
From tough to tender, the men between these covers stop at nothing to get what they want. These sweat-soaked tales show just how bad boys can really get.

CALDWELL/EIGHNER
QSFX2
$5.95/278-7
Other-worldly yarns from two master storytellers—Clay Caldwell and Lars Eighner. Both eroticists take a trip to the furthest reaches of the sexual imagination, sending back ten scalding sci-fi stories of male desire.

CLAY CALDWELL
SOME LIKE IT ROUGH
$6.95/544-1
A new collection of stories from a master of gay eroticism. Here are the best of Clay Caldwell's darkest tales—thrilling explorations of dominance and submission. Hot and heavy, Some Like It Rough is filled with enough virile masters and willing slaves to satisfy the the most demanding reader.

JOCK STUDS
$6.95/472-0
Scalding tales of pumped bodies and raging libidos. Swimmers, runners, football players—whatever your sport might be, there's a man here waiting to work up a little sweat, peel off his uniform, and claim his reward for a game well-played....

ASK OL' BUDDY
$5.95/346-5
Set in the underground SM world—where men initiate one another into the secrets of the rawest sexual realm of all. And when each stud's initiation is complete, he takes part in the training of another hungry soul....

STUD SHORTS
$5.95/320-1
"If anything, Caldwell's charm is more powerful, his nostalgia more poignant, the horniness he captures more sweetly, achingly acute than ever."
—Aaron Travis

A new collection of this legend's latest sex-fiction. Caldwell tells all about cops, cadets, truckers, farmboys (and many more) in these dirty jewels.

TAILPIPE TRUCKER
$5.95/296-5
Trucker porn! Caldwell tells the truth about Trag and Curly—two men hot for the feeling of sweaty manflesh. Together, they pick up—and turn out—a couple of thrill-seeking punks.

SERVICE, STUD
$5.95/336-8
Another look at the gay future. The setting is the Los Angeles of a distant future. Here the all-male populace is divided between the served and the servants—guaranteeing the erotic satisfaction of all involved.

QUEERS LIKE US
$4.95/262-0
For years the name Clay Caldwell has been synonymous with the hottest, most finely crafted gay tales available. *Queers Like Us* is one of his best: the story of a randy mailman's trek through a landscape of available studs.

ALL-STUD
$4.95/104-7
This classic, sex-soaked tale takes place under the watchful eye of Number Ten: an omniscient figure who has decreed unabashed promiscuity as the law of his all-male land. Love is outlawed—and two passionate men find themselves pitted against an oppressive system.

BUY ANY 4 BOOKS & CHOOSE 1 ADDITIONAL BOOK, OF EQUAL OR LESSER VALUE, AS YOUR FREE GIFT

MASQUERADE BOOKS

CLAY CALDWELL & AARON TRAVIS
TAG TEAM STUDS
$6.50/465-8

Wrestling will never seem the same, once you've made your way through this assortment of sweaty studs. But you'd better be wary—should one catch you off guard, you might spend the night pinned to the mat....

LARRY TOWNSEND
LEATHER AD: M
$5.95/380-5

John's curious about what goes on between the leatherclad men he's fantasized about. He takes out a personal ad, and starts a journey of discovery that will leave no part of his life unchanged.

LEATHER AD: S
$5.95/407-0

The tale continues—this time told from a Top's perspective. A simple ad generates many responses, and one man puts these studs through their paces....

1 800 906-HUNK

Hardcore phone action for real men. A scorching assembly of studs is waiting for your call—and eager to give you the headtrip of your life! Totally live, guaranteed one-on-one encounters. (Must be over 18.) No credit card needed. $3.98 per minute.

BEWARE THE GOD WHO SMILES
$5.95/321-X

Two lusty young Americans are transported to ancient Egypt—where they are embroiled in warfare and taken as slaves by barbarians. The two finally discover that the key to escape lies within their own rampant libidos.

MIND MASTER
$4.95/209-4

Who better to explore the territory of erotic dominance than an author who helped define the genre—and knows that ultimate mastery always transcends the physical. One gifted man exploits his ability to control others.

THE LONG LEATHER CORD
$4.95/201-9

Chuck's stepfather never lacks money or male visitors with whom he enacts intense sexual rituals. As Chuck comes to terms with his own desires, he begins to unravel the mystery behind his stepfather's secret life.

THE SCORPIUS EQUATION
$4.95/119-5

The story of a man caught between the demands of two galactic empires. Our randy hero must match wits—and more—with the incredible forces that rule his world.

MAN SWORD
$4.95/188-8

The *trés gai* tale of France's King Henri III, who encounters enough sexual schemers and politicos to alter one's picture of history forever! Witness the unbridled licentiousness of one of Europe's most notorious courts.

THE FAUSTUS CONTRACT
$4.95/167-5

Another thrilling tale of leather lust. Two cocky young hustlers get more than they bargained for in this story of lust and its discontents.

CHAINS
$4.95/158-6

Picking up street punks has always been risky, but here it sets off a string of events that must be read to be believed. The legendary Townsend at his grittiest.

RUN, LITTLE LEATHER BOY
$4.95/143-8

The famous tale of sexual awakening. A chronic underachiever, Wayne seems to be going nowhere fast. While exploring the gay leather underground, he discovers a sense of fulfillment he had never known before.

RUN NO MORE
$4.95/152-7

The sequel to *Run, Little Leather Boy*. This volume follows the further adventures of Townsend's leatherclad narrator as he travels every sexual byway available to the S/M male.

THE SEXUAL ADVENTURES OF SHERLOCK HOLMES
$4.95/3097-0

A scandalously sexy take on the notorious sleuth. Via the diary of Holmes' horny sidekick Watson, experience Holmes' most challenging—and arousing–adventures! An underground classic

THE GAY ADVENTURES OF CAPTAIN GOOSE
$4.95/169-1

Jerome Gander is sentenced to serve aboard a ship manned by the most hardened criminals. In no time, Gander becomes one of the most notorious rakehells Olde England had ever seen. On land or sea, Gander hunts down the Empire's hottest studs.

DONALD VINING
CABIN FEVER AND OTHER STORIES
$5.95/338-4

"Demonstrates the wisdom experience combined with insight and optimism can create."
—*Bay Area Reporter*

Eighteen blistering stories in celebration of the most intimate of male bonding, reaffirming both love and lust in modern gay life.

MASQUERADE BOOKS

DEREK ADAMS

MILES DIAMOND AND THE CASE OF THE CRETAN APOLLO
$6.95/381-3
Hired to track a cheating lover, Miles finds himself involved in a highly unprofessional capacity! When the jealous Callahan threatens not only Diamond but his studly assistant, Miles counters with a little undercover work—involving as many horny informants as he can get his hands on!

THE MARK OF THE WOLF
$5.95/361-9
The past comes back to haunt one well-off stud, whose desires lead him into the arms of many men—and the midst of a mystery.

MY DOUBLE LIFE
$5.95/314-7
Every man leads a double life, dividing his hours between the mundanities of the day and the pursuits of the night. Derek Adams shines a little light on the wicked things men do when no one's looking.

HEAT WAVE
$4.95/159-4
Derek Adams sexy short stories are guaranteed to jump start any libido—and *Heatwave* contains his very best.

MILES DIAMOND AND THE DEMON OF DEATH
$4.95/251-5
Miles always find himself in the stickiest situations—with any stud he meets! This adventure promises another carnal carnival, as Diamond investigates a host of horny guys—each of whom hides a secret Miles is only too willing to expose!

THE ADVENTURES OF MILES DIAMOND
$4.95/118-7
The debut of this popular gay gumshoe. To Diamond's delight, "The Case of the Missing Twin" is packed with randy studs. Miles sets about uncovering all as he tracks down the delectable Daniel Travis.

KELVIN BELIELE

IF THE SHOE FITS
$4.95/223-X
An essential volume of tales exploring a world where randy boys can't help but do what comes naturally—as often as possible! Sweaty male bodies grapple in pleasure.

JAMES MEDLEY

THE REVOLUTIONARY & OTHER STORIES
$6.50/417-8
Billy, the son of the station chief of the American Embassy in Guatemala, is kidnapped and held for ransom. Billy gradually develops an unimaginably close relationship with Juan, the revolutionary assigned to guard him.

HUCK AND BILLY
$4.95/245-0
Young lust knows no bounds—and is often the hottest of one's life! Huck and Billy explore the desires that course through their bodies, determined to plumb the depths of passion. A thrilling look at desire between men.

FLEDERMAUS

FLEDERFICTION: STORIES OF MEN AND TORTURE
$5.95/355-4
Fifteen blistering paeans to men and their suffering. Unafraid of exploring the furthest reaches of pain and pleasure, Fledermaus unleashes his most thrilling tales in this volume.

VICTOR TERRY

MASTERS
$6.50/418-6
Terry's butchest tales. A powerhouse volume of boot-wearing, whip-wielding, bone-crunching bruisers who've got what it takes to make a grown man grovel.

SM/SD
$6.50/406-2
Set around a South Dakota town called Prairie, these tales offer evidence that the real rough stuff can still be found where men take what they want despite all rules.

WHiPs
$4.95/254-X
Cruising for a hot man? You'd better be, because these WHiPs—officers of the Wyoming Highway Patrol—are gonna pull you over for a little impromptu interrogation....

MAX EXANDER

DEEDS OF THE NIGHT: Tales of Eros and Passion
$5.95/348-1
MAXimum porn! Exander's a writer who's seen it all—and is more than happy to describe every inch of it in pulsating detail. A whirlwind tour of the hypermasculine libido.

BUY ANY 4 BOOKS & CHOOSE 1 ADDITIONAL BOOK, OF EQUAL OR LESSER VALUE, AS YOUR FREE GIFT

MASQUERADE BOOKS

LEATHERSEX
$4.95/210-8
Hard-hitting tales from merciless Max. This time he focuses on the leather clad lust that draws together only the most willing and talented of tops and bottoms—for an all-out orgy of limitless surrender and control....

MANSEX
$4.95/160-8
"Mark was the classic leatherman: a huge, dark stud in chaps, with a big black moustache, hairy chest and enormous muscles. Exactly the kind of men Todd liked—strong, hunky, masculine, ready to take control...."

TOM CAFFREY
TALES FROM THE MEN'S ROOM
$5.95/364-3
Male lust at its most elemental and arousing. The Men's Room is less a place than a state of mind—one that every man finds himself in, day after day....

HITTING HOME
$4.95/222-1
Titillating and compelling, the stories in *Hitting Home* make a strong case for there being only one thing on a man's mind. Hot studs via the imagination of this new talent.

"BIG" BILL JACKSON
EIGHTH WONDER
$4.95/200-0
"Big" Bill Jackson's always the randiest guy in town—no matter what town he's in. From the bright lights and back rooms of New York to the open fields and sweaty bods of a small Southern town, "Big" Bill always manages to cause a scene!

TORSTEN BARRING
CONFESSIONS OF A NAKED PIANO PLAYER
$6.95/626-X
Frederic Danton is a musical prodigy—and currently the highest paid and most sought-after concert pianist in the world. At the height of his fame, Frederic withdraws from the limelight, and many fear he will never return. And why would he? Frederic books passage on the *S. S. Yeoman*, bound for the isle of Corrigia—home of the most depraved gay sex resort known to man!

GUY TRAYNOR
$6.50/414-3
Some call Guy Traynor a theatrical genius; others say he was a madman. All anyone knows for certain is that his productions were the result of blood, sweat and outrageous erotic torture!

SHADOWMAN
$4.95/178-0
From spoiled aristocrats to randy youths sowing wild oats at the local picture show, Barring's imagination works overtime in these steamy vignettes of homolust.

PETER THORNWELL
$4.95/149-7
Follow the exploits of Peter Thornwell and his outrageously horny cohorts as he goes from misspent youth to scandalous stardom, all thanks to an insatiable libido and love for the lash. The first of Torsten Barring's popular SM novels.

THE SWITCH
$4.95/3061-X
Some of the most brutally thrilling erotica available today. Sometimes a man needs a good whipping, and *The Switch* certainly makes a case! Packed with hot studs and unrelenting passions, these stories established Barring as a writer to be watched.

BERT McKENZIE
FRINGE BENEFITS
$5.95/354-6
From the pen of a widely published short story writer comes a volume of highly immodest tales. Not afraid of getting down and dirty, McKenzie produces some of today's most visceral sextales.

CHRISTOPHER MORGAN
STEAM GAUGE
$6.50/473-9
This volume abounds in manly men doing what they do best—to, with, or for any hot stud who crosses their paths.

THE SPORTSMEN
$5.95/385-6
A collection of super-hot stories dedicated to the all-American athlete. These writers know just the type of guys that make up every red-blooded male's starting line-up....

MUSCLE BOUND
$4.95/3028-8
Tommy joins forces with sexy Will Rodriguez in a battle of wits and biceps at the hottest gym in town, where the weak are bound and crushed by iron-pumping gods.

SONNY FORD
REUNION IN FLORENCE
$4.95/3070-9
Follow Adrian and Tristan an sexual odyssey that takes in all ports known to ancient man. From lustful Turks to insatiable Mamluks, these two spread pleasure throughout the classical world!

MASQUERADE BOOKS

ROGER HARMAN
FIRST PERSON
$4.95/179-9
Each story takes the form of a confessional—told by men who've got plenty to confess! From the "first time ever" to firsts of different kinds....

J. A. GUERRA, ED.
SLOW BURN
$4.95/3042-3
Torsos get lean and hard, pecs widen, and stomachs ripple in these sexy stories of the power and perils of physical perfection.

DAVE KINNICK
SORRY I ASKED
$4.95/3090-1
Unexpurgated interviews with gay porn's rank and file. Get personal with the men behind (and under) the "stars," and discover the hot truth about the porn business.

SEAN MARTIN
SCRAPBOOK
$4.95/224-8
From the creator of *Doc and Raider* comes this hot collection of life's horniest moments—all involving studs sure to set your pulse racing!

CARO SOLES & STAN TAL, EDS.
BIZARRE DREAMS
$4.95/187-X
An anthology of voices dedicated to exploring the dark side of human fantasy. Here are the most talented practitioners of "dark fantasy," the most forbidden sexual realm of all.

MICHAEL LOWENTHAL, ED.
**THE BADBOY EROTIC LIBRARY
Volume 1**
$4.95/190-X
Excerpts from *A Secret Life, Imre, Sins of the Cities of the Plain, Teleny* and others.
**THE BADBOY EROTIC LIBRARY
Volume 2**
$4.95/211-6
This time, selections are taken from *Mike and Me, Muscle Bound, Men at Work, Badboy Fantasies,* and *Slowburn.*

ERIC BOYD
MIKE AND ME
$5.95/419-4
Mike joined the gym squad to bulk up on muscle. Little did he know he'd be turning on every sexy muscle jock in Minnesota! Hard bodies collide in a series of horny workouts.
MIKE AND THE MARINES
$6.50/497-6
Mike takes on America's most elite corps of studs! Join in on the never-ending sexual escapades of this singularly lustful platoon!

ANONYMOUS
A SECRET LIFE
$4.95/3017-2
Meet Master Charles: eighteen and quite innocent, until his arrival at the Sir Percival's Academy, where the lessons are supplemented with a crash course in pure sexual heat!
SINS OF THE CITIES OF THE PLAIN
$5.95/322-8
indulge yourself in the scorching memoirs of young man-about-town Jack Saul. Jack's sinful escapades grow wilder with every chapter!
IMRE
$4.95/3019-9
An extraordinary lost classic of gay desire and romance in a small European town on the eve of WWI. An early look at gay love and lust.
THE SCARLET PANSY
$4.95/189-6
Randall Etrange travels the world in search of true love. Along the way, his journey becomes a sexual odyssey of truly epic proportions.

HARD CANDY

ELISE D'HAENE
LICKING OUR WOUNDS
$7.95/605-7
"A fresh, engagingly sarcastic and determinedly bawdy voice. D'Haene is blessed with a savvy, iconoclastic view of the world that is mordant but never mean." —*Publisher's Weekly*

This acclaimed debut novel is the story of Maria, a young woman coming to terms with the complexities of life in the age of AIDS. Abandoned by her lover and faced with the deaths of her friends, Maria struggles along with the help of Peter, HIV-positive and deeply conflicted about the changes in his own life, and Christie, a lover who is full of her own ideas about truth and the meaning of life.

BUY ANY 4 BOOKS & CHOOSE 1 ADDITIONAL BOOK, OF EQUAL OR LESSER VALUE, AS YOUR FREE GIFT

MASQUERADE BOOKS

CHEA VILLANUEVA
BULLETPROOF BUTCHES
$7.95/560-3

"...Gutsy, hungry, and outrageous, but with a tender core... Villanueva is a writer to watch out for: she will teach us something."
—Joan Nestle

One of lesbian literature's most uncompromising voices. Never afraid to address the harsh realities of working-class lesbian life, Chea Villanueva charts territory frequently overlooked in the age of "lesbian chic."

KEVIN KILLIAN
ARCTIC SUMMER
$6.95/514-X

A critically acclaimed examination of the emptiness lying beneath the rich exterior of America in the 50s. With the story of Liam Reilly—a young gay man of considerable means and numerous secrets—Killian exposes the complexities and contradictions of the American Dream.

STAN LEVENTHAL
BARBIE IN BONDAGE
$6.95/415-1

Widely regarded as one of the most clear-eyed interpreters of big city gay male life, Leventhal here provides a series of explorations of love and desire between men.

SKYDIVING ON CHRISTOPHER STREET
$6.95/287-6

"Positively addictive." —Dennis Cooper

Aside from a hateful job, a hateful apartment, a hateful world and an increasingly hateful lover, life seems, well, all right for the protagonist of Stan Leventhal's latest novel. An insightful tale of contemporary urban gay life.

MICHAEL ROWE
**WRITING BELOW THE BELT:
Conversations with Erotic Authors**
$7.95/540-9

"An in-depth and enlightening tour of society's love/hate relationship with sex, morality, and censorship."
—James White Review

Award-winning journalist Michael Rowe interviewed the best and brightest erotic writers and presents the collected wisdom in *Writing Below the Belt*. Includes interviews with such cult sensations as John Preston, Larry Townsend, Pat Califia, as well as new voices such as Will Leber, Michael Lowenthal and others. An illuminating look at some of today's most challenging writers.

PAUL T. ROGERS
SAUL'S BOOK
$7.95/462-3
Winner of the Editors' Book Award

"A first novel of considerable power... Speaks to us all."
—New York Times Book Review

The story of a Times Square hustler, Sinbad the Sailor, and Saul, a brilliant, self-destructive, dominating character who may be the only love Sinbad will ever know. A classic tale of desire, obsession and the wages of love.

PATRICK MOORE
IOWA
$6.95/423-2

"Full of terrific characters etched in acid-sharp prose, soaked through with just enough ambivalence to make it thoroughly romantic." —Felice Picano

The tale of one gay man's journey into adulthood, and the roads that bring him home.

LARS EIGHNER
GAY COSMOS
$6.95/236-1

An analysis of gay culture. Praised by the press, *Gay Cosmos* is an important contribution to the area of Gay and Lesbian Studies.

WALTER R. HOLLAND
THE MARCH
$6.95/429-1

Beginning on a hot summer night in 1980, *The March* revolves around a circle of young gay men, and the many others their lives touch. Over time, each character changes in unexpected ways; lives and loves come together and fall apart, as society itself is horribly altered by the onslaught of AIDS.

BRAD GOOCH
THE GOLDEN AGE OF PROMISCUITY
$7.95/550-6

"The next best thing to taking a time-machine trip to grovel in the glorious '70s gutter." —San Francisco Chronicle

"A solid, unblinking, unsentimental look at a vanished era. Gooch tells us everything we ever wanted to know about the dark and decadent gay subculture in Manhattan before AIDS altered the landscape." —Kirkus Reviews

RED JORDAN AROBATEAU
DIRTY PICTURES
$5.95/345-7

Dirty Pictures is the story of a lonely butch tending bar—and the femme she finally calls her own.

MASQUERADE BOOKS

LUCY AND MICKEY
$6.95/311-2

"A necessary reminder to all who blissfully—some may say ignorantly—ride the wave of lesbian chic into the mainstream."
—Heather Findlay

The story of Mickey—an uncompromising butch—and her long affair with Lucy, the femme she loves.

DONALD VINING
A GAY DIARY
$8.95/451-8

"*A Gay Diary* is, unquestionably, the richest historical document of gay male life in the United States that I have ever encountered...."
—Body Politic

Vining's *Diary* portrays a vanished age and the lifestyle of a generation frequently forgotten. An unprecedented look at the lifestyle of a pre-Stonewall gay man.

FELICE PICANO
AMBIDEXTROUS
$6.95/275-2

"Makes us remember what it feels like to be a child..."
—The Advocate

A highly acclaimed volume, and the first of the author's novelistic memoirs. Picano tells all about his formative years: home life, school face-offs, the ingenuous sophistications of his first sexual steps.

MEN WHO LOVED ME
$6.95/274-4

"Zesty...spiked with adventure and romance...a distinguished and humorous portrait of a vanished age." —*Publishers Weekly*

In 1966, Picano abandoned New York, determined to find true love in Europe. He becomes embroiled in a romance with Djanko, and lives *la dolce vita* to the fullest. Upon returning to the US, he plunges into the city's thriving gay community of the 1970s.

THE LURE
$6.95/398-8
A Book-of-the-Month-Club Selection
After witnessing a brutal murder, Noel is recruited by the police, to assist as a lure for the homophobic killer. Undercover, he moves deep into the freneticism of gay highlife in 1970s Manhattan—where he discovers his own hidden desires. A hypnotic, highly-acclaimed whodunnit, enlivened with period detail.

WILLIAM TALSMAN
THE GAUDY IMAGE
$6.95/263-9

"To read *The Gaudy Image* now...it is to see first-hand the very issues of identity and positionality with which gay men were struggling in the decades before Stonewall. For what Talsman is dealing with...is the very question of how we conceive ourselves gay." —from the introduction by Michael Bronski

ROSEBUD

THE ROSEBUD READER
$5.95/319-8
Rosebud has contributed greatly to the burgeoning genre of lesbian erotica, introducing new writers and adding contemporary classics to the shelves. Here are the finest moments from Rosebud's runaway successes.

DANIELLE ENGLE
UNCENSORED FANTASIES
$6.95/572-7
In a world where so many stifle their emotions, who doesn't find themselves yearning for a little old-fashioned honesty—even if it means bearing one's own secret desires? Danielle Engle's heroines do just that—and a great deal more—in their quest for total sexual pleasure.

LESLIE CAMERON
WHISPER OF FANS
$6.50/542-5
A thrilling chronicle of love between women, written with a sure eye for sensual detail. One woman discovers herself through the sensual devotion of another.

RACHEL PEREZ
ODD WOMEN
$6.50/526-3
These women are sexy, smart, tough—some say odd. But who cares! An assortment of Sapphic sirens proves once and for all that comely ladies come best in pairs.

RED JORDAN AROBATEAU
THE BLACK BIKER
$6.95/624-3
The further adventures of the Outlaws. Once again, the Oils Club witnesses the outrageous antics of these ultimate rebels, banded together against a hostile world. One day, a mysterious biker walks into Oils, looking for love, driven by lust, and hoping to leave a sorry past behind.

BUY ANY 4 BOOKS & CHOOSE 1 ADDITIONAL BOOK, OF EQUAL OR LESSER VALUE, AS YOUR FREE GIFT

MASQUERADE BOOKS

STREET FIGHTER
$6.95/583-2
Another blast of truth from one of today's most notorious plain-speakers. An unsentimental look at the life of a street butch—Woody, the consummate outsider, living on the fringes of San Francisco.

SATAN'S BEST
$6.95/539-5
An epic tale of life with the Outlaws—the ultimate lesbian biker gang. Angel, a lonely butch, joins the Outlaws, and finds herself loving a new breed of woman and facing a new brand of danger on the open road....

ROUGH TRADE
$6.50/470-4
Famous for her unflinching portrayal of lower-class dyke life and love, Arobateau outdoes herself with these tales of butch/femme affairs and unrelenting passions.

BOYS NIGHT OUT
$6.50/463-1
Incendiary short fiction from this lesbian literary sensation. As always, Arobateau takes a good hard look at the lives of everyday women, noting well the struggles and triumphs each experiences.

RANDY TUROFF
LUST NEVER SLEEPS
$6.50/475-5
Highly erotic, powerfully real fiction. Turoff depicts a circle of modern women connected through the bonds of love, friendship, ambition, and lust with accuracy and compassion.

K. T. BUTLER
TOOLS OF THE TRADE
$5.95/420-8
A sparkling mix of lesbian erotica and humor. An encounter with ice cream, cappuccino and chocolate cake; an affair with a complete stranger; a pair of faulty handcuffs; and more.

ALISON TYLER
THE SILVER KEY: Madame Victoria's Finishing School
$6.95/614-6
In a Victorian finishing school, a circle of randy young ladies share a diary. Molly records an explicit description of her initiation into the ways of physical love; Colette reports on a ghostly encounter. Eden tells of how it feels to wield a switch; and Katherine transcribes the journey of her love affair with the wickedly wanton Eden. Each of these thrilling tales is recounted in loving detail....

COME QUICKLY: For Girls on the Go
$6.95/428-3
Here are over sixty of the hottest fantasies around. A volume designed a modern girl on a modern schedule, who still appreciates a little old-fashioned action.

VENUS ONLINE
$6.95/521-2
Lovely Alexa spends her days in a boring bank job, saving her energies for the night—when she goes online. Soon Alexa—aka Venus—finds her real and online lives colliding sexily.

DARK ROOM: An Online Adventure
$6.50/455-0
Dani can't bring herself to face the death of her lover, Kate. Determined to keep the memory of her lover alive, Dani goes online under Kate's screen alias—and begins to uncover the truth behind Kate's death....

BLUE SKY SIDEWAYS & OTHER STORIES
$6.50/394-5
A variety of women, and their many breathtaking experiences with lovers, friends—and even the occasional sexy stranger.

DIAL "L" FOR LOVELESS
$5.95/386-4
Katrina Loveless—a sexy private eye talented enough to give Sam Spade a run for his money. In her first case, Katrina investigates a murder implicating a host of lovely, lusty ladies.

THE VIRGIN
$5.95/379-1
Seeking the fulfillment of her deepest sexual desires, Veronica answers a personal ad in the "Women Seeking Women" category—and discovers a whole sensual world she had only dreamed existed!

LOVECHILD
GAG
$5.95/369-4
One of the bravest young writers you'll ever encounter. These poems take on hypocrisy with uncommon energy, and announce Lovechild as a writer of unforgettable rage.

ELIZABETH OLIVER
THE SM MURDER: Murder at Roman Hill
$5.95/353-8
Intrepid lesbian P.I.s Leslie Patrick and Robin Penny take on a really hot case: the murder of the notorious Felicia Roman. The circumstances of the crime lead them through the leatherdyke underground, where motives—and desires—run deep.

MASQUERADE BOOKS

LAURA ANTONIOU, ED.

LEATHERWOMEN III:
The Clash of the Cultures
$6.95/619-7
Laura Antoniou gathers the very best of today's cutting-edge women's erotica—concentrating on multicultural stories involving characters too infrequently seen in this genre. More than fifteen of today's most daring writers make this a compelling testament to desire.

LEATHERWOMEN
$6.95/598-0
"...a great new collection of fiction by and about SM dykes."
—SKIN TWO

A groundbreaking anthology. These fantasies, from the pens of new or emerging authors, break every rule imposed on women's fantasies. The hottest stories from some of today's newest writers make this an unforgettable exploration of the female libido.

LEATHERWOMEN II
$4.95/229-6
Another volume of writing from women on the edge, sure to ignite libidinal flames in any reader. Leave all taboos behind when exploring these pages, because these Leatherwomen know no limits....

VALENTINA CILESCU

MY LADY'S PLEASURE:
Mistress with a Maid, Volume 1
$5.95/412-7
Claudia Dungarrow, a lovely, powerful professor, attempts to seduce Elizabeth Stanbridge, setting off a chain of events that eventually ruins her career. Claudia vows revenge—and makes her foes pay deliciously....

DARK VENUS:
Mistress with a Maid, Volume 2
$6.50/481-X
Claudia Dungarrow's quest for ultimate erotic dominance continues in this scalding second volume! How many maidens will fall prey to her insatiable appetite?

BODY AND SOUL:
Mistress with a Maid, Volume 3
$6.50/515-8
Dr. Claudia Dungarrow returns for yet another tour of depravity, subjugating every maiden in sight to her sexual whims. Though many young women have fallen victim to her unquenchable lusts, she has yet to hold Elizabeth in submission. Will she ever?

THE ROSEBUD SUTRA
$4.95/242-6
A look at the ultimate guide to lesbian love. The Rosebud Sutra explores the secrets women keep from everyone—everyone but one another, that is...

MISTRESS MINE
$6.50/502-6
Sophia Cranleigh sits in prison, accused of authoring the "obscene" *Mistress Mine*. What she has done, however, is merely chronicle the events of her life under the hand of Mistress Malin.

AARONA GRIFFIN

LEDA AND THE HOUSE OF SPIRITS
$6.95/585-9
Two steamy novellas in one volume. Ten years into her relationship with Chrys, *Leda* decides to take a one-night vacation—at a local lesbian sex club. In the second story, lovely Lydia thinks she has her grand new home all to herself—until dreams begin to suggest that this *House of Spirits* harbors other souls, determined to do some serious partying.

PASSAGE & OTHER STORIES
$6.95/599-9
"A tale of a woman who is brave enough to follow her desire, even if it leads her into the arms of dangerous women."
—Pat Califia

Nina finds herself infatuated with a woman she spots at a local café. One night, Nina follows her, only to find herself enmeshed in an maze leading to a mysterious world where women test the edges of sexuality and power.

LINDSAY WELSH

BAD HABITS
$6.95/625-1
"If you like hot lesbian erotica, run—don't walk—and pick up a copy of *Bad Habits*."
—Lambda Book Report

When some dominant and discerning women begin to detect tell-tale signs of poor training in their servants, they know there's only one remedy—careful, correct re-instruction. And in no time, a certain group of wayward young ladies is back in school, joyfully learning the real, burning truth of submission to Woman.

SEXUAL FANTASIES
$6.95/586-7
A volume of today's hottest lesbian erotica. A dozen sexy stories, ranging from sweet to spicy, *Sexual Fantasies* offers a look at the many desires of modern women.

BUY ANY 4 BOOKS & CHOOSE 1 ADDITIONAL BOOK, OF EQUAL OR LESSER VALUE, AS YOUR FREE GIFT

MASQUERADE BOOKS

SECOND SIGHT
$6.50/507-7
The debut of lesbian superhero Dana Steel! During an attack by a gang of homophobic youths, Dana is thrown onto subway tracks. Miraculously, she survives—and finds herself possessing powers that make her the world's first lesbian superhero.

NASTY PERSUASIONS
$6.50/436-4
A hot peek into the behind-the-scenes operations of Rough Trade—one of the world's most famous lesbian clubs. Join Slash, Ramone, Cherry and many others as they bring one another to the height of ecstasy.

MILITARY SECRETS
$5.95/397-X
Colonel Candice Sproule heads a specialized boot camp. Assisted by three dominatrix sergeants, Colonel Sproule takes on the submissives sent to her by military contacts. Then along comes Jesse—whose pleasure in being served matches the Colonel's own.

THE BEST OF LINDSAY WELSH
$5.95/368-6
Welsh was one of Rosebud's early bestsellers, and remains one of our most popular writers. This sampler is set to introduce some of the hottest lesbian erotica to a wider audience.

NECESSARY EVIL
$5.95/277-9
One lovely submissive decides to create a Mistress who'll fulfill her heart's desire. Little did she know how difficult it would be—and, in the end, rewarding....

A VICTORIAN ROMANCE
$5.95/365-1
A young woman realizes her dream—a trip abroad! Soon, Elaine comes to discover her own sexual talents, as a hot-blooded Parisian named Madelaine takes her Sapphic education in hand.

A CIRCLE OF FRIENDS
$6.50/524-7
A close-knit group of women pair off to explore all the possibilities of lesbian passion, until finally it seems that there is nothing—and no one—they have not dabbled in.

ANNABELLE BARKER
MOROCCO
$6.50/541-7
A lovely young woman stands to inherit a fortune—if she can only withstand the ministrations of her guardian until her twentieth birthday. But Lila finds that liberty has its own delicious price....

A.L. REINE
DISTANT LOVE & OTHER STORIES
$4.95/3056-3
In the title story, Leah Michaels and her lover, Ranelle, have had four years of blissful, smoldering passion together. When Ranelle is out of town, Leah records an audio "Valentine:" a cassette filled with erotic reminiscences....

A RICHARD KASAK BOOK

LARRY TOWNSEND
THE LEATHERMAN'S HANDBOOK
$12.95/559-X
With introductions by John Preston, Jack Fritscher and Victor Terry
A special twenty-fifth anniversary edition of this guide to the gay leather underground, with additional material addressing the realities of sex in the 90s. A volume of historical value, the *Handbook* remains relevant to today's reader.

ASK LARRY
$12.95/289-2
For many years, Townsend wrote the "Leather Notebook" column for *Drummer* magazine. Now read Townsend's collected wisdom, as well as the author's careful consideration of the way life has changed in the AIDS era.

SIMON LEVAY
ALBRICK'S GOLD
$20.95/518-2/Hardcover
"Well-plotted and imaginative... [Levay's] premise and execution are original and engaging." —*Publishers Weekly*

From the man behind the controversial "gay brain" studies comes a tale of medical experimentation run amok. Is Dr. Guy Albrick performing unethical experiments in an attempt at "correcting" homosexuality? Doctor Roger Cavendish is determined to find out, before Albrick's guinea pigs are let loose among an unsuspecting gay community...

PAT CALIFIA
DIESEL FUEL: Passionate Poetry
$12.95/535-2
"Dead-on direct, these poems burn, pierce, penetrate, soak, and sting.... Califia leaves no sexual stone unturned, clearing new ground for us all." —*Gerry Gomez Pearlberg*

Pat Califia's first collection of verse. A volume of extraordinary scope, and one of this year's must-read explorations of underground culture.

MASQUERADE BOOKS

SENSUOUS MAGIC
$12.95/458-5

"*Sensuous Magic* is clear, succinct and engaging even for the reader for whom S/M isn't the sexual behavior of choice.... When she is writing about the dynamics of sex and the technical aspects of it, Califia is the Dr. Ruth of the alternative sexuality set...." —*Lambda Book Report*

"Captures the power of what it means to enter forbidden terrain, and to do so safely with someone else, and to explore the healing potential, spiritual aspects and the depth of S/M." —*Bay Area Reporter*

"Don't take a dangerous trip into the unknown—buy this book and know where you're going!" —*SKIN TWO*

SHAR REDNOUR, ED.
VIRGIN TERRITORY 2
$12.95/506-9

Focusing on the many "firsts" of a woman's erotic life, *VT2* provides one of the sole outlets for serious discussion of the myriad possibilities available to and chosen by many lesbians.

VIRGIN TERRITORY
$12.95/457-7

An scintillating anthology of writing by women about their first-time erotic experiences with other women. A groundbreaking and influential examination of contemporary lesbian desire.

MICHAEL BRONSKI, ED.
TAKING LIBERTIES: Gay Men's Essays on Politics, Culture and Sex
$12.95/456-9

Lambda Literary Award Winner

"Offers undeniable proof of a heady, sophisticated, diverse new culture of gay intellectual debate. I cannot recommend it too highly." —Christopher Bram

An essential look at the state of the gay male community. Some of the gay community's foremost essayists—from radical left to neo-conservative—weigh in on such slippery topics as outing, identity, pornography, pedophilia, and much more.

FLASHPOINT:
Gay Male Sexual Writing
$12.95/424-0

Over twenty of the genre's best writers are included in this thrilling and enlightening look at contemporary gay porn. Accompanied by Bronski's insightful analysis, each story illustrates the many approaches to sexuality used by today's gay writers.

HEATHER FINDLAY, ED.
A MOVEMENT OF EROS:
25 Years of Lesbian Erotica
$12.95/421-6

Tracing the course of the genre from its pre-Stonewall roots to its current renaissance, Findlay examines each piece, placing it within the context of lesbian community and politics.

MICHAEL FORD, ED.
ONCE UPON A TIME:
Erotic Fairy Tales for Women
$12.95/449-6

How relevant to contemporary lesbians are traditional fairy tales? Some of the biggest names in lesbian literature retell their favorites, adding their own sexy twists.

HAPPILY EVER AFTER:
Erotic Fairy Tales for Men
$12.95/450-X

Adapting some of childhood's beloved stories for the adult gay reader, the contributors to *Happily Ever After* dig up the erotic subtext of these hitherto "innocent" diversions.

CHARLES HENRI FORD & PARKER TYLER
THE YOUNG AND EVIL
$12.95/431-3

"*The Young and Evil* creates [its] generation as *This Side of Paradise* by Fitzgerald created his generation."—Gertrude Stein

Originally published in 1933, *The Young and Evil* was a sensation due to its portrayal of young gay artists living in Greenwich Village. From drag balls to bohemian flats, these characters followed love wherever it led them.

BARRY HOFFMAN, ED.
THE BEST OF GAUNTLET
$12.95/202-7

Gauntlet has always published the widest possible range of opinions. The most provocative articles have been gathered by editor-in-chief Barry Hoffman, to make *The Best of Gauntlet* a riveting exploration of American society's limits.

AMARANTHA KNIGHT, ED.
LOVE BITES
$12.95/234-5

A volume of tales dedicated to legend's sexiest demon—the Vampire. Not only the finest collection of erotic horror available—but a virtual who's who of promising new talent.

BUY ANY 4 BOOKS & CHOOSE 1 ADDITIONAL BOOK, OF EQUAL OR LESSER VALUE, AS YOUR FREE GIFT

MASQUERADE BOOKS

MICHAEL ROWE
WRITING BELOW THE BELT: Conversations with Erotic Authors
$19.95/363-5

"An in-depth and enlightening tour of society's love/hate relationship with sex, morality, and censorship."
—*James White Review*

Rowe speaks frankly with cult favorites such as Pat Califia, crossover success stories like John Preston, and up-and-comers Michael Lowenthal and Will Leber.

MICHAEL LASSELL
THE HARD WAY
$12.95/231-0

"Lassell is a master of the necessary word. In an age of tepid and whining verse, his bawdy and bittersweet songs are like a plunge in cold champagne." —Paul Monette

The first collection of renowned gay writer Michael Lassell's poetry, fiction and essays. As much a chronicle of post-Stonewall gay life as a compendium of a remarkable writer's work.

WILLIAM CARNEY
THE REAL THING
$10.95/280-9

"Carney gives us a good look at the mores and lifestyle of the first generation of gay leathermen." —Pat Califia

With a new introduction by Michael Bronski. *The Real Thing* returns from exile more than twenty-five years after its initial release, detailing the attitudes and practices of an earlier generation of leathermen.

RANDY TUROFF, ED.
LESBIAN WORDS: State of the Art
$10.95/340-6

"This is a terrific book that should be on every thinking lesbian's bookshelf." —Nisa Donnelly

The best of lesbian nonfiction looking at not only the current fashionability the media has brought to the lesbian "image," but considerations of the lesbian past via historical inquiry and personal recollections.

ASSOTTO SAINT
SPELLS OF A VOODOO DOLL
$12.95/393-7
Lambda Literary Award Nominee.
"Angelic and brazen." —Jewelle Gomez

A spellbinding collection of the poetry, lyrics, essays and performance texts by one of the most important voices in the renaissance of black gay writing.

EURYDICE
F/32
$10.95/350-3

"It's wonderful to see a woman...celebrating her body and her sexuality by creating a fabulous and funny tale."
—Kathy Acker

A funny, disturbing quest for unity, *f/32* tells the story of Ela and her vagina—the latter of whom embarks on one of the most hilarious road trips in recent fiction. An award-winning novel.

FELICE PICANO
DRYLAND'S END
$12.95/279-5
The award-winning author's first sci-fi novel. *Dryland's End* takes place in a fabulous techno-empire ruled by intelligent, powerful women. While the Matriarchy has ruled for over two thousand years and altered human society, it is now unraveling. Military rivalries, religious fanaticism and economic competition threaten to destroy the mighty empire.

LUCY TAYLOR
UNNATURAL ACTS
$12.95/181-0
"A topnotch collection..." —*Science Fiction Chronicle*

A disturbing vision of erotic horror. Unrelenting angels and hungry gods play with souls and bodies in Taylor's murky cosmos: where heaven and hell are merely differences of perspective; where redemption and damnation lie behind the same shocking acts.

TIM WOODWARD, ED.
THE BEST OF SKIN TWO
$12.95/130-6
Provocative essays by the finest writers working in the "radical sex" scene. Including interviews with cult figures Tim Burton, Clive Barker and Jean Paul Gaultier.

JOHN PRESTON
MY LIFE AS A PORNOGRAPHER AND OTHER INDECENT ACTS
$12.95/135-7

"...essential and enlightening... *My Life as a Pornographer*] is a bridge from the sexually liberated 1970s to the more cautious 1990s, and Preston has walked much of that way as a standard-bearer to the cause for equal rights...." —*Library Journal*

A collection of author and social critic John Preston's essays, focusing on his work as an erotic writer, and proponent of gay rights.

MASQUERADE BOOKS

LAURA ANTONIOU, ED.
LOOKING FOR MR. PRESTON
$23.95/288-4/Hardcover
Interviews, essays and personal reminiscences of John Preston—a man whose career spanned the gay publishing industry. Ten percent of the proceeds from this book will go to the AIDS Project of Southern Maine, for which Preston served as President of the Board.

SAMUEL R. DELANY
THE MOTION OF LIGHT IN WATER
$12.95/133-0
"A very moving, intensely fascinating literary biography from an extraordinary writer....The artist as a young man and a memorable picture of an age." —William Gibson

Samuel R. Delany's autobiography covers the early years of one of science fiction's most important voices. A self-portrait of one of today's most challenging writers.

THE MAD MAN
$23.95/193-4/Hardcover
"Delany develops an insightful dichotomy between [his protagonist]'s two worlds: the one of cerebral philosophy and dry academia, the other of heedless, 'impersonal' obsessive sexual extremism. When these worlds finally collide ... the novel achieves a surprisingly satisfying resolution...."
—Publishers Weekly

The legendary Samuel Delany's most provocative novel. For his thesis, graduate student John Marr researches the life and work of the brilliant Timothy Hasler: a philosopher whose career was cut tragically short over a decade earlier. Marr notices parallels between his life and that of his subject—and begins to believe that Hasler's death might hold some key to his own life as a gay man in the age of AIDS.

CARO SOLES, ED.
MELTDOWN!
An Anthology of Erotic Science Fiction and Dark Fantasy for Gay Men
$12.95/203-5
Meltdown! contains the very best examples of the increasingly popular sub-genre of erotic sci-fi/dark fantasy: stories meant to send a shiver down the spine and start a fire down below.

GUILLERMO BOSCH
RAIN
$12.95/232-9
In a quest to sate his hunger for some knowledge of the world, one man is taken through a series of extraordinary encounters that change the course of civilization around him.

CECILIA TAN, ED.
SM VISIONS:
The Best of Circlet Press
$10.95/339-2
Circlet Press, publisher of erotic science fiction and fantasy genre, is now represented by the best of its very best—a most thrilling and eye-opening rides through the erotic imagination.

DAVID MELTZER
THE AGENCY TRILOGY
$12.95/216-7
"...'The Agency' is clearly Meltzer's paradigm of society; a mindless machine of which we are all 'agents,' including those whom the machine supposedly serves...." —Norman Spinrad

A vision of an America consumed and dehumanized by a lust for power.

MICHAEL PERKINS
THE GOOD PARTS: An Uncensored Guide to Literary Sexuality
$12.95/186-1
A survey of sex as seen/written about in the pages of over 100 major fiction and nonfiction volumes from the past twenty years.
COMING UP: The World's Best Erotic Writing
$12.95/370-8
Michael Perkins has scoured the field of erotic writing to produce an anthology sure to challenge the limits of the most seasoned reader.

MICHAEL LOWENTHAL, ED.
THE BEST OF THE BADBOYS
$12.95/233-7
The best Badboy writers are collected here, in this testament to the artistry that has catapulted them to bestselling status. A virtual primer of contemporary gay erotic writing, including work by John Preston, Clay Caldwell, Aaron Travis, and others.

BUY ANY 4 BOOKS & CHOOSE 1 ADDITIONAL BOOK, OF EQUAL OR LESSER VALUE, AS YOUR FREE GIFT

MASQUERADE BOOKS

LARS EIGHNER
ELEMENTS OF AROUSAL
$12.95/230-2
A guideline for success with one of publishing's best kept secrets: the novice-friendly field of gay erotic writing. Eighner details his craft, providing the reader with sure advice.

MARCO VASSI
THE EROTIC COMEDIES
$12.95/136-5
"The comparison to [Henry] Miller is high praise indeed.... But reading Vassi's work, the analogy holds—for he shares with Miller an unabashed joy in sensuality, and a questing after experience that is the root of all great literature, erotic or otherwise...."
—David L. Ulin, *The Los Angeles Reader*

Scathing and humorous, these stories reflect Vassi's belief in the power and primacy of Eros in American life.

A DRIVING PASSION
$12.95/134-9
Famous for the lectures he gave regarding sexuality, *A Driving Passion* collects these lectures, and distills the philosophy that made him a sensation.

THE STONED APOCALYPSE
$12.95/132-2
Vassi's autobiography, financed by the other erotic writing that made him a cult sensation.

THE SALINE SOLUTION
$12.95/180-2
The story of one couple's affair and the events that lead them to reassess their lives.

CHEA VILLANUEVA
JESSIE'S SONG
$9.95/235-3
"It conjures up the strobe-light confusion and excitement of urban dyke life.... Read about these dykes and you'll love them."
—Rebecca Ripley

Touching, arousing portraits of working class butch/femme relations. An underground hit.

STAN TAL, ED.
BIZARRE SEX AND OTHER CRIMES OF PASSION
$12.95/213-2
Over twenty stories of erotic shock, guaranteed to titillate and terrify. This incredible volume includes such masters of erotic horror as Lucy Taylor and Nancy Kilpatrick.

ORDERING IS EASY

MC/VISA orders can be placed by calling our toll-free number
PHONE 800-375-2356/FAX 212-986-7355
HOURS M-F 9am—12am EDT Sat & Sun 12pm—8pm EDT
E-MAIL masqbks@aol.com
or mail this coupon to:
MASQUERADE DIRECT
DEPT. BMMQ98 801 2ND AVE., NY, NY 10017

BUY ANY FOUR BOOKS AND CHOOSE ONE ADDITIONAL BOOK, OF EQUAL OR LESSER VALUE, AS YOUR FREE GIFT

QTY.	TITLE	NO.	PRICE
			FREE

DEPT. BMMQ98 (please have this code available when placing your order)

We never sell, give or trade any customer's name.

- SUBTOTAL
- POSTAGE AND HANDLING
- TOTAL

In the U.S., please add $1.50 for the first book and 75¢ for each additional book; in Canada, add $2.00 for the first book and $1.25 for each additional book. Foreign countries: add $4.00 for the first book and $2.00 for each additional book. No C.O.D. orders. Please make all checks payable to Masquerade/Direct. Payable in U.S. currency only. NY state residents add 8.25% sales tax. Please allow 4–6 weeks for delivery. Payable in U.S. currency only.

NAME _____

ADDRESS _____

CITY _____ STATE _____ ZIP _____

TEL( ) _____

E-MAIL _____

PAYMENT: ☐ CHECK ☐ MONEY ORDER ☐ VISA ☐ MC

CARD NO. _____ EXP. DATE _____